WHEN SHE UNRAVELS

A DARK MAFIA ROMANCE

GABRIELLE SANDS

THE FALLEN

CHAPTER 1

VALENTINA

MAMMA MARRIED one of the most important New York City dons when she was only eighteen. Marriages like that are never easy, but everyone said she was born for the role. Her stoicism in the face of every struggle Papà threw her way gave her a reputation of being reliable, unbreakable, and utterly unflappable. Even her name, Pietra, means stone in Italian.

I was raised to be just like her—the perfect mafia wife—but in my marriage to Lazaro, I'm crumbling. If my mother is granite, I must be soapstone. Every night spent in the basement with my husband chips away at me.

Soon, there will be nothing left.

I tear my gaze off my wedding ring and take in my surroundings. I always thought the private dining room of La Trattoria was ostentatious. The luxury is so in your face it would make most honest people blush, but as it happens, few of those make it past the heavy wooden doors. Blue silk-covered walls, stuccoed ceiling, a three-tier chandelier, and that ridiculous floor. An intricate floral design made of granite, marble, and travertine. The floor alone is worth more than most people's homes. It belongs in a sitting room of a royal palace. Instead, it decorates what is effectively Papà's favorite meeting room.

Given how his meetings often go, I wouldn't be surprised if that floor has seen more dead bodies than a morgue, but today, there are no signs of impending bloodshed.

After all, the women of the Garzolo clan are here for a bridal shower—a joyous occasion. Or what should be one, if Belinda, my cousin and the bride-to-be, would stop crying into her plate.

"Are we going to keep ignoring the fact that she's bawling her eyes out?" Gemma asks as she plucks a piece of gluten-free bread out of a basket.

I glance at the women sitting around the table—an assortment of aunts, cousins, sisters, and grandmothers. Only Nonna and Belinda's mother seem to notice her distress. They trade an apprehensive look with each other before plastering on insincere smiles.

"We're not ignoring it. We're pretending those are tears of happiness," I say to my sister.

The table can comfortably seat twenty, but we have a big family and a few distant cousins who absolutely refused to be left out, so there's twenty-six of us squished side by side.

I'm sandwiched between Gemma on my right and Mamma on my left. Mamma is giving Belinda her best stink-eye. If that wasn't enough to communicate her disapproval, the clench in her jaw ought to do it. I know exactly what she's thinking—it's above Garzolo women to be this emotional.

Mamma hates crying, whining, and complaining, and as her eldest daughter, I've had plenty of tutelage on how to avoid doing any of those at all costs.

A skill that's been tested frequently since I got married two months ago.

The thing is, poor eighteen-year-old Belinda hasn't had the same training, and her reaction to her situation is understandable. Next month, she's set to marry one of Papà's most senior capos, who happens to be *three times* her age. Papà arranged it, and as I've learned, he isn't in the business of brokering happy marriages.

"This is so awkward," Gemma says. "I'd rather be at a funeral."

Mamma overhears—how can she not when she's sitting close enough for her elbow to brush mine every time she reaches for her water glass—and sticks her neck out to look at Gemma. The expression on her face isn't a full-fledged frown, but anyone who knows her knows that the tiny line between her botoxed brows means she's *pissed*. "Take Belinda to the bathroom, and don't come out until she's calmed down."

My sister's face pales. "*Me*? How am I supposed to calm her down?" She shoots me a pleading look. "Send Vale instead."

Mamma's gaze lands on me for a moment before she shakes her head. "Go, Gemma. Don't take too long." There's a subtle edge to her tone that tells us there's no point in arguing.

Gemma lets out a long sigh, rises out of her seat, and

smooths her hands over her knee-length linen skirt. "If I'm not back in ten, it means I need back up."

Her departure is like a flick of a switch. The uncomfortable tension that appeared between Mamma and I soon after my wedding day snaps into place. My spine straightens. Her jaw works.

"You don't think I'm capable of giving advice to Belinda on her upcoming marriage?" I ask. I should keep my mouth shut, but I can't. My heartbreak at her and Papà's betrayal is too fresh. How could they give me, their eldest daughter, to someone like Lazaro?

Mamma twirls her *spaghetti-al-limone* on her fork and raises it off her plate. "I know you're still adjusting."

A bitter smile twitches across my lips. "Is that what I'm doing?"

"I hope so. I prepared you for this."

She has to know that's a ludicrous statement. "Nothing you taught me remotely prepared me to deal with my current situation."

Her chews slow. She swallows her food and turns her face to me. "Have you forgotten our lessons?"

I tighten my hand around my fork. "Which ones? I don't believe any of them covered how to handle being forced to—"

"Let me remind you of one," she interrupts. "Garzolo women never complain about circumstances they can't change."

My lungs constrict. "Ah, of course. That's a classic."

"You're a married woman with a husband you must support in whichever way he requires. We already have one insolent child at this table, Valentina. We don't need another one."

It's ridiculous that after everything that's happened recently, receiving criticism from her still feels like a sharp sting.

"You can face any challenge this life throws at you," she continues. "That's how I raised you. Do not insult me with your weakness."

I draw my elbows in. I suddenly can't stand the thought of coming into contact with her. My appetite is gone. I move my food around my plate until Mamma exhales with frustration.

"Go check on your sister," she snaps.

I don't need to be told twice.

The bathroom is down the hall, and when I turn the corner, a slightly calmer-looking Belinda hurries past me. She gives me a watery smile.

"Where's Gemma?" I ask.

"She's fixing her makeup."

In the bathroom, Gemma's leaning over the counter to get closer to the mirror as she reapplies her lipstick.

"Good work," I say, stepping to her side and slapping my purse on the marble surface. "Belinda seems way better."

"I told her he won't be able to get it up at his age."

I sputter a surprised laugh. "How would you know that?"

"I don't. What else was I supposed to tell her? Not everyone can get as lucky as you and get themselves a handsome young enforcer for a husband. I'm sure Lazaro has no problems in that department."

A sour taste appears inside my mouth. If only she knew that Lazaro had little interest in fucking me. Besides doing his duty on the night of our wedding, he hasn't touched me in bed.

He gets off on something entirely different.

I school my features into a mask, but it's harder around Gemma. We're only two years apart, and we've always been close. She was the first person I told about my betrothal when Papà informed me I'd be marrying his best enforcer. I later found out from Mamma that I was Lazaro's reward for uncovering a big plot to overthrow Papà—one that ended with a capo and ten of his soldiers dead. Papà always made a point to reward loyalty in his men, but that approach didn't appear to extend to his daughters.

Gemma closes her lipstick tube and meets my gaze in the mirror. "Speaking of, how are things? We've barely talked since you two came by for brunch a few weeks ago."

I pretend I'm suddenly very interested in my own reflection. "I'm fine." My sister can never know the details of my marriage—the things Lazaro does and makes me do. It would shatter all her illusions about our parents and about me. "Why didn't Mamma bring Cleo?"

"Cleo's not allowed out of the house, so you'll have to come over if you want to see her," Gemma says as she adjusts a strand of her hair.

She looks perfect, as always. Her hair is a sleek hazel bob that frames her oval face, and today she's wearing the diamond earrings I'd gifted to her for her nineteenth birthday a few months ago. She has lush lashes, stunning gray eyes, and a body toned to perfection with the help of her five private Pilates classes a week. Unlike her, I've never been into fitness, so the few extra pounds I carry in my ass and hips are here to stay.

"What did our little sister do now?" I ask.

"She ran away from her guard while they were at the mall, and when he found her fifteen minutes later, she was at a tattoo parlor. The tattoo artist had just finished stenciling the words *We did it* on her back."

Did what? She couldn't be possibly referring to... "Freed Britney?"

Gemma rolls her eyes. "Her idol. Papà told Mamma they never should have allowed Cleo to go to all those rallies. He thinks she's brainwashed, and now Mamma is set on putting her through a reeducation, whatever the heck that means. In the mornings, they spend hours in the kitchen. Mamma's teaching her how to cook traditional Italian dishes. And in the afternoons, there's a constant stream of tutors in and out of the house. I think she's making her sit through etiquette classes. Cleo's been complaining nonstop."

It's so ridiculous, and I can't help but laugh. My youngest sister has always been the most rebellious out of the three of us. It used to worry me. Now, I hope she won't let Mamma dim that spark. "I give it a week, at most, before the prison sentence is over. Mamma has always had a soft spot for Cleo."

"I don't know," Gemma says, turning to me. Her expression slides into a frown. "Something's going on with Papà. He's upped the security detail for all of us. At first, I thought it was because of what Cleo did, but that doesn't explain why he added more men to his detail as well. He seems...off."

"Have you asked Mamma about it?"

"She won't tell me anything. Says I should stay focused on the party next month." Her shoulders slump. "They want to give me to one of the Messeros, Vale. I swear, they've invited that entire clan so that they can parade me around like I'm some piece of meat."

The Messeros run upstate New York. As far as I know, we've always managed to co-exist with them without much trouble. They deal in racketeering and construction, while Papà's primary business is in cocaine—not a ton of overlap. If Papà wants to give Gemma to one of them, it means he wants to forge an alliance. What for?

"You know their reputation," Gemma says. "The men of that family act like it's still the Stone Age. I wouldn't be able to leave the house without an escort, even as a married woman. I'm sure Papà wants to give me to the don's son, Rafaele. He's pretty, but his reputation is as black as it gets. Apparently, he became a made man at thirteen. *Thirteen.*"

The Messeros are famous for their brutal initiation ceremonies. They require aspiring members to kill for their capo. It's how they ensure their members won't hesitate to do what needs to be done when someone doesn't pay their protection fees.

Anger flares inside my chest. Papà wants to do to Gemma exactly what he did to me—marry her off to a killer. I don't know how I'll be able to stand aside and watch it happen.

Mamma's voice sounds inside my head. *You may not understand your father's ways, but everything he does is to protect our family.*

Every day I repeat that sentence like a prayer, and every day its power wanes.

What happens when I stop believing it entirely? It goes against everything I've been taught, but I constantly daydream about running away from Lazaro. It would be a real scandal. The end of my life as I know it. I'd be caught and handed to my husband for punishment, and he'd enjoy making me scream.

A barbed wire squeezes around my heart at the thought of what my husband would do in retaliation. If it was only my life at risk, it would be one thing, but he's made it clear that others would pay for any hint of disobedience I display.

"I'll talk to Mamma about the Messeros," I say.

Gemma waves me off. "Don't bother. You know she won't listen. Just come to the party, please. I really need you there."

I nod. "We should head back. They'll wonder where we are."

When we reappear in the dining room, our cousin Tito is there. There's no way he was invited to the shower. It's girls only. He's hovering behind where Nonna's sitting, eyeing the giant spread of mortadella on the table, but when he sees me, he seems to forget about it.

"I came looking for you," he says.

"Is everything okay?"

"Lazaro called. He asked me to take you home." Tito jingles his car keys in his pocket.

Alarm bells ring inside my head. "What happened?"

"He just said he needs you home."

The face of the large clock hanging on the wall reads five pm. It's early. Too early for Lazaro's games. The things he does—the things he makes me do—they belong in the dark. But what else could he want me for?

I float through the room, patting my aunts on their arms and kissing their cheeks. After a quick goodbye to Belinda and a hug to Gemma, I make my way to the exit. I can feel my mother's gaze on my back. She's upset I didn't say goodbye to her, but I can't handle her right now.

Humid May air wraps around my shoulders like a blanket as soon as Tito and I step through the back door. The puddles on the ground tell me it must have just stopped raining. His car, a bulletproof G-Wagon, is parked only a few steps away. He helps me into the backseat before slamming the door shut and sliding in the front. "We haven't seen you in a while."

I like Tito. We've always gotten along. Unlike most of my male relatives, he doesn't talk to me like I'm some brainless Barbie. "I'm adjusting to married life," I say.

Tito huffs. "Tell Lazaro he needs to let you out more often. Just because he doesn't know how to have any fun, doesn't mean you can't have any either."

Despite Tito's assumptions, it isn't Lazaro keeping me from family functions. I'm the one who's been declining invitations whenever I can. I simply don't have the energy to pretend like everything is fine. Most days I can hardly get out of bed. Today, I came because Mamma told me it wasn't optional.

Lazaro wouldn't care if I was out of the house for most of the day. He's frigid and emotionless. The only time I've seen him affected in any way is when—

No. Don't think about it.

I change the topic. "How have you been, Tito?"

His long fingers tap against the wheel. "Exhausted. There's a lot of work."

"I thought you were a bunch of workaholics," I tease, shooting him a tired smile in the rearview window.

He eyes me for a moment, and then his shoulders relax by a minuscule amount. "Yeah, sure we are. You know what I say, Vale. I'll sleep when I'm dead. But it's one thing to kill myself for the family, and a whole other thing to do some assholes' bidding." He stuffs a cigarette in his mouth and grabs his lighter off the dashboard. "I'm no one's lapdog." The words come out muffled as he lights his smoke. "And I'm not about to bury my nose in anyone's shit."

I try to unpack that statement. "Papà's having you working for someone else?"

Tito rolls down the window and blows out a cloud of smoke. "Me, my father, Lazaro, even Vince. We're chasing down shit that doesn't make any sense. I think it's all a fucking distraction, but no one listens to me."

At the mention of my older brother, my ears perk up. Vince is in Switzerland, working at one of the banks and managing a large chunk of the clan's capital. If he's involved, it means something major is afoot. Some kind of a business deal?

"Who's the other party?" I ask.

Tito puffs on his cig and shakes his head. "Don't worry yourself about it. Have you seen that new movie on Netflix about aliens? It's a real mindfuck."

We chat about TV for the rest of the ride, and I try to mask the suffocating dread I feel the closer we get to Lazaro's house. I refuse to call it my home. I've never felt at home there. For me, it's a prison with no way out.

We pass through the gate and pull into the long driveway. Tito kisses me goodbye on the cheek. "Take care of yourself, Vale. And let me know if you find anything good to watch."

I promise him I will and pass through the front door.

My husband stands in the kitchen, looking down at his iPad, his back turned to me. He's in a steel-blue button-up shirt, a pair of black slacks, and a leather belt, his usual business attire. My muscles soften with relief. Lazaro always changes into something more comfortable before we begin. Maybe nothing will happen tonight.

"Welcome home," he says, his gaze not leaving the screen. "How was the bridal shower?"

He doesn't really give a shit, but he likes to go through the motions. I don't know why. It's not like there's anyone here he needs to convince we have a normal marriage.

"Fine." I move to the sink and grab an empty glass to fill with water. "Tito said you needed me back here." There's a small leather backpack on the counter by the sink. That's not mine. Did Lorna, our housekeeper, leave it there?

Lazaro lifts his gaze to me and watches as I drink. When I finish, he smiles softly and hands me the iPad. Cold dread curls inside my gut. I know that look. It can only mean one thing.

"I have something special for you," he says in a low voice, bringing his hand to my face. His fingers trace my cheek. "Take a look."

I swallow and look down.

On the screen is the camera feed to our basement.

And curled up in fetal position on the cold concrete floor is a woman.

CHAPTER 2

VALENTINA

MY SURROUNDINGS DIM. There's a film of cold sweat on my palms. Beneath my skin, a million little worms start to buck and crawl.

Whenever Lazaro brings a new victim, it always starts like this. Adrenaline surges through my veins and makes me want to vomit. Sometimes, I wish my brain and body would just switch off.

I call them victims even though most of them are bad men. They're thieves and criminals and killers with resumes as varied as a box of crayons. But they all die the same way.

At my hand.

"Who is she?" I ask.

My husband's lips rise at the corners as he stares at the woman on the screen. "A little Casalese mouse. We might get to keep her for a while."

I frown. What does that mean? And that strange nickname... He never calls the people he brings here any special names.

He extends his hand. "Let's go meet her."

He must feel how sweaty my palm is in his cool and dry one, but he doesn't say anything about it. I've never figured out if he's only pretending not to notice my discomfort, or if it genuinely doesn't register with him. I've cried, I've screamed, I've begged—nothing. His soft smile never leaves his face as he gives me my commands. It doesn't budge even when he tells me what he'll do to me and Lorna if I don't obey.

The skirt of my long flower-patterned dress rustles around me as Lazaro and I descend into the basement. The soles of my expensive flats are thin. I can feel the biting cold of the concrete through them. The woman on the floor must be freezing.

She comes into sight, and my heart pounds out an erratic beat. Her face isn't visible beneath a veil of long blond hair. She's wearing a pair of jeans and a button-up blouse that's ripped in a few places.

Where did they catch her and how? Was Lazaro the one who got her?

Sometimes his victims are brought to us, and other times he plays the role of both hunter and executioner. It's the latter role that he's famous for among the criminal circles. The men of the New York underworld know that if they get on Stefano Garzolo's bad side, he only needs to say the word, and my husband will come for them. And that's enough to keep most of them in line.

The woman stirs. There's a small movement, followed by a pained moan. She's not bleeding anywhere as far as I can see, but she must have been sedated.

Lazaro moves with purpose. He grabs her wrists and pulls her hands over her head. She begins to struggle sluggishly, but its fruitless. Lazaro is strong. It doesn't take him more than thirty seconds to tie her wrists together with a thick rope. When he's finished, he lifts her by her waist and links the rope on a metal hook hanging from the ceiling. The woman sways, suspended by her arms. At last, her hair falls away from her face, and I see her narrowed hazel eyes.

I press my palm over my mouth. My God, she's just a girl. No more than eighteen. Around Cleo's age. A current of nausea slams into my gut and tosses it from side to side.

She starts to pant, but she's still pretty out of it. Her head lolls from side to side.

"Why is she here?" I ask quietly. There has to be an explanation. Everything Papà does is to keep our family safe, so she must be a threat.

Lazaro shrugs. "It's just a job."

"A job?"

"Someone wants her. She happened to be in our territory. A favor was called, so we took her, and now me and you get to play with her for a bit. Someone's picking her up tomorrow evening."

My breathing turns uneven. Picking her up dead or alive? Either way, "play" is Lazaro's code word for torture. Is this somehow connected to what Tito was telling me earlier? "But what did she do?"

"Nothing. She was born with the wrong last name."

There is no gravity to his words. No indication he realizes the horror of what he just uttered. My husband doesn't care about why someone ends up in his basement, but I do. I need reasons—excuses—for what we do to these people. I use the crumbs he gives me to justify my actions.

He was a rapist, and now he's getting what he deserves.

He stole money from the clan, and he could have killed Tito if the shot had landed where he'd intended it to.

He cut the cocaine with enough levamisole to give the buyers seizures.

But this reason is so flimsy it can't even be used by someone as practiced in mental gymnastics as me.

Suddenly, a scream pierces the air. The sedative must have worn off. The girl starts bucking so hard I'm afraid she'll dislocate her shoulders. A vein in Lazaro's neck ticks. He's not worried anyone will hear her. The basement is sound-proofed, and the neighbors know better than to stick their nose in his business. But Lazaro hates when they scream for no reason.

"Quiet now," he says, pulling out a syringe.

The girl's screams turn into whimpers. "No, please. Please don't stick me with that," she says in a subtle Italian accent.

My husband smiles at her the way he would at a delivery boy. All friendly and good humored. "Are you done? If you promise to be quiet, I'll put the needle away."

The girl's eyes flit from the syringe to my husband to me. She holds my gaze for a second, confusion flickering across her expression. I don't look like a killer, especially when I'm dressed for a bridal shower. She's probably wondering what the hell I'm doing here.

"I won't scream," she says in a shaking, pleading voice. Her chest rises and falls with her rapid, shallow breaths, and once again, I'm struck by how young she is. Not a single wrinkle on her face, not a hint of a gray hair.

This girl doesn't seem like the type to hurt anyone.

I shut my eyes as horror swells inside my belly.

"Please, this is a mistake," she says, trying to keep her voice calm. "I don't know who you think I am, but I'm just a tourist. I'm in New York for two weeks with my friend." Her lips wobble. "Is Imogen..."

Lazaro sticks his hands into the pockets of his slacks and leans back against the wall. "Your friend is dead."

The girl's features contort.

Lazaro's smile grows, and he shakes his head, as if he's in on some secret joke. "Trust me, out of the two of you, your friend's the lucky one."

It takes her a second to process his meaning, but when she does, silent tears stream down her cheeks. "I don't understand," she babbles. "Why is this happening?"

"It's not your fault," he says calmly. "Don't blame yourself. There really was nothing you could have done."

It's like he's trying to mess with her. This is part of the punishment, I realize. Whoever asked Papà to capture this girl wanted her to suffer.

My husband turns to me. "I'm going to go change. You two can use the time to get to know each other."

The girl and I both watch him leave up the stairs, and then it's just us. The back of my throat starts to ache. I know what's coming. She'll beg. They all do.

"Please, you have to help me," she croaks out. "He's wrong. He's got the wrong girl."

I take a step toward her. She flinches away, obviously not knowing what to expect from me. She's got a dusting of freckles across her button nose and plump cheeks.

"He's never wrong," I say. My mouth is so dry that my tongue feels like sandpaper.

She must be thirsty too.

"Do you want some water?" I ask.

She nods.

I grab a bottle of water from the mini fridge and bring it to her. She gulps the water down while I do my best to pour it into her mouth. Up close, I can smell her. Lemon-verbena, mint, and dust. She even smells like innocence. This girl is not a threat. She doesn't deserve to feel excruciating pain.

I look away as a shudder cascades through me. Images flash inside my head like an old slide show. Lazaro's bliss-filled eyes when they take their last breaths. The way his pants tent at the crotch. The proud look he gives me while I'm shaking on the floor with blood all over my hands.

"Please help me," she begs.

There's a dull pain in my throat. "I don't have a choice."

I wish I did. I wish I could stop being so afraid.

"There's always a choice. You can choose to help me." Another tear spills down her right cheek and drips off her chin onto her shirt. "I can see you're a good person."

My teeth dig into my bottom lip. A good person? If I was one, I'd find a way to be brave.

Lazaro told me what he'd do if I stop.

He'll kill Lorna, and he'll torture me.

He knows me well enough to know my desire to protect our innocent housekeeper would keep me in line.

But this girl is innocent too.

She holds my gaze, her young eyes shining with desperate determination that feels all too familiar... Cleo. She reminds me of my little sister.

She might be someone's sister too. A daughter. Maybe a mother one day.

How can I take that away from her?

And that's when the realization slams into me.

I can't.

If there's even a small chance I can get her out of this, I have to take it.

My lungs expand with a deep breath. It's the first one I've taken in weeks.

"You don't want to hurt me," the girl says in a hushed voice.

No, I don't. I think I've always known it would come to this one day. I held on for as long as I could, but I can't do it anymore.

I'm going to get her out of here.

Which means I need a plan, and I need it *fast*.

My surroundings come into sharper focus as I come to terms with what I'll have to do.

Lazaro must be neutralized.

I prowl to the drawers along the wall and start flinging them open one by one.

"What are you doing?" the girl asks.

"Helping you. Be quiet." I find a knife and tuck it into the back of my skirt. It's not hard to find weapons down here, but it would be nice if there was a...

Gun. I pick it up from the bottom of a drawer and check to see if it's loaded. I've been to the shooting range three times. Papà thinks it is a basic skill everyone in the family should know, even the girls. I thought it was progressive of him, but that was before he married me to a sadistic killer.

"What are you going to do with that?" the girl asks.

"Shoot him."

She swallows. "And then? How do we get out of here?"

That's a great question. If we can get past Lazaro, she can escape out the back entrance. It's never guarded when Lazaro is around. No one is crazy enough to try to attack Garzolo's main executioner in the comfort of his home. If she runs across the backyard, she can cross through the narrow wooded area and end up outside the neighborhood, on the side of the road.

And then what? No, she needs a car. But Michael, the guard at the entrance of the neighborhood, is on Lazaro's payroll, and he'll sound an alert if he sees some unknown woman driving one of our vehicles.

He won't if it's me who's driving. I can say I'm going to the grocery store to pick up something for dinner. That will buy us an hour at least. Is that enough time for me to get the girl to safety?

I swap the knife tucked into my skirt with the gun and rush over to start cutting the rope binding her hands. She's breathing hard, but there's a spark in her eyes now.

"Do you have anyone in New York who can help you?" I ask.

"No. My friend was the only one who came with me, but if I get my phone back, I can call someone."

"They're going to be after us quickly," I tell her. "You need to be far away before they realize you're gone."

My thoughts race. I'll put her in the trunk and get as far away as possible, but she needs to flee somewhere farther than where a car can take her.

"I need to get to the airport," she says, as if sensing my thoughts. "I need to get home to—"

"Don't tell me," I interrupt. If I'm caught, it's better I don't know where she went. "Do you have your passport?"

"It was in my backpack," she says. "But I don't have that anymore."

The backpack on the counter must be hers. "I know where it is." I finish cutting through the rope, and the girl staggers into me.

"You'll be okay," I mutter, even though I have no idea if that's true. "I'm going to knock him out when he returns, and then you need to follow me upstairs. We'll grab your things and take the car out. You'll get in the trunk. I'll drive directly to the airport. From the moment I drop you off, you're on your own."

Relief and anxiety dance across her face. "Okay."

The gun's cold, but it burns through the clothes on my back. I take it into my hand and motion for her to move behind me.

The minutes that we wait for Lazaro to return are agonizing. My guts move so loudly I'm afraid he'll hear them as soon as he opens the door to the basement. But I also know that my husband will never expect this from me. In his eyes, I'm powerless. Hardly a threat. I can use that to my advantage.

Finally, the door opens with a muffled creak. We're standing out of sight, so when he gets to the bottom of the stairs, it's his back I'm looking at. There's no time for hesitation. I can't allow him to process the fact that the girl is no longer tied up. My finger presses against the trigger, and just as he whirls around, I shoot.

CHAPTER 3

VALENTINA

THE GUN RECOILS. Lazaro falls. The sound of the shot vibrates my eardrums. The moment expands, absorbing more and more observations until it finally bursts, and I jump into motion.

"Let's go," I say, grabbing the girl by her wrist.

"Is he dead?" she asks as I drag her up the stairs.

"I don't know." There's no time to check where I hit him, all I know is he's down and not moving. The thought I may have killed him barely registers. I doubt it. I'm not that lucky.

I run so fast up the stairs I nearly trip. Somehow, I have enough sense left in me to lock the door to the basement once we're out. We round the corner and burst into the kitchen.

"Here." I throw the backpack to the girl.

She rummages through it and makes a frustrated sound. "My passport is here but my phone and wallet are gone."

How is she going to pay for her flight? We need cash. If I give her my credit card, Papà will easily be able to track her down.

"Come with me," I tell her as I start toward Lazaro's office on the second floor. He has a safe filled with money, weapons, and other valuables. My flats skid to a stop on the polished hardwood floor as we reach the safe. It's a mighty thing, nearly as big as a fridge.

"You know the code?" the girl asks.

I don't bother answering her as I key in the passcode. Like time, words feel precious. Every sound we make is a risk, a chance for someone to hear us. The house is empty at this hour, Lorna left in the early afternoon, but I'm paranoid. I look over my shoulder as I pull open the safe's heavy door. Half of me expects to see a bleeding Lazaro right behind us with a knife in his hand, but he's not there.

I reach in and grab a stack of cash, and then after a moment, I take my passport too. I have no idea what I'm going to do once I drop her off, but returning here isn't an option, and I won't get far without any documents.

Everything is quiet as we make our way to the garage, but my hands shake as I press the button to open the trunk.

"Get in," I tell the girl.

I temper the urge to speed through the neighborhood. That might tip Michael off that something's wrong. When I pull up outside his booth, I plaster on my most relaxed smile, even though I'm hyper aware of the drops of sweat collecting along my hairline. Michael steps out and motions for me to lower the window. We've always been cordial, but no more than that. I hope he's not in the mood for conversation.

"Heading out?" he asks, dragging his gaze over the inside of the car. He's just doing his job. There's nothing here that should arouse his suspicion.

"Yep. Need to grab a few things for dinner at the store," I say.

His eyes narrow. "What's that in your bag?" he asks, pointing to where my purse is lying on the seat beside me.

My heart jumps up into my throat. For a split second, I think the passport slipped out, and he's wondering why I need it to go to the store. Instead, when I look down, it's the knife that I stuffed in there that has fallen out.

I let out an embarrassed laugh. "Oh, that must be Lazaro's. He always forgets his things in the car."

Michael sniffs. "Might want to put that away in the glove compartment while you're out."

"You're absolutely right."

He stares at me while he waits for me to do it. Crap, I stashed the gun there. I open the compartment just an inch and slide the knife in as quickly as I can.

He sniffs again and then steps away from the car. "I'll open the gate."

I hold my breath until I turn a corner and he disappears out of sight. We're out. We actually made it out.

There's a very short-lived moment of relief until I realize I have another dilemma. I don't know how to get to the closest airport, Newark, without the GPS, which means I need to keep my phone on, but that means Papà's men will be able to track me once they know I'm gone. Shit.

I pull up the maps app, quickly type in our destination, and scan over the route. It's not too bad. As soon as we get close to the airport, there'll be signs everywhere. With one final look, I pry open the SIM card compartment and toss the chip out the window. Then I turn off my phone.

My thoughts race as I get onto the highway. I have a short window of time to decide what the hell I should do. Michael will sound the alarm as soon as he realizes I've been gone too long. It will be only a matter of time before Papà's men have me trapped.

If Lazaro is alive, they'll hand me right back to him. If he's dead, Papà will be the one in charge of my punishment. I squeeze my hands tighter around the wheel. He won't treat me kindly for interfering in his business, freeing one of his prisoners, and killing one of his best men. Papà hates traitors. He won't show me any mercy.

Three loud thuds drift over from the back of the car.

I take the next exit and pull into the parking lot of an abandoned Target. This stop is time we can't waste, but I'm worried she's suffocating in there. I pop open the trunk and help her get out.

"I was going to puke if I stayed in there for a minute longer," she says as she swings her legs over the edge.

"We need to keep driving," I tell her. "We're still about ten minutes from the airport." I take my phone out and jog to a nearby garbage can. There's no way I can keep the device. Even without the SIM card, I'm sure they'll be able to track me as soon as I turn it back on. I'm about to run back to the car when my gaze catches on my wedding ring. After a moment, I slip it off my finger and throw it away too.

The girl takes the seat beside me and we get back on the road. "What are we going to do when we get there?" she asks.

"You're going to buy a seat on the first flight out," I say. "You need to be on a plane as soon as possible."

In my periphery, I see her nod. I can't imagine what she's feeling and thinking. How much of this will she remember when the adrenaline wears off? She's holding it together, but just barely.

Not like I'm doing much better, to be honest.

We drive in silence for a few minutes, but I can feel her pensive gaze on me. "Why did you decide to help me?" she asks.

Despite the many reasons that immediately pop into my head, I struggle giving her an answer.

Because you're innocent.

Because you remind me of my little sister.

Because if I hurt someone one more time, I might kill myself right after.

And I want to live, even if I don't deserve to. For some reason, I'm not ready to say goodbye to this ugly world.

"Because I can," I say finally.

There are signs for Newark Airport now. "Drop me off at the international terminal," the girl says.

It's a good idea to leave the country. Papà's influence goes far, but he's not omnipotent.

"The cash is in my purse," I say. "Take whatever you need."

She grabs the bag from where it's wedged between her feet and pulls out the wad of cash. Then she counts it. "I'll take four grand. That'll be enough to get me home." She continues to count. "That leaves you with six."

Six grand, a knife, a gun, and the clothes on my back. That's all I have left to my name.

"What are you going to do?" the girl asks.

Run.

Run and hope they don't find me.

My sisters won't understand why I left because they don't know anything about Lazaro's sadistic games. My parents won't ever tell them, but maybe this will be their wake-up call to not do to Gemma and Cleo what they've done to me. I wonder how they'll explain my disappearance. Cleo will be skeptical no matter what they say, but Gemma might believe them. She's loyal. Committed. Just like I used to be. Before my wedding, Mamma told me she was pleased with how well I absorbed all of her lessons.

Sorry, Mamma. I'm about to become your biggest disappointment. I couldn't handle the life you wanted for me. No one's going to call me a perfect wife after this.

"Did you hear me?"

I glance over at my companion. She's gnawing on her nails. She looks so scared. It makes an ache appear in my chest.

Is she going to make it on her own? What if I shot my husband only for her to get taken by someone else? I have no idea what her story is, or why Lazaro was ordered to take her. What if he wasn't the only one after her?

"I don't know what I'm going to do," I say.

A tangled strand of hair falls into her face. "Will you come with me to buy my ticket?" Her voice shakes. "I don't want to look suspicious to the airline workers. You can say you're my sister and that you're buying me a last-minute trip."

I don't want to know where she's going, but she has a point. She looks young and she's travelling with no luggage. What if they think she's in trouble and don't allow her to board?

"Okay, I'll go with you. As soon as you get past security, buy yourself a change of clothes and wear a hat. Don't talk to anyone unless you have to."

"Do you think they're following us?"

"If they're not already, they will be."

The international terminal is right here. I pull to a stop in a no-parking zone, and we get out.

"Won't they tow your car?" she asks.

"We'll be quick." Let them tow it. I'm not coming back to it. Once we get the girl's ticket, I'll buy my own to somewhere far from here.

We stop by the departures screen, and she points to a flight to Barcelona. "That one. I'll be able to get picked up from there."

It's leaving in an hour.

"Let's go," I say and lead her to the ticket counter.

For all our worrying, the agent doesn't bat an eye as she issues the girl her ticket.

Clutching her passport in her hand, she turns to me. Her hazel eyes meet mine.

There's one last thing left for me to say. "Don't ever come back to New York. Ever."

She sucks in a ragged breath. "This city can go to hell."

Her pink-soled Converse shoes slap against the floor as she jogs to the security line.

I wait until she's out of sight and then walk over to a different agent.

When I tell him I'll take any flight leaving in the next hour besides the one to Barcelona, he shakes his head. "Every other flight we have leaving in the next hour is full," he tells me. "You can try going to a different airline to check what they have. Terminal two."

I grind my teeth. There's no time to run around the airport. Papà might already be figuring out what happened. "But there's availability on the flight to Barcelona?"

"We have one seat left in business class," he confirms.

Converse girl managed to get the last economy seat. I've started calling her that in my head, because it feels strange to have lived through the most intense hour of my life with someone who's name I don't even know. She's Converse girl from now on.

"How much is it?"

"It's three thousand five hundred and two dollars."

My eyes bulge. Jesus, it's expensive, but that's what I get for buying a ticket minutes before the flight boards. I don't want to go where she's going, but I don't really have a better choice. I hand him the money.

The two and a half grand I have left in my purse feel like nothing, especially since I don't know what I'm going to do once I get to Europe. How long is that going to last me? I have no idea how to find a job. The only "job" I've ever had was helping Mamma organize charity events, and I didn't have to interview for that. What skills do I have? I don't think keeping secrets, cooking a mean lasagna, and looking pretty screams "hire me".

The agent's voice saves me from descending into a total meltdown.

"Here's your boarding pass." He hands me a slip of paper. "You should hurry to the gate."

I bolt through the airport, pass through security, and duck into a store to get myself a hoodie and a hat. My dress is too recognizable, and I don't want Converse girl to see me and think that I'm tailing her.

At the gate, I spot her sitting in one of the seats, so I make sure I'm not in her line of sight. It's all families and excited tourists mulling around, but every time I see a single male, my heart skips a beat. Is he reaching into his jacket for his phone? Who's he calling? Did he just look at me for a second too long?

The paranoia is brutal. I force myself to take deep breaths. There's no way Papà could've tracked me down this quickly. Even if I only inflicted a flesh wound on Lazaro and he got up as soon as we left the house, he'd need some time to track me down. He can't know where I went.

Unless they tracked the car.

Oh God. I'm so stupid. *Of course*, they'd track the car's GPS signal. If Lazaro can see I dropped the vehicle off at the airport, that means he knows I'm here. He's probably on his way now. He might be at the terminal already.

By the time they start boarding, I'm barely holding it together.

I stay back until the very last group and move through the boarding procedure in a daze. My body is firmly stuck in fight-or-flight mode, but I'm forced to wait in one line and then the next. I'm jittery and sweaty. If anyone asks, I'll tell them I have flight anxiety.

When I get on the plane, I see Converse girl in one of the far rows in economy. She's got a hat pulled low over her face, and she's not even trying to look at anyone. Good. I slide into my window seat in row five and turn my face to the window. I'll be off the plane before her, so as long as I stay in the business section during the flight, there's no chance she'll see me.

When the door to the plane shuts and we start to move, a moan of relief moves past my lips. With it go the remnants of my energy. I thought I'd be on pins and needles the entire flight, but my body shuts down, and I plunge into sleep.

CHAPTER 4

VALENTINA

Turbulence wakes me some time later. Outside my window, the sky is painted with magenta and orange strokes, and fluffy white clouds stretch below us, as far as the eye can see. The screen on the back of the seat in front of me says we're forty minutes from landing in Barcelona.

I didn't dream, but now that I'm back in the land of the living, images explode inside my head. Converse girl curled in a fetal position on the hard basement floor. My palm squeezed around the cold gun. Lazaro collapsed on the ground, thick blood seeping from beneath him.

Maybe I did manage to kill him.

This thought calms me. The calm reaches inside of me and takes up residence inside my body for the first time in months.

Each morning I woke up beside Lazaro marked the beginning of another endless day. I'd eat my breakfast, choke on my lunch, and have a panic attack or two in the hours leading up to Lazaro's return.

I never knew if he'd bring someone with him that day or not. He didn't operate on a regular schedule, because the business of the clan doesn't have one either. It's all chaos, governed by blood and white powder, and just when you think you've learned the rules, they change.

There were ten of them. An average of one per week since the day after our wedding. I don't know most of their names, but I'll remember their faces forever.

I stretch my cold, aching feet and rub my palms along my arms to get some blood flowing to my extremities. I resist the urge to get up to use the bathroom and peek at Converse girl. She's fine. She said she can get picked up from the airport, which means she must have friends or family in Spain. Was her accent Spanish or Italian? Now that I think about it, it might have been either. If she knows I'm on her plane, she'll only get freaked out.

The light flicks on, and the captain announces we're about to begin our descent. As the plane fills with sounds of seatbelts being fastened and sleepy conversations, the clouds part to reveal land and the unmistakable glitter of the sea.

When I step off the plane onto the jet bridge, I'm hit with an oppressive wave of heat. The signs are written in English and Spanish, and I follow them to customs. I just want to get out of the restricted zone so that I can figure out my next move.

I've been to Spain once for a wedding in Seville. Carolyn, someone I knew from high school. The only reason Papà allowed me to go was because her father was a senator. It was four days of drinking, eating tapas, and lounging in beautiful palaces built for old kings.

My brother, Vince, was my chaperone, but he didn't stick around much after another female guest caught his eye. I wasn't about to do anything stupid, anyway, not when I was already engaged to Lazaro. I was nervous about marrying him, but it's not like I could have said no to Papà when he told me Lazaro was to be my husband. As soon as the words had left his mouth, it was assumed to be a done deal. Any hint of disagreement would have been met with harsh discipline.

The customs agent stamps my passport and hands it back to me. "Welcome to Spain," he says and waves me through.

The Barcelona airport is huge and sprawling. I exchange my dollars to euros, get myself a pastry and an espresso, and sit down at a small table in the cafe.

I need to keep moving so that I'm harder to track down, but where should I go? I don't have a phone anymore, so I can't even research anything online.

There are two giant screens above me that rotate through what appears to be an endless list of flights. I scan them over as I chew, and just as I manage to get through the entire list once, a group of young British men sit down at the table beside me.

"I can't wait to see Solomun," one of them says excitedly. "He'll be playing tomorrow night at Revolvr, and everyone says it's the wildest party."

His friend nudges his shoulder. "Did you forget? We already promised Addie we'd see her at Amnesia. She's working there for the summer as a server."

This elicits a chorus of hoots from his companions. "Are you still trying to get with that chick?" one of them exclaims. "Forget it, mate. She's in fucking Ibiza, she's not thinking about you."

I take a sip of my espresso and glance back to the board.

There's a flight to Ibiza in an hour and a half.

The only thing I know about Ibiza is what everyone else does. It's an island known for hardcore partying. Like the European version of Vegas, I suppose. A place where people constantly come and go. A place it might be easy for a girl to get lost in...

I drum my fingertips against the edge of the table. What have I got to lose? It's not like I have any better ideas for where to go.

Twenty minutes later, I'm at the gate.

The rest of my journey is a blur. After I disembark the plane in Ibiza, my mind registers a series of snapshots—the row of taxis at the terminal, the billboards advertising DJs along the road, the palm trees that line the sidewalks.

The driver takes me to Sant Antoni de Portmani—a town he says is far cheaper than downtown Ibiza. I'm so tired that when I finally get out of the car, I don't think twice about walking into the first hostel I find.

The tiny lobby smells like incense and wood. Photos of the island cover most of the walls, and there are shelves everywhere with candles and travel books for sale. A jug of water sits on a tiny table with a few stacked cups by its side.

Whenever I'd travel with my family, we'd always stay in five-star hotels. Shiny marble floors, high ceilings, concierges in crisply pressed uniforms, and chocolates on our pillows. I remember getting picky about the stupidest things—the thread count on the sheets and the firmness of the mattress.

Now, I'm so exhausted, I'd be fine sleeping on a wooden palette.

I ask for a private room for two nights. That should be enough for me to figure out what's next.

The receptionist eyes me curiously while she types some stuff on her computer. I'm worried she'll ask me questions I can't answer, but besides asking to see my passport, she holds her tongue. What are the chances the tech geniuses Papà has on his payroll will be able to track me down in the hostel's system? It's a long shot, even for them.

"Here you go." She hands me my receipt and a key attached to a simple metal keychain. Engraved on it is the number five. "You're all the way at the end of the hall. Last door on the right."

"Thanks."

Inside, my room is simple but clean. I collapse on the bed and try to take a nap, but even though I'm deathly tired, sleep won't come. The anxiety of not knowing what I'm going to do here gnaws at me. My wallet is one hundred euros lighter after paying for my room, and I have no way to replenish my cash.

I sit back up and catch a whiff of myself. Jesus, I stink. I'm definitely not going to find a job if I look like I haven't showered in two days. Dragging myself into the bathroom, I freshen up the best I can and then head out to buy myself some toiletries and a few changes of clothes.

The town unfurls around me like a colorful tapestry. It's a

bit run down, but the shore and the azure-blue water more than make up for it.

I walk around for a bit, but as the afternoon creeps in, the dial on the sun turns way up. It's incredibly hot. The humidity makes my skin sticky, and the money I stuffed inside my bra because I didn't want to leave anything at the hostel is giving me an itch. I take most of it out and move it to my purse.

There's a small shopping area the receptionist recommended and marked with an X on my tourist map. She said I'd find whatever I needed there, so I make my way over.

I pick up three tops, a pair of shorts, a light dress, a pair of sneakers, some underwear, and a backpack to hold it all. After I pay for everything, I stop by the entrance of the store and do a quick count of the money left in my purse. One thousand eight hundred and thirty-four euros, plus the little bit left in my bra. It's fine. I'll make it work.

By now, my family must know that I'm gone. It's been nearly twenty-four hours. If Lazaro's dead, the maid must have found him. If he's alive, he would have told Papà what happened.

As I start walking back to the hostel, images of Lazaro splayed on the floor flash inside my mind. I don't feel an ounce of pity for him. I don't really feel anything at all.

A shiver runs through me. That's wrong, isn't it? I should have *some* feelings about the fact that I might have murdered my husband. What if something inside of me is permanently damaged? Is this my punishment? Being condemned to live the rest of my life numb? Unable to feel normal human emotions and incapable of empathy or love?

I helped Converse girl. That has to count for something. When I saw her there, so young and terrified, I couldn't do it. Yet that one act doesn't make up for the other people I harmed. Not even close. I could have chosen to help any one of them, and I didn't.

A body collides into me hard enough to push the air out of my lungs.

"What the hell?"

All I see is a whirl of black clothing and a flash of a male face.

"*Disculpe!*" he says, and then he's running away from me.

It takes me a grand total of three seconds to catch onto what just happened.

My purse is gone.

I break out into a sprint in my flimsy flats with my new backpack bouncing painfully against my lower back and shout after the thief, but the distance between us only grows.

He's faster than me.

Passersby stop and stare, some even try to grab the man, but none of them succeed. Eventually, I stop, my breath coming out in raged pants. My hands press against my thighs, and whatever bubble of hope I had left bursts.

My money is gone.

I feel sick.

When I get back to the hostel and tell the receptionist what happened, she's sympathetic.

"Do you want to file a police report?" she asks.

"Do you think it will help?"

She winces apologetically. "Honestly? No. In my five years of working here, I've seen about a dozen guests get robbed, and only one managed to get her purse back. Empty."

I sigh and lean against the counter. Of course, I can't go to the police. I can't show them my passport, which I still have because I moved it into my backpack. Why the hell didn't I do that with the cash?

I'm left with a few crumpled bills inside my bra. What will I do when it runs out?

Everything is going wrong.

I'm close to tears when the door that leads to the women's dorm room opens and two young women walk out. They're dressed in short shorts and graphic T-shirts. One of them, a tall pretty blonde with big blue eyes, gives me a pitying look.

"We overheard what happened," she says. "That's so shitty."

Her friend nods in agreement. "I got robbed last year in Barcelona. They got my ID, my phone, everything. It was the worst." She tucks a strand of dark, curly hair behind her ear. She's shorter than the blonde, and her green T-shirt says *You can be whatever you want.*

"I should have been more careful," I say. "I dropped my guard."

"How about we get you a drink?" the blonde asks. "We were just about to go to a bar down this street."

Alcohol. Yes, that sounds far better than the other thing I'm considering—jumping under the wheels of a truck.

I give them a tired smile. "Sure, that'll be nice."

They introduce themselves while we walk. The blonde is Astrid, and the brunette is Vilde.

"What's your name?" Vilde asks.

Crap. The receptionist knows my real name, so I can't give them something totally random in case they use it in front of her, but the less people know my real name the better. "It's Ale," I say. Good enough. In theory, it could be an unusual nickname for Valentina. "Where are you from?"

"Sweden." Astrid pulls open a door to what appears to be a bar. Above the door is a sign that reads *Caballo Blanco*. "What about you? Are you here on vacation?"

I really should have prepared my answers ahead of time instead of giving them off the cuff. "I'm from Canada. Just travelling around for a few months. What about you?"

"We're seasonal workers," Vilde says as we take our seats at a free table. "We just got hired last week."

"What kind of work do you do?" I ask after a server takes our order for a pitcher of sangria.

"I'm a dancer," Astrid says. "And Vilde is a bartender." A wide grin spreads across her face. "It's been a dream of ours for a while to spend a season working in Ibiza."

"It's work, but it's also a lot of fun," Vilde says.

My mood improves a tiny bit when the sangria arrives. I didn't drink much before getting married to Lazaro, but during our marriage, I worked my way up to a bottle of wine a day. I throw the entire glass back in two gulps and pray the alcohol kicks in quickly. I need something to take the edge off.

"Do you think I could get a job here?" I ask as Astrid refills my glass. "I'm not picky. That guy took most of my money, and if I don't figure out how to get more, I don't know what I'll do. I need to save up a bit before I can go anywhere else."

Astrid groans and shakes her head. "What a nightmare. Can't believe that asshole ruined your trip. But listen, there's always work for pretty girls in Ibiza."

My spine straightens. "You think so?

"The clubs hire a ton of people for high season, and it's just getting started."

"I can't dance, and the only drink I know how to make is a martini," I say.

"Please, you'll find a job." Astrid pats my shoulder. "One look at you, and the club managers are going to be eating out of your hand."

"She's right," Vilde says. "They go through people like crazy, because a lot of the workers party too much and just stop showing up. They're always hiring. Come to our club tonight. We work at Revolvr. We'd put in a good word, but since we're so new, it won't count for much. You should just try talking to one of the managers."

What do I have to lose? I don't have much to offer, but I'm willing to learn.

There's another problem though. "I don't know if I'm legally allowed to work here."

Astrid tsks. "You'll find a way around it."

"I had a friend from Argentina who worked here three summers in a row under the table," Vilde says. "It's not uncommon here."

Working illegally in Ibiza—wow, life sure does take sharp turns. But if I can get a job without documents, I'll be practically untraceable.

"It's worth a try," I say.

Astrid gives me an encouraging grin. "Get there around one," she says before laughing at my puzzled expression. "The party goes all night and all morning here."

Sounds like I'm about to become a creature of the night. It could be a good thing.

After all, in the dark there are more places to hide.

CHAPTER 5

VALENTINA

THERE ARE times in life when one becomes untethered. The things we take for granted are ripped away from us. Conditions we assume to be permanent reveal themselves to be as temporary as a beautiful sunset. The familiar disappears, and we are forced to confront the unknown.

When I open my eyes, I don't recognize anything around me. The walls are yellow, while I'm used to them being blue. The spring bed is lumpy and makes squeaking sounds every time I move. The bathroom smells like lemons.

"You're in Spain," I mumble quietly. "You got away."

It doesn't feel real. Maybe if I keep talking to myself, it will eventually click.

It's dark outside. The cheap clock hanging on the wall says it's twelve am, which means I need to start getting ready for Revolvr.

I shower and pull on the microscopic dress I bought after saying goodbye to Vilde and Astrid. They recommended I wear something showy to fit in. It has a deep V cut at the front, an even deeper one at the back, and the hem just barely covers my butt.

I've never worn anything like this in my entire life. I'm so uncomfortable in it, I can't help but constantly tug it in place as I wait for a cab. When the taxi arrives, I maneuver my body inside the car and somehow manage to avoid a nip slip.

The girls told me earlier that I should just ask one of the servers if a manager is around when I arrive. It's not much of a plan, especially since I don't know what I'm going to say even if I'm able to find someone to talk to. All I know is that I'm ready to beg for a job if I have to.

"We're here," the driver announces as we pull to a stop.

When he tells me the amount, I groan inwardly. I didn't trust myself to figure out the bus schedule in the middle of the night, but it looks like I'll have to on my way home.

I pay the driver and get out to look around. The beach is nearby. I can't see it, but I smell the salt in the air. There are a few apartment buildings, nothing too attention grabbing, except for a giant neon sign on top of a boxy structure that says Revolvr.

When I step inside the property, my jaw drops.

It's way bigger than what it looked like from the outside. I'm lost immediately. I pass by at least three bars before entering the main area where a DJ is playing bass-heavy dance music. It's a cavernous space with balconies, multiple levels, and a massive dance floor. You could fit thousands of people here, easy.

My head spins, and not just because of the strobe lights or the fast-paced Japanese cartoon playing on a big screen. They'll never find me here, I realize with relief. If I get a job at the club, no one will notice me working in these masses of gyrating bodies and blinking lights.

I approach a small bar tucked against one of the walls and try to catch the attention of a server. "Excuse me!"

He doesn't hear me. The music coming through the sound system is too loud.

I try again, and it feels uncomfortable. I've always been told to be soft spoken and demure, but I can't afford to be like that anymore. *Literally*. If I want to survive on my own, I need to step way outside my comfort zone.

The server finally notices me. "*Hola*," he says, eyeing me up and down. "*Dime*."

"I'm sorry, I'm looking for a manager. Is there one here tonight?"

His brows scrunch together. "A manager? I don't know, I just started my shift. Look, we're really busy."

I clear my throat. "Who's in charge tonight?"

The server purses his lips. "The boss is here, so he's in charge. You see that small balcony way up there?"

I turn to look in the direction he's pointing, and that's when I see *him*.

A lone man stands on a balcony high above the dance floor, flickering lights dancing over his form.

The hairs on the back of my neck stand straight.

The server's voice comes in muffled, as if someone placed a glass container over my head. "That's Señor De Rossi."

Even from this far away, he's intimidating. Tall, straight-backed, and impeccably dressed. He's wearing a meticulous three-piece suit that molds to his body as if it's made of putty. I've spent my life around men dressed in suits like that, and I know what they mean.

Power. Prestige. Brutality.

My eyes widen as his dark gaze slides my way.

Stop. You're projecting.

My paranoid mind is still seeing danger everywhere. He's a club owner, not a made man.

But he's looking at me as if I exist solely for his consumption. As if I'd been bought and paid for by him, and today's the day he takes possession.

I shake the feeling off.

I'm not here to be claimed.

"He's looking at you," the server says, sounding a little perplexed, as if this isn't a normal occurrence. "Do you know each other?"

"No," I say. "But I need to talk to him."

There's wry laughter behind me. "Good luck."

I turn back to ask the server what he means by that, but he's already gone, pouring someone else a drink. I could use some liquid courage, but I'm not in a position to afford a fifteen-euro cocktail.

When I look back at the balcony, De Rossi's attention is somewhere else. There's a bearded man with dark slicked-back hair standing beside him.

The newcomer has an impressive physique—brawny and muscular. He's got a walkie-talkie clipped to his belt like the bouncers, but he's not wearing a Revolvr branded T-shirt like the others I've seen mulling around. He pats De Rossi on the back in a familiar greeting and says something to the man. I get the feeling that the two of them are friends.

What if they leave somewhere together? I can't waste any time.

To the surprise of absolutely no one, I get stopped by a bouncer at the bottom of the stairs that lead to the balcony.

"Staff only," he says in a monotone voice.

"I need to speak to Mr. De Rossi."

He gives me a cursory look, sniffs, and shakes his head. "And I need to go home and fuck my wife. We've all got our dreams."

My cheeks redden, but I pull my shoulders back. "Please, this is very important."

"I doubt it."

"I just need a few minutes."

His eyes narrow. "I said, staff only. Do you want to be escorted out?"

My nails dig into my palms. Shit. What am I supposed to do?

"Let her pass."

I glance in the direction of the voice. It's the brawny guy who was talking to De Rossi. He's just come down the stairs, and now he's looking at me with curious eyes. On his left earlobe is a small dangly silver earring.

"Ras," the bouncer says. "You sure?"

"Ella llamó su atención."

The bouncer gives me a cross look, sighs heavily, and lifts the velvet rope. "Go."

I can't believe my luck. I have no idea what this Ras guy said to the bouncer, but that doesn't stop me from giving him a bright smile. "Thank you."

He shakes his head as if my gratefulness is misplaced.

A frisson of fear erupts inside of me, but I ignore it. I've made it this far. I'm not turning back.

The closer I get to De Rossi, the harder my heart pounds. I can feel it beating in my neck, my fingers, even my feet. If I mess this up, I'm screwed.

There's a hidden booth on the balcony that can't be seen from below. De Rossi's sitting there now, his arms spread over the back of the seat. Broad shoulders, trim waist, and a few inches of flowing hair that's pushed back from his brutally handsome face. His brows are furrowed as he watches the crowd. A clip glints on his tie.

I hesitate. It's like De Rossi's a king holding court in his castle.

I suppose that's exactly what this is.

As I slide into the booth and take a seat on the edge, those eyes find their way back to me. There's a lethal charge about him. He tries to hide it beneath the crisp lines of his suit and his unruffled demeanor, but his eyes betray him. They seem older than the rest of him, with crow's feet visible on his otherwise unlined face. What have those eyes seen?

I take a deep breath and regret it immediately. This man's cologne is designed to make you want to drape yourself over him.

"Can I help you?" His powerful tenor slides over my skin like a silk robe. I pick up on a very mild accent.

"Hi, I'm Ale."

"Ale...?"

"Romero."

"What are you doing here, Romero?" He takes a spare glass from a tray in front of him, splashes what looks like whiskey into it, and slides the glass to me.

I take it and clutch it to my chest. "I needed to speak to you."

He takes a sip of his own caramel-colored drink. His eyes flick down to my glass, and then past it to the revealing cut of my dress. His gaze lingers unabashedly. "Then speak."

My hands itch to adjust my clothing, but I force myself not to and scramble for something to say. "De Rossi is an Italian name, isn't it?"

He nods.

"I'm Italian too. Italian-Canadian," I clarify. "My family immigrated a long time ago. I haven't been back in many years."

His brows furrow at my rambling.

Okay, time to lay it all out. I clear my throat. "I'm looking for work. I was hoping I could convince you to hire me."

Lines appear on his forehead. I think I managed to surprise him. "You're looking for work?"

"Correct. I'm willing to do anything." My cheeks warm when I realize what that sounded like. "I mean, I'll take any position you have available."

His lips twitch, but it takes him only a moment to grow stern again. "We hired all of our employees weeks ago."

"Ah. Well, I just got here." The prospect of being homeless makes dread solidify at the bottom of my belly. *Think, damn it. Convince this man!* "This place is gigantic. I'm sure you can always use some extra help. People must come and go all the time." I'm fishing. Deep water.

"What do you want to do here exactly?"

I smooth my palms over my lap. "To be honest, I don't have any specific skills per se."

"You don't say," he interrupts before taking another sip of his whiskey.

I pretend I didn't hear him. "But I'm the hardest worker you'll ever meet."

At this, his serious demeanor cracks, and he barks a laugh.

If he wasn't laughing at me, I might take a moment to appreciate the rumbly sound, but I'm too busy trying to keep my composure.

"Why is that funny?" I ask.

He swipes his hand over his mouth and skewers me with a no-bullshit stare. "*Principessa*, you don't look like you've worked a day in your life. What do you know about hard work?"

His words may as well be a punch in the gut.

I swallow down the burn in my throat from his insult and force the next words out of my mouth. "That's a presumptuous thing to say. You don't know anything about me."

"No, but I've got eyes and a brain. What I see is that you like to show off your key assets." His gaze licks over my chest. "You seem to think that's all it takes for you to have men do whatever you say. Maybe it's worked back home, but unfortunately for you, in Ibiza, beautiful women are a dime a dozen. If I hired all of them, I wouldn't have a night club. I'd have a harem."

Embarrassment coats my skin with heat. "That's unfair."

"Life's unfair. If I was wrong about anything I just said, you would have learned that lesson by now." He looks away from me, signaling his dismissal.

A foreign feeling starts to build inside my chest.

No. No way. He doesn't get to dismiss me like that. I'm not going to let him. I've let others walk all over me my entire life, but that ends now.

I don't even know what I'm doing as I slam my glass down on the table with a loud clank to draw his attention back to me. I've never stood up to a man like this, never dared to, but it must be my desperation snapping my backbone into place.

"I know life is unfair," I say angrily. "It's unfair that men like you get to look down on women like me because of misguided first impressions. Must be nice to have the privilege to shit all over people trying to find honest work."

He scoffs. "You don't need honest work when you've got a trust fund. Those flats on your feet cost over a thousand euros. Did Daddy get tired of footing your bills? Maybe you should consider reconciling with him before trying to live out some half-baked attempt at independence on *fucking Ibiza*."

"Bold statement for someone who's Daddy probably bought this club for him."

De Rossi's expression tightens. "My daddy's dead. This club is the product of my own blood, sweat, and tears. Which is why it irks me when spoiled little girls like yourself walk in expecting everyone to give them exactly what they want for just putting their tits on display."

I shoot up to my feet. "You're a pig."

He stands up and steps into my space. "No, I'm a wolf. And you're a sheep that wandered into the wrong pasture."

My hands curl into fists as I crane my neck to look at his face. Does he think he can intimidate me by unfurling to his full height and towering over me? What De Rossi doesn't know is that I've lived my whole life surrounded by men far more terrifying than him. Physically, I might not be his match, but if he thinks he can make me cower with his words alone, he's about to be very disappointed.

"I'm no sheep," I say, enunciating every word. "And I don't want you to give me anything for just showing up. I want a fair chance, that's all. Let me work here for a week as a trial.

If it works out, hire me. If I don't meet your standards, I'll leave when the week is up."

He trails his bottom lip with his teeth. "Why would I agree to that?"

"Because if you don't, you're just a judgmental jerk who gets off on putting other people down. Don't you want to know if you're right about me? Or are you scared to be proven wrong?"

"Hardly."

"Then take the deal."

A beat drops, and the crowd below us erupts in excited shouts, but De Rossi is still as he considers my offer. I peer into his eyes. Now that he's finally shut that unbearable mouth, I am once again aware that he's a very, *very* attractive man. He really doesn't deserve those damn cheekbones or that broad forehead or those lips that seem like they'd be surprisingly soft to touch.

My stomach flutters.

A steady pulse appears between my legs.

My God, what's wrong with me? I'm not here to admire him. I'm here to get a job so that I can keep a roof over my head.

His own gaze slithers over my body, as if I finally convinced him I'm worth a second glance.

His jaw works, and then he nods. "Fine. One week. Be here on Monday, eleven am."

A slow, triumphant smile spreads across my lips. "I'll be here."

"Fine."

"Great."

He gives me one final weary look and then makes a small gesture with his hand at someone behind me.

Ras appears at the top of the stairs.

"She's ready to leave," De Rossi says after a moment.

"I'll walk you out." Ras extends his hand my way.

I take it, and De Rossi frowns. He's probably already regretting our deal. As I descend the steps, I can feel his devilish black eyes boring a hole through the back of my head.

I already know he's not going to make it easy, but I've survived two months of hell with Lazaro. I can make it through a week with De Rossi, no matter what he throws my way.

CHAPTER 6

DAMIANO

I'M NOT MYSELF TONIGHT.

The weight in my chest is heavy. The pain inside my head is the kind that has no simple cure.

When I close my eyes, I see flames racing up my mother's legs as she stands in the kitchen of my childhood home on the outskirts of Casal di Principe. Whenever I smell gasoline, I think of that night.

Whenever I suffer a failure, I remember the screams she made.

"You didn't need to come in."

I blink. Ras is sitting on the other side of the desk. We're in my office, about a hundred meters from the main dancefloor of Revolvr, but the soundproof walls ensure no sound seeps in. How is it that I didn't hear him come in? *Cazzo*.

"If I wasn't here, I'd be climbing the walls back home," I say to my right-hand man. It's true. I had no distractions to keep me occupied. Which begs the question—why the fuck did I let that girl walk away earlier when I had every intention of making her into my distraction tonight?

Ale Romero. When I saw her down by the bar, I swear, I felt chills. In ancient times, kings would have waged wars over a woman like her. Exquisite face, shapely tits, tight ass, and shiny black hair that nearly reached her trim waist. I could feel the stirrings of madness inside of me. I had a strong suspicion she regularly drove men insane.

My sour mood had lifted when I saw her moving to the entrance of my balcony. I'd been sure she wanted to fuck me right there. It wouldn't have been the first time.

Most nights, all I have to do is show up, and the women appear. That's just how it works when you own half of the world's most famous island—in my portfolio of clubs, hotels, and restaurants, Revolvr is just the crown jewel.

Instead, she'd asked for a job.

That had taken me aback, which doesn't happen often. I'm usually good at reading people's intent, but even that skill of mine appeared to be compromised after my shitshow of a morning. It pissed me off. I'd wanted her, but I could *just tell* she'd make me work for it. Normally, I'd love the challenge, but tonight, I'm in no fucking mood to play games.

I went off on her despite already being hard for her. When she showed a bit of backbone instead of backing down, I did something I could only attribute to my agitated state of mind.

I gave in.

Ras props his ankle on his knee. "If you're thinking about what happened, maybe we should talk ab—"

"I'm done talking about it," I bite out. "Did they clean up the garage?"

"Yes, the body's gone."

"Good. There's nothing more to do until we get more information." Ras knows it as well as me. Hypotheses and suspicions aren't enough to make an accusation against our don.

He studies me for a moment and then narrows his eyes. "Then what the fuck is on your mind? You're fixated on something."

I glare at him. Sometimes, he's able to read me too well.

I shouldn't have let her leave. I should have leaned into the wicked thought I had when she said she'd do anything to get the job. *Peel off that dress, climb onto my cock, and bounce.*

That visual sends a pulse to my groin. It feels particularly filthy, because that's not how I hire my employees. My morals might be loose by most standards, but I wouldn't get to where I am by doing stupid shit like that at my legitimate businesses. Reputation is everything in Ibiza.

"It's that girl, isn't it?" Ras asks, studying my sullen expression. "If you wanted her, why did you let her go?

"I didn't," I say. "She'll be here Monday."

That throws him off. "What do you mean?"

"She's going to audition for a job. I agreed to a week-long trial."

Ras touches his fingers to his forehead and looks up at me. "Are you fucking serious?"

"I'm really not in a joking mood."

This earns me a frustrated groan. "What trial? You know I don't have time for this with everything going on."

Ras is the only person who's allowed to speak to me that way. Without each other, we'd both be dead ten times over. Plus, he's family. Still, when I give him a dark look, he straightens his back and makes a tiny nod. It's his way of acknowledging now's not the time to test my patience.

He's not wrong though. Why the fuck did I agree to this stupid trial? I can call it off, but I don't like breaking my word. I might as well have a bit of fun tormenting Romero the way the memory of her is tormenting me now. She won't last more than a few days. If she's a hard worker, then I'm a fucking priest.

"I don't want you to spend time on it. Give her to Inez."

He arches a brow. "Inez? If the girl's going to be working here, we might as well make her a dancer. She'll do well with the VIPs."

The thought of her dancing in front of groups of drunk men spreads a burning sensation through my chest. No *fucking* way. "I said give her to Inez. If she lasts a week, I might reconsider, though I don't expect her to."

He lets out a long breath through his lips. "*Va bene.*"

"Did you talk to Napoletano?"

"A few hours ago," he says. "The construction project was greenlighted by Sal this morning."

"*Merda.*" Sal's going to be pouring concrete for a factory that's on another clan's territory. Our don is a fucking idiot. I know it, Ras knows it, everyone fucking knows it. And yet no one speaks up. "We're going to have a war on our hands."

Ras shakes his head. "You already made your opinion known last month. Leave it."

I don't like his tone. "You think I should have stayed silent at the meeting?"

Ras sighs. "You know Sal will never listen to you, even if you're one hundred percent right and he's one hundred percent wrong. Speaking up will only make things worse. You pissed him off by questioning his judgement in front of all the other capos at the meeting, and now we have Nelo and Vito here, sticking their ugly noses into our business. Who knows how far he's willing to go to bring you in line?"

Our eyes meet. Yes...how far?

I lean back into my chair and look at the picture hanging on my wall. Ras, his parents, Martina, and I. It would have been a different photo if Sal hadn't killed my father and taken his place as the don of the Casalesi clan, one of the most powerful in the Camorra *sistema*.

My mother would still be alive.

My family would be intact.

I would be next in line.

"He's going to turn our clan to dust," I mutter.

"They'll turn on him before it comes to that."

I flex my hand. "They need to turn on him faster." We might have a way to turn the tide, but only if we get the proof we need.

Ras knows what I'm thinking. "I'm on it."

"Put extra protection on your parents," I say as I rise to leave. "Just in case." If it wasn't for Ras's father—Uncle Julio—Sal would have killed me the same day my parents died. I was eleven years old, still a kid whose balls hadn't dropped, but even back then Sal saw me as a threat. Killing me would put his worries to rest, but it wouldn't be well received by the capos. Clan children were generally off-limits, something Uncle Julio made sure to remind to everyone in Sal's vicinity.

I was spared.

But the first chance he got, Sal sent me away. To Ibiza.

It's always been one of the clan's foreign strongholds—there is no Ibiza without the drugs we provide. Being capo here sounds fine on paper, until one realizes it's the equivalent of being in exile. Clan business doesn't happen over the phone or the Internet. It happens in person, in Casal di Principe.

And Sal really doesn't like it when I go back home.

I bid goodbye to Ras and make my way to the parking lot.

"Take me to the house," I tell the driver as I climb into the car. Beyond the window, the sky is still dark but soon it will begin to lighten. We pass by the long line of green taxis outside Revolvr, and I catch myself looking for Romero in the queue. She's not there.

When we drive past the bus stop, I scoff. No way she'd take one of those to wherever she's staying. What the fuck is she doing looking for a job in Ibiza? A part of me is curious. I'm ninety-five percent convinced she's just a hot rich girl who decided to rebel and prove something to her family. Grass is always greener. Once she sees what I have planned for her, she'll run right back to Daddy with her tail between her legs.

But there's one thing that makes me pause. Inside her eyes, I thought I saw a glimpse of real desperation. Maybe even fear.

What could she be scared of?

I twist one of my rings. When someone's never been truly desperate, it doesn't take much to bring that feeling on. That must be it. She's probably just scared of getting her ego bruised.

With a sigh, I run my hand over my lips. Why the fuck am I analyzing her? Enough. I can't remember the last time I spent this much time thinking about a woman my dick hasn't even met.

The closer we get to home, the darker my thoughts turn. I don't know for sure who's behind what happened last night, but it's got Sal's paranoia spelled all over it. If we can prove our don is the culprit, he won't have long to live.

A made man outside of the sitting don's bloodline can take over the position by strangling the sitting don to death with his bare hands. It's barbaric, but that's how it's always been with the Casalese. It takes intelligence and strategy to get into the same room as the don—there's no one better protected. I'll have to turn some of his closest friends to my side first, and if I don't do it right, they'll run straight to him. I need to show them definitively that Sal is no longer fit to rule.

I flex my hands. It's a high bar.

But if I want to protect the person most important to me, it's what I have to do.

People have always told me my level headedness is my biggest strength. I don't make rash decisions. I don't act out without thinking the consequences through.

A weaker man would have gone after Sal by now, but I know better. I'll wait until the perfect moment.

And then I'll take back everything he stole.

CHAPTER 7

VALENTINA

On Monday, I disembark the bus that stops across the street from Revolvr at ten forty-five am. The surroundings look so different in broad daylight I have to convince myself I've come to the right place.

I'm nervous. All weekend, I tossed and turned at night, worrying about De Rossi changing his mind and putting me right back where I started. I managed to spend barely any money in the past two days, surviving on ramen and free breakfast at the hostel, and taking up Astrid and Vilde on their invitation to move into their cheaper shared dorm. Still, neither of those things change the fact that I'm practically broke.

I make my way inside the club through the main entrance.

"Over here."

I turn in the direction of the voice. It's Ras. He's sitting on a stool by one of the bars, a sweating beer in his hand. Dressed in a pair of well-worn jeans and a washed-out gray

T-shirt, he almost seems approachable...that is until I register the weary look on his face.

"Hi," I say in a voice that comes out like a squeak. "Thanks for meeting me. I really appreciate this opportunity."

He looks like he's trying really hard not to roll his eyes. "Just doing my job," he says gruffly. "The scope of which apparently keeps expanding."

"You don't usually do this?"

"You mean take on a new staff member after we've already hired everyone for the season? No. I don't."

Heat blankets my cheeks. "De Rossi agreed to a trial."

"I know what De Rossi agreed to. Lucky for you, I just transferred an employee over to Laser. You'll be replacing them."

My brows knot in confusion. "Laser?"

"Another one of the boss's clubs."

"He owns more than one club?"

"He owns half the big clubs on the island. Along with more hotels, restaurants, and condominiums than you and I can count."

Great. De Rossi is some kind of Ibizan business magnate. If I screw this up, my job prospects here might all but disappear. I bite my lip to suppress a groan. The stakes just got higher.

"You got lucky," Ras says, jumping off his stool and motioning for me to follow him. "The boss must have been in a particularly kind mood when you met him."

"Are you trying to be funny?"

That earns me a deep laugh. "You couldn't tell?" Amusement dances in his eyes. "You wouldn't be here otherwise."

I bite back a retort. De Rossi may have been rude, but he's giving me a chance nonetheless. I'm not going to complain about him to one of his employees.

Speaking of... "So what do you do here?" I ask Ras.

"My official title is the general manager and head of security at Revolvr, but I do all kinds of things." He draws to a halt by the women's bathroom, where a gray-haired cleaner is fussing around a cart filled with cleaning supplies.

"Here we are," Ras says. "Ale, meet Inez. She's the daytime shift manager for our custodian team." He gives a warm smile to the short middle-aged woman. "Inez, this is Ale Romero. She's just joined your team."

"Nice to meet you," I say without missing a beat, and shake Inez's hand. I was expecting De Rossi would have me work as one of those bottle service girls, but custodian will do just fine. I know how to clean. I often helped Lorna back at Lazaro's house even though she chastised me about it. Is this the best De Rossi's got?

"Great," Ras says as he reaches into the cart. "Here's your uniform. Your shift starts in ten minutes."

By the time I come out dressed in a matching combo of sky-blue slacks and a short-sleeved button-up shirt, Inez is already waiting with another cart for me.

She peers at me over a pair of clear rimmed glasses. "Señor Ras tells me to put you in the Mannequin room."

"Fine by me." I have no idea what the Mannequin room is, but as far as I'm concerned, one room is the same as any other.

"All of the supplies are here." She pushes the cart toward me. "Go past the pink doors over there. If you have any questions, come to the main room, I'll be working there."

"Thank you."

She gives me a smile—does it seem a little pitying?—and walks away with a slight limp.

Once I make it inside the room, her parting smile makes a lot more sense.

The space isn't large, maybe big enough for a hundred or so people, but the floor is covered in confetti. It's mush in places where liquor was spilled over it, and in one of the corners, I discover a wet pile of what could only be vomit.

It's disgusting, but what De Rossi doesn't know is that I've seen enough disgusting things to harden my stomach to steel.

I get to work. The cart has all the supplies I could possibly need. First, I sweep the floor, and then I get out the mop. When I open up the bottle of bleach, the smell makes memories come up, but I temper them down.

De Rossi's voice floats into the room. "I can barely recognize you in that uniform, Romero. Had enough yet?"

I whirl around and land my gaze on De Rossi's luxuriously suited form. Suddenly, I'm all too aware of the hair sticking to my damp forehead and the ill-fitting uniform made out of fabric that doesn't breathe. He gives me a sardonic look, as if he thinks all he has to do is nudge me a bit and I'll break.

"Not at all," I say, giving him a tight smile. "This has been a great day so far."

His lips twitch, and he peers down at the floor of the room. "You missed a bit here."

"Where?"

"Right here." He points. "Quality, Romero. I don't hire people who half-ass their work."

He wants to humiliate me. Go right ahead. After the things I've done for Lazaro, I don't have any pride left.

I lower to my knees in front of De Rossi, making sure to keep that smile frozen on my face. "Thank you for your feedback. I'll get it taken care of."

His expression shifts, and for a moment, he looks kind of disturbed. Or maybe he's just disappointed his negging is not having the effect he was hoping for.

I grab a rag and start rubbing at the spot. There's some perverse part of me that's enjoying this entire thing. Let's be frank here, I want to live, but I know I'm scum. A murderer, a torturer, a morally bankrupt coward. I'll never forgive myself for what I did to those people, criminals or not.

If De Rossi wants to lay it on even thicker, he can go ahead. He can't break someone who's already broken.

There's a sudden tightness in my throat. I swallow past it and force myself out of my head. I better distract myself with something. "I thought things like you only come out at night," I say. I'm still getting used to my ability to talk back to him. Despite him holding my fate in his hands, he doesn't scare me like Lazaro or Papà.

"Things like me?"

"Demons, vampires, soul-sucking Dementors..."

He chuckles. "I see. You've elevated me to something super-human. Do I really strike you as so formidable?"

"You would take that as a compliment," I grumble as I get back on my feet. "How's that? See any other spots I missed?"

De Rossi smooths his hand over his tie. "You sure this is the kind of work you want to be doing?"

I dip the mop in the bucket before squeezing it out in the plastic basket. "This work suits me just fine."

"Let's see if that's how you feel by the end of the week," he says, pulling a protein bar out of his pocket and tearing it open.

Honestly, I'm surprised. He didn't strike me as the snacking type, but I guess he's got to maintain all that muscle somehow.

For some time, he just stands there, leaning against the bar and watching me work while he eats.

My stomach emits a loud growl. I was so anxious this morning, I skipped breakfast.

De Rossi hears it. "Hungry?"

I heave a sigh. "Don't you have somewhere else to be?"

He approaches and stops very close to me. My stomach tightens when he raises his bar to my lips. "Here."

I eye the protein bar. I would have asked if it was poisoned if I didn't just see him take a bite.

He cocks a brow. "Open your mouth. I can't have my employees passing out on the job."

"Open my mouth? What are you going to do, feed *ungh*—"

He silences me by shoving the bar past my lips.

For a millisecond, I think I can taste him on the surface. Whiskey and chocolate and something brutally decadent.

I push the ridiculous thought away. It doesn't matter to me what he tastes like.

He watches me chew, his gaze falling to my lips for a brief moment.

I lick my bottom lip to sweep up a crumb. His eyes narrow.

"Better get back to work." He hands me the bar. I guess he's done with feeding me like I'm some wild animal. "This room better be spotless if you want to return tomorrow."

I don't dignify that with a response.

By the time I'm done, six hours later, I can see my reflection in the floor in nearly every surface. Inez comes by to inspect my work.

"*Vale, bien hecho*," she says after checking the corners for dust with her index finger. "You did a good job."

"Thank you. What else can I do?"

She appraises me, and when her thin lips curl into a slight smile, I feel a small triumph. At least I'm winning her over.

"You're done for today. Come back tomorrow at eleven."

One day down, four more to go.

CHAPTER 8

VALENTINA

THE REST of the week ticks by. I keep my head down and do whatever Inez tells me to—clean the toilets, mop the floors, polish the mirrors, vacuum the VIP section, and on and on. By the time Friday rolls around, I've learned the entire layout of the club, and it doesn't feel so massive anymore. The daytime staff start to recognize me and even say hello.

Then comes Friday, and with it, my final assignment. De Rossi's office.

I have to admit, I'm a bit curious to see where he spends his time. Ras meets me when I arrive and walks me down a hall I've only passed through a few times before. We stop in front of a heavy-looking door, and he knocks. No response.

"Guess we'll have to come back later," I say.

"I have a spare key. Don't touch anything you're not supposed to." Ras turns his key inside the lock and holds open the door for me.

Well, it's definitely way fancier that I expected it to be. The room reminds me of my Papà's office back home, with dark oak shelves laden with books and a massive desk adorned with geometrical paperweights. My attentions snags on a picture frame hanging on one of the walls. I make a note to examine it more closely once Ras leaves.

"He wants everything dusted, the floor swept and mopped. Said something about a big cobweb in the corner behind his desk."

"Lovely," I mutter. "Have you been working for him for a while?"

Ras nods. "He's the only boss I've ever had."

"How did you get your job? Did he have you scrub floors too?"

"No, that's just for you."

"I feel so special."

"Him and I go way back," Ras says vaguely, clearly trying to end this conversation. "I've got somewhere else I need to be. Any questions before I leave?"

"Yeah, one."

He cocks his head. "Why do I have a feeling I'm not going to like it?"

He's wary of me. I wonder why? What has De Rossi said to him about me? "It's Friday. Do you think I passed the trial?"

"You've still got one shift left."

"But you know De Rossi. Which way is he leaning?"

Ras looks behind me. "You'll have to ask him yourself."

I turn around and see De Rossi enter the room. He slaps Ras on the shoulder as he passes him, which Ras takes as a signal to leave.

"Did Ras tell you what you need to do?" he ask once we're alone in the room.

"Yes, he gave me all the instructions for cleaning your lair."

"My lair?" De Rossi asks. He leans against the desk and gives me a smirk. "It's more of a torture chamber, as far as you're concerned. If you think I'm going to give you a break just because it's Friday..."

His words pass by me as my brain latches on to *torture chamber*. Lazaro's basement flashes in front of my eyes. The torn, bloodied flesh. The glint of the knife I'm holding in my hand. And the worst of it, his voice penetrating my ears with cruel commands to inflict unimaginable pain. *"Take his hand, Vale. I want you to cut off his fingers for me."*

"Ale."

De Rossi's voice snaps me out of it. He's standing very close to me now.

"I'm sorry," I say as I take a step back. I can't let my thoughts wonder like that, damn it. I need to get through the next few hours without giving De Rossi a reason not to hire me.

His expression is strange. If I didn't know any better, I might think there's a hint of concern reflected in his eyes. "Were you having some kind of a moment, or were you just ignoring me?"

"I was ignoring you."

He doesn't look convinced. "Why did you apologize?"

Why do you care? I want to scream. Instead, I say, "I can't remember."

He's not impressed with my response. "Do you need to sit down?" he asks, surprising me.

"I'm fine." I begin to rummage through the cart for a clean cloth. "Can I get started now?"

De Rossi flexes his jaw and nods, but he doesn't leave like I hoped he would. He sits down at his desk and watches me as I climb up the step ladder and begin to dust his shelves. His gaze heats my skin, and a drop of sweat rolls down the valley of my spine.

"There must be something more important for you to do," I exclaim when I can't take it anymore.

"Nothing more important than quality control."

"Don't tell me you can see an errant speck of dust from all the way over there."

"Do you want me to come closer?"

"No, thanks." I climb down the ladder and move it over to the next bookshelf. This guy has thousands of books in here, mostly classics and non-fiction. Rows and rows of tomes on business, strategy, marketing...

"You really built your business by yourself?" De Rossi looks fairly young for a business mogul. No more than thirty. How does one become so successful in such a short amount of time?

He leans back in his chair. "I had an investor when I got started. I doubled his money in three years."

"What was the company?"

"Concrete."

I yawn. "Boring."

Amusement flickers over his face. "Nightclubs are a lot more fun."

"Fun? All I see you do is sulk on your balcony."

"You saw me doing that *once*."

"I'm sure I'd see it again if I came back here after midnight."

"Is that what you're planning to do tonight?"

"No. I'm going to crash as soon as I get home. This week has been—" I stop myself. No way I'm going to admit that I'm exhausted.

The glint in his eyes tells me he's onto me. "Better get started on the floor soon. You need to rub it with a special wood cleaner after you mop," he advises.

"Of course, your highness. I'll be sure to rub your wood just the way you like it." I realize how that sounded the moment the words leave my mouth. My eyes meet De Rossi's.

He tips his chin up and gives me a very male smirk. "You *really* want to ace your trial week."

"You know what I meant," I grumble as I reach for the vacuum.

"Sounded like you were propositioning me."

"I'd rather proposition a deflated balloon."

The sound of his chuckle settles somewhere low inside my belly. The sensation is not completely unpleasant. "Someone ought to teach you how to talk to your superiors."

I glance at him over my shoulder. "You're not my boss yet."

His eyes flare. I think he'll hire me just to torment me some more. I get the sense that some part of him enjoys the fact that I talk back to him.

I begin to vacuum, and after a while, I no longer feel his attention on me. He works on something on his laptop and eats a green apple while I use the long attachment of the vacuum to get into every corner of the room. It's not that dirty to begin with. I wonder if Inez was the one who put it all in order before me.

When I pass by the framed photo, my curiosity gets the best of me, and I stop to look at it. It's a family. A man and a woman with three kids. There's a young boy—maybe twelve or eleven—in the center of the picture, and he's holding a small child. Beside him is an older boy, with his arm slung over the shoulders of the smaller one. It's a weird family picture. No one is smiling.

I squint at the boy in the middle. "Is this your family, De Rossi?"

A pen clicks. "Yes."

"You have siblings."

"I do."

"Your mom is very beautiful."

"She's my aunt."

My brows furrow together as I turn to him. "You said this was your family. I assumed they were your parents."

"My parents died when I was young," he says evenly. "My mother's sister and her husband took me and my sister in."

I face the photo once again. "So who's the other..." Wait, he looks a little familiar. "Is that Ras? You two are related?"

"He's my cousin."

Ah. So De Rossi's most trusted employee is related to him. Maybe besides all the violence and murder, being a businessman is not so different from being a mafioso after all.

The image of little De Rossi holding his sister tugs at my heart. "That must have been hard. Losing them at that age."

"Romero, I'm not looking for a therapist. Drop the audition."

Who would have thought that sweet little boy in the picture would grow into this six-foot something menace? I glare at him and turn the vacuum back on.

When I'm done with the rest of the room, I approach his desk. "I need to get behind your chair. Ras said there's a cobweb."

De Rossi scoots over just enough for me to squeeze by.

As I move past him, I inhale a lungful of his scent. As much as I hate to admit it, he smells incredible. Salt and sea and something smokey, as if he'd smoked a cigar earlier today.

I push that dangerous line of thinking away and get down on my knees. The cobweb is not nearly as bad as Ras had made it seem. I crawl forward to get a better look. There are two dead flies caught inside of it.

De Rossi clears his throat. I ignore him. Maybe he's prepping his next biting remark. Wouldn't want to interrupt his creative process.

I take down the web with a wet cloth. De Rossi's polished leather shoe is in my line of sight, and he's tapping it on his precious wood floor, probably spreading dirt he brought in from outside everywhere.

"Worried about something?" I ask him.

His foot stops. "Just considering how strange it is that you keep ending up on your knees around me."

I resist the urge to slap his ankle with the cloth. "That's what happens when my job is literally to be on the floor. Get your mind out of the gutter."

Is he looking at my ass? The thought that he might be makes me lick my lips. And arch my back.

De Rossi clears his throat and takes a loud bite of his stupid apple. I smile.

My little victory is cut short when I move to get up and instead end up falling back down on my butt.

"Ouch!" I wrap my palms around my calf. Goddamn charley horse. It must be all the physical labor this week.

"What happened?" De Rossi gets out of his seat and kneels beside me. "Are you hurt?"

"Spasm," I grit out as I rub my tense muscles. Tears spring to my eyes.

"Let me see," he demands.

"There's nothing to see, I just need to work it out."

"Stop being stubborn."

The protest dies on my tongue when he wraps his big hands around my calf and smooths both of his thumbs down the back. He's stronger than me, applies more pressure, and it feels so much better than whatever I was doing to myself. The sensation is enough to work a small moan out of me.

"How's that?" he asks in a low tone.

"Better."

"Hmm."

I drop my head to rest against the edge of his desk while he keeps going. My lids lower. It's hot today, and now that I'm not in motion, the tiredness sets in. De Rossi hadn't been totally wrong about me when he deduced I hadn't had to work a day in my life. Food, shelter, and money had always been a given. Not anymore. I've worked hard this week, harder than I've ever had to, and my body hasn't had time to adjust to it yet.

He digs his fingers into just the right spot, and I bite my bottom lip to hold back another moan. A completely unwanted tendril of heat swirls in my core. I was attracted to him before he opened that cruel mouth—a fact I'd love to forget. This is De Rossi, for God's sake. He saw someone in pain and decided to help out. It doesn't change anything.

But when I crack open my lids, the look on his face makes sparks crackle across my skin. It's downright wolfish. He meets my gaze and holds it. I suck in a breath.

"It doesn't hurt anymore," I whisper.

His fingers slow, his touch turns gentler. "You're probably dehydrated."

"A businessman and a doctor. How do you find the time?"

He drops his hands away from me and rises. A second later, I'm handed a bottle of water from his desk. "Drink this."

I do because... Well, he's probably right. I haven't had anything to drink since this morning. I've forgotten how to take care of myself, and I'm still trying to remember.

"Thanks," I say after I finish the water. "Take a look around. Let me know if I missed anything."

He passes a cursory glance around the room. "It looks fine."

"Fine's not good enough for you, De Rossi. It needs to be excellent."

I think I see a flicker of respect in his eyes. I give him a tired smile. "I'm a quick learner. And as I tried to tell you, I work hard."

He tilts his head slightly to the side, and after a moment, he extends his hand. "Let me help you up."

His hand is warm and steady. I rise to my full height, putting my eyes on the same level as his collarbones. When he appears in no rush to let me go, I tip my head back and meet his gaze.

He's wearing a thoughtful expression. "I talked to Inez. She told me you're one of the best employees she's ever trained."

My body feels light with relief. Inez put in a good word for me? I'm going to give her a long hug next time I see her. "She's good at directions."

He inhales and then lets out a resigned breath. I can tell he's not thrilled with having to utter his next sentence. "I'll admit, I may have been wrong about you."

I swallow, trying to tempter my premature excitement. "Does that mean..."

His smile is a mere flicker. He drops my hand, walks behind his desk, and closes his laptop. "It means this won't be the last time you clean this office."

A grin overtakes my face. "Yes, boss."

"On Monday, bring your documents. Ras will arrange your contract."

Documents?

Crap.

CHAPTER 9

VALENTINA

WHEN I GET BACK to the hostel, Astrid and Vilde are in our room, and I tell them I got the job.

"Welcome to the team," Astrid exclaims. "We should celebrate tonight."

"Don't you need to work?" I ask. De Rossi didn't give me more than a moment to enjoy my achievement before flinging another problem in my face, so I'm not in the most celebratory mood.

I don't have any papers to show him on Monday, and I have no idea how I'm going to weasel out of that. I still have my real passport—tucked under my mattress—but it's useless to me now.

"We're both scheduled on Saturday this week," Vilde says. "And we were already planning on taking advantage of our day off. One of the other dancers told us about an incredible seafood restaurant that's right on the water."

"I don't know. I'm pretty exhausted after the week I've had," I say.

"We're in Ibiza. The entire point is to go out and have fun and meet people. Maybe I could get laid tonight," Astrid says wistfully. "It's been too long. I broke up with Matthew two—no, three—months ago, and after him there was that one guy, but he was really awful in bed. He was poking around down there like I was a TV remote or something."

Vilde and I grimace at the vivid image.

"What about you?" Astrid asks. "You have a boyfriend back in Canada that you've been quiet about?"

Lazaro's face appears in my mind. "No boyfriend." Just a possibly dead psycho ex-husband who's only slept with me once. I've spent so much time hating Lazaro for what he forced me to do to his victims, that I've barely considered the other ways he's harmed me. I'm not a virgin, but I'm not far off from it. My marriage was a hideous farce in more ways than one.

My one sexual interaction with Lazaro lasted all of three minutes. He took off my dress, put his fingers inside of me, and after a few seconds replaced them with his dick. I held on to him for dear life, forcing my tears back, praying the pain between my legs would go away quickly. It didn't. It didn't stop until he finished and pulled out.

You know what would really go against everything my family taught me? Casual sex.

Oh God, they would lose their minds if they knew their daughter not only ran away, but also became a whore. In the clan, being called a whore was the worst thing a woman could be labeled. Whores are disloyal. They can't be trusted.

They certainly shouldn't be loved. Only fools fell for them, men that didn't know any better.

Papà and Lazaro might find me at any moment—why not take advantage of my current freedom to really put that whole perfect mafia wife thing to rest?

I tell Vilde and Astrid they've won me over, and a few hours later, we start to get ready.

Astrid lets me borrow one of her provocative outfits. Unlike that first night at Revolvr, I decide to embrace showing off a generous amount of skin.

When I look in the mirror, I see a stranger. A woman with silky black hair pulled back in a knot at the nape of her neck. She's in a blue bandeau top that's a bit too small for her breasts, and a matching blue miniskirt. Red lips painted on a canvas of pale skin. She blinks at me with long eyelashes that fan over a pair of gray eyes. The eyes seem familiar, like they belong to someone I used to know a long time ago.

When I look into them for too long, other reflections start to flash. The faces of all the people I've killed. One layered on top of another, until the composite product is me.

I turn away from the mirror.

Astrid and Vilde pick the perfect moment to tumble out of the bathroom and provide me with a distraction. They take me in.

"You look fucking hot," Astrid comments, before popping a gum bubble. "I need three more minutes, and then we'll head out."

We leave the hostel and get on a bus. The restaurant is called Aromata, and when we reach our stop, I see that it's right on the beach and overlooks a small bay with calm waters.

The weather is pleasant, with warm air and a slight breeze. Astrid talks to the hostess, while I crane my neck to see past her into the open-air restaurant. It's bustling, filled with conversation and the steady beat of laid-back techno music.

The hostess grabs a few menus. "This way, please."

We follow her to the edge of the bar where there are exactly three empty chairs. "Is this all right?" she asks.

"We'll take whatever we can get," Astrid says. "We're lucky. They look completely full," she adds after the hostess walks away.

I glance at some of the nearby plates. "Food looks great."

"That bar looks even better," Vilde says as she studies the bottles on the shelves behind the bar.

A cute male bartender with dark, curly hair comes over to take our orders. "What can I get you, señoritas?"

"A pitcher of cava sangria, heavy on the fruit," Astrid orders.

"You got it."

"And we're from Revolvr," Vilde says.

The bartender nods. "Can I see your employee cards?"

I give the girls a quizzical look. "What is this for?"

"Oh, we get amazing discounts here because it's one of GR's restaurants," Astrid says as she hands the bartender her card. "Groupo De Rossi."

My mood immediately darkens.

"I don't have one yet," I tell the bartender.

"I'm sorry, but without the ID, I can't honor the discount."

"Oh, come on," Astrid whines.

"My manager will have my head," he says with an apologetic grimace. "He's going crazy because the owner's here tonight. Wants everything to be perfect."

It's as if someone tightens a screw in my brain, making everything around me come into sharper focus.

I exhale loudly and spin around.

Four tables ahead of us sits De Rossi.

And he's staring at me.

"You've got to be kidding me," I say under my breath.

He's at a table with Ras, three other men I don't know, and three stunning women dressed in expensive clothes and enough fine jewelry to make them sparkle.

De Rossi lifts his glass of red wine and takes a long sip, all the while drinking me in with his eyes. I feel him on my cheeks, my décolleté... My nipples grow hard from a particularly sharp breeze, and I shiver.

Vilde elbows me. "Maybe you can ask Ras to vouch for you."

I shake my head and turn back around. "Don't worry about it, I'm fine."

When the waiter hands us the menus, my eyes bulge. Twenty-five euros for a salad? Fifty euros for a piece of fish? I slam the menu closed and put it on the bar.

The girls feel bad that they didn't realize I wouldn't have my ID, so they kindly offer to pay for me, but I tell them I'm not hungry. They've been generous enough to me as is. I should have asked to get paid for the week I worked before I left Revolvr, but I was so distracted by the mention of a contract, it slipped my mind.

When the food arrives, my stomach starts to growl, so I excuse myself and go to the bathroom. The second I come out, I slam right into a hard, warm body.

"Oof!"

Strong hands wrap around my waist. Immediately, I know it's him.

"What are you—"

"Tell me, what did you hope to accomplish by showing up here dressed like this?" he says close to my ear. Close enough for his breath to caress my neck.

My pulse speeds. "What—"

"If you wanted attention, you got it."

I tug his hands off me. "You have no idea what I want."

"You like having men's hungry eyes on you. Is that it?"

"I think you're just upset I caught *you* looking."

My words slam his mouth shut. I think he might leave me alone, but instead, his hand cinches my wrist.

"What now?" I demand as he pulls me in the direction of the bar. People are staring at us, but if he notices it, he doesn't care. In fact, it's almost like he *wants* them to see us together. Instead of taking the most direct route, he walks me all the way around the dining room.

"I don't need an escort," I tell him.

"You have no idea what you need."

We make it to the bar, and when he lets go of me, he leaves behind a bracelet of heat wrapped around my wrist. Astrid and Vilde slide off their stools and stammer out a few panicked hellos, but he barely acknowledges them. He's about to walk away, but then he notices there's no plate for me on the counter. He shoots me a furious glare I can't begin to comprehend and waves the bartender over. The young man nearly trips over his feet.

"*Si, Señor De Ross—*"

"Put their bill on my tab," he snaps.

My jaw drops. Excuse me? Does he think I'm some charity case? Didn't I just prove to him I don't need any handouts? "You can't do this," I say.

"Keep telling me what I can't do."

The warning in his voice is impossible to miss. I meet his dark eyes and swallow. "I'm not going to order anything."

He turns back to the bartender. "Have the chef prepare the catch of the day, the octopus, ceviche, and all the sides." Then he leans into my ear again. "If you don't eat what I ordered, I'm going to come back and feed it to you. Think hard about whether you want me to do that in front of the entire restaurant."

My heart slams against my ribcage, and I tell myself it's due to my outrage and definitely *not* because of all the other feelings swirling inside my chest. "You wouldn't."

"I have, and I would." He steps away and waits for me to piece it together. Damn it, he's not lying. That stupid granola bar.

"You are infuriating," I hiss, but I don't think he hears me. He's already turned on his heel and is stalking away.

Astrid and Vilde gape at me.

"I didn't ask for him to do this," I say.

Astrid lets out a disbelieving laugh. "What did you do to get so under his skin?"

"Nothing. I have no idea what possessed him." Maybe he just gets some perverse joy from bossing me around.

When the food De Rossi ordered arrives, I insist they dig in with me. Everything tastes so incredibly good that my irritation eases. I can still feel the ghost of his touch on my wrist, and when I remember how he drank me in with his eyes, heat flickers on at the pit of my belly. Still, I make a point to not to look at De Rossi's table.

The hours tick by. It doesn't take long for Astrid and Vilde to get comfortable with our new open tab, and soon we're all well on our way past tipsy. When the dance floor opens up, we're the first ones on it.

They turn up the music so that it drowns out most conversation. Now that I'm heavily buzzed and well fed, I'm in a surprisingly good mood. Was I too stubborn with De Rossi? All the man wanted to do was pay for my meal, even if he acted like a brute. Maybe I should at least give him my thanks.

I look around, but I can't see him. Just as I'm sure he left the restaurant, an arm wraps around my waist.

My blood surges through my veins like lava. "Still looking?" I ask over my shoulder.

"Only at you."

I freeze. It's not De Rossi's voice. For a split second, everything around me cancels out, and Lazaro's face flashes in my mind.

I whirl around and nearly laugh with relief. A tall stranger. He's dangerous looking. There's a knife tattoo on his face, to the side of his left eye, and a nose that's been broken one too many times, but to me he is no one. Fear leaves me like a retreating wave.

Whatever he sees in my face excites him. He steps closer, pressing his chest to my breasts and planting his palms just above the curve of my ass. "What's your name, *bella*?"

"I don't give it out to strangers," I say, trying to pull away.

"We won't be strangers for much longer," he says an inch away from my lips. His breath is rotten. He's moving my hips with his hands, grinding me into his crotch like I'm some fuck toy. From the bulge pressing against my leg, it's clear what he wants.

Everything suddenly feels dirty and sick. The alcohol—a mix of wine, tequila, and God knows what else—splashes inside my stomach, and my clothes feel too tight. I'm sweaty from the dancing, some of my hair has fallen out of my bun, and it's sticking to my neck.

The stranger won't let me go, and I discover I don't have any will to fight him.

You wanted to be a whore tonight, a voice says inside my head. *It's what you deserve.*

His eyes turn liquid with desire. "Come with me, *bella*." He turns me in the direction of the restroom. Then he starts to push me that way, his big active body overwhelming my smaller passive one.

I glance to the side, toward the bar. Astrid and Vilde are chatting to the bartender, the three of them laughing at some joke. Maybe they'll still be there when this man is done with me. Maybe they'll never know what I invited upon myself with my wickedness. When days, weeks, months later they talk about this night, it will be one thing in their minds and another thing in mine. A creeping loneliness wraps around the entirety of my thoughts and squeezes hard.

Just then, the bulk of the man pressed against me disappears.

I open my eyes—I must have closed them at some point—and try to orient myself. The bathroom is to my right, the dance floor to my left, and ahead of me stands De Rossi, holding the other man by the collar of his shirt.

"You're still here," I say numbly.

He ignores me. "She's drunk," he says to the tattooed man. "Leave."

The stranger sneers. "Fuck you."

"Careful."

"Who's she to you?"

My heart picks up speed.

De Rossi's expression is a blank mask. "No one. But this is my fucking territory, and you've overstayed your welcome."

A jolt of surprise travels through me. The word territory comes with all kinds of connotations from my old life. Then I remember it's his club, his private property.

De Rossi flexes his fists. "Don't make me say it twice, Nelo."

Whatever Nelo senses in De Rossi's body language makes him grimace impotently. "I was bored out of my fucking mind in this shithole anyway," he says with a sniff. His cold gaze passes over me, before he shakes his head at De Rossi. "You should find a few more easy sluts like her to improve the entertainment."

I gasp as if I'd been struck.

De Rossi hears it. He pulls his fist back and breaks Nelo's nose.

CHAPTER 10

DAMIANO

MY HAND STINGS, but I barely notice the pain over the buzzing sound inside my head. The fury that flooded my brain the moment I saw Nelo on her made me feel like a different man. I'm not some low-level soldier salivating for a fist fight to show everyone how tough I am. I deal with my problems with a lethal combination of ruthlessness, strategy, and stealth.

But there was nothing strategic about punching Nelo—the guy Sal sent to spy on me—right in the fucking face.

I lost control.

All because of Ale.

My gaze lands on her head of silky black hair, and a shiver runs up my spine. So it begins. I fucking knew I'd regret keeping her around me.

She turns to me, her lips parted in shock.

I cast one look at Nelo on the ground, gesture to Ras that he needs to sort this shit out, and take her arm to drag her out of the restaurant.

"Are you out of your mind?" Ale demands once we manage to push through the crowd of observers. "Who asked you to get involved?"

"Everything that happens on my properties is my business," I grind out.

"You're clinically insane. Punching a customer. Get ready for a slew of scathing reviews."

"He's not a customer. He's my cousin."

She throws up a hand. "Another one? As if that makes it any better."

We're in the parking lot. Where the hell is my driver? He needs to take her home and out of my sight. This woman is messing with my head, and I don't have time for this shit with everything else that's going on.

"Oh my God." She starts squirming out of my grip. "Astrid and Vilde are still there. We need to go back."

"We are not going back."

"Damn it, De Rossi! I can't leave them. You may have started a brawl."

I let out a frustrated groan and jerk my phone out of the pocket of my slacks. "I'll tell Ras to make sure they get home safe, all right? Happy?"

"Happy? *Happy?* No, I'm not happy."

I release her arm and send a text to Ras. She's overreacting. There's not going to be a brawl. I knocked Nelo out cold, and I saw who he came in with—just a couple of low-level dealers, his new friends on the island. If he was with his brother, it may have been an entirely different thing.

"Why did you intervene?"

"Nelo is a shithead. You don't want to get involved with him."

She laughs in disbelief. "I don't need you to police who I get involved with."

Doesn't she? Does she even know what was likely to happen if I allowed Nelo to take her into that bathroom? It's like she got a few drinks in her and suddenly lost all sense of self-preservation.

"You want to know why I got involved?" I growl. "I thought you were maybe being pressured into doing something you didn't want to. I saw how he grabbed you, how he moved you around. You didn't look very interested to me."

She grows still, and suddenly, I can't bring myself to meet her eyes.

Cazzo. I should punch myself in the mouth. Did I really just admit to her I was trying my hand at being a knight in shining armor? I don't know what the ever-loving-fuck I'm doing when I'm around this woman.

"You don't know me," she finally says, her voice so low I barely pick up on it.

"No, I don't," I snap. "Maybe Nelo knows you better. Maybe he was right when he called you a—" I slam my mouth shut.

"Called me a what? A slut?"

I grind my jaw in response. No one is allowed to call her that. No one.

She sighs. "There are far worse things to be than a slut, De Rossi. You didn't need to take such offense on my behalf."

My driver appears from behind the restaurant.

"I'm sorry, señor, I was grabbing a bite to eat in the kitchen."

I jerk my head in Ale's direction. "Take her home. I need to go back there." This conversation is done. I need to go clean up my mess, down a strong drink, and figure out what I'm going to do about this woman.

Either I make her mine or completely erase her from my mind.

When I walk back into the restaurant, I see that Nelo's gone, and the customers have dispersed. The staff are cleaning up for the night, and no one dares to look at me.

Ras comes to my side. "We comped everyone's meals. One guy got it on camera, but I made him delete it in front of me. This isn't going to get out."

Maybe it won't make it to the news, but Nelo will complain to Sal. Sal might start asking questions about Ale. Questions I can't answer.

"I want him and his brother off my island."

"After tonight, that's unlikely to happen. Let's get out of here. The staff will close the place down."

We get into Ras's car, and he starts driving in the direction of my house. When I don't say anything, he sniffs and gives me a sideways glance. "Care to offer an explanation?"

"There's nothing to explain."

He cracks his neck. "My job is to mitigate risk. I can't do my job if you don't tell me what the hell is going on between you and that girl."

"I already told you I hired her."

"Last time we talked, you said that was highly unlikely to happen."

"I didn't expect her to get through the week, but she did." I begrudgingly have to admit I was wrong about her. She had a tough week—I told Inez she had to go hard on her—but Ale took everything in stride. Even the most disgusting tasks weren't beneath her. "There was no reason for me not to give her the job."

"Is a bodyguard part of her benefits package?"

I run my hand over my face. "No."

"Then what the fuck was that?"

"Nelo was asking for it." He was, but that doesn't mean I had to deal with it in public. If I had kept my cool, I could have used his behavior as an excuse to kick him off Ibiza. Now, I'll have to call Sal with a convincing lie about what happened. If he thinks I have a woman, he'll use it against me. I'll have to tell him Nelo was harassing a customer, and I couldn't allow that to happen on my property.

"This isn't like you," Ras says. "You've always kept your temper on a tight leash."

Because that's what I've had to do to survive and to keep those I care for safe. As far back as I can remember, I've been in the crosshairs of the Casalese don. I don't know how many wrong moves I have until he decides to pull the trigger.

When I don't say anything, he turns to me. "Is that girl going to be more than just an employee?"

Who is Ale Romero? Ever since I shook her hand in my office, I've had that question on my mind. I don't know anything about her. I could ask Ras to look into it, but that will only feed into my growing obsession.

I need to maintain my tentative peace with Sal until I have what I need to make a real move against him. That means what happened tonight cannot happen again.

"No," I say. But something tells me it won't be long before my conviction is tested again.

On Monday, I'm in my office signing a batch of contracts when a knock comes.

"Come in," I call out, lifting my gaze off the papers.

It's her.

Cazzo. What is she doing here? I told Inez not to send her back to my office again. All weekend, I forced myself not to think about her. Every time she popped into my head unbidden, I did one hundred pushups. My arms are fucking killing me.

All that effort, for fucking nothing. The sun streams through the window, leaving a long patch of light on the ground, and she steps right into it. *Madonna*. She looks unreal. That hair. What I would do to twist it like a rope around my fist while I bury myself inside of her.

She brushes something off her uniform and sends me a guarded look.

I lower my pen. "What is it?"

"I wanted to apologize for what happened on Friday. You were right. I was drunk."

I lean back in my chair. "I didn't expect an apology."

"I can admit when I'm wrong."

Can she? Interesting. With the attitude she likes to give me, I would have expected her to be the type that doubles down. "It's a rare quality."

"I wasn't behaving like myself that night," she says. "And you're my boss now. I'd like to put it behind us."

My lips twitch with amusement. She wants me to know she's not planning on getting herself into another mess like that again. Good. She learned her lesson. "You surprise me, Romero. I thought it would take far longer for you to get used to calling me boss."

Instead of jumping into our usual bickering, she clears her throat. "You said on Friday we'd talk about my contract today."

"Yes. Ras prepared it." I open a drawer and pull out a few sheets of paper held together by a paper clip while she slides into the chair across from me. "Take a look."

She flips through it without reading it. Then she meets my gaze. "There's a small problem."

"What kind of a problem?"

"I don't have my passport."

My body grows tense. Was she getting trafficked? It's the first suspicion that crosses my mind and it turns my mood sour. "Why's that?"

"I got robbed when I first got here. They took most of my money and my passport," she says.

Not an unusual occurrence in Ibiza, but I don't buy it. She's not telling me the full truth. If she ran away from traffickers, she won't be safe here. I need to find out who took her and make sure they won't find her again.

"You said you're Canadian."

"That's right."

"Unless you have a work visa, you don't have the right to work in Spain even with a passport."

"People do it all the time."

"Illegally."

"I'm not sure," she says.

"I am." I can feel her panic as she deflates before my eyes.

"Is there something you can do? I really need this job."

I lean forward and clasp my hands on top of the desk. She shifts under my gaze, more uncomfortable than I've ever seen her. "I want you to be honest with me," I say.

"I'm not lying. I was robbed."

"Are you in trouble?"

"What trouble? Of course not."

More lies.

"Why are you here, Romero?"

"Why does anyone come to Ibiza?"

"I don't care about anyone. I'm asking about *you*."

When she just stares at me with scared wide eyes, I decide to be direct. "Did someone bring you here by force?"

Her brows furrow. "No. Why would you ask that?"

"Sometimes girls are brought here against their will."

She purses her lips and gives her head a shake. "No one brought me. I chose to come here."

The words ring true this time. I relax a bit. No need for a manhunt after all.

"But why Spain? Why Ibiza? Canada can't be that bad. Friendly people."

"Cold as hell."

Her deadpan response draws a chuckle out of me, and some of the tension in the room eases.

She sighs. "You want honesty?"

"Yes."

"I ran away from my family. They weren't good to me. I wanted to put as much distance as I could between us. An ocean, ideally. So I came here. There's not much else to be said."

What did her family do to her? I study her carefully. "You're afraid of something."

"No." Her answer comes too quickly.

"Who are you afraid of?" I press.

"Look, it doesn't matter. I get paranoid sometimes, that's all."

"If you tell me who, I'll make sure they don't step foot on this island."

My offer shocks her, but she only considers it for a moment before she shakes her head.

"Thank you," she says. "But that won't be necessary. There's no way for them to know I'm here."

I'm tempted to argue. For someone with resources, there are many ways to track a person down. If I ask Ras to look into her, I could probably find out who her family is in a day or two. But I won't ask him, and it's for a good reason. With everything that's going on in my life, Ale Romero can't be my priority.

Still, I can't kick her to the curb when she's hiding from someone. It's untenable.

I hand her my pen. "Sign the papers."

She nearly rips it out of my hand. "Thank you."

"Not a word about this to anyone," I say once she slides the contract back to me.

"Of course. Thank you again. I mean it."

Our fingers brush when I take the pen back. Since when do I even notice shit like that?

She leaves, and I rake my fingers through my hair. There's something about Ale that pulls me to her. Something I don't understand.

But it's something that I *must* learn how to control.

CHAPTER 11

VALENTINA

MY SECOND WEEK working at Revolvr is far easier than the first. With the documents fiasco no longer hanging over me, I jump into my work with vigor. My body begins to adjust to the manual labor, and when I get home on Thursday, I have enough energy to put on my bathing suit and take a walk down to the beach.

I slip off my flip-flops and dig my toes into the warm sand. A boy runs past me and screams with delight at his colorful kite. The intensely blue water shimmers like an enormous veil of tiny diamonds. It's beautiful.

Gemma would love suntanning here while drinking a glass of cool prosecco and reading a mystery novel she picked up at the airport. Whenever we flew anywhere, it was a tradition for her to buy one and crack it open on the plane. And Cleo would have been intrigued by all the nightlife. She'd beg me to get permission from Mamma and Papà to take her out, and when she inevitably got her way, she'd make a big deal out of finding us the perfect outfits. My youngest sister loves dressing up.

God, I miss them. What I would do to squeeze them and give them both a kiss.

Instead of moping, I place my canvas bag on the ground, stuff my dress inside, and make my way toward the water. The cool waves lick at my ankles. I bite the bullet and run into the sea as fast as I can.

I haven't seen De Rossi since Monday. The fact that he hired me despite the situation with my documents, combined with his concern about me on Friday, makes me feel all sorts of strange things. Maybe he's not as bad as he seems. I'm starting to detect an actual human being beneath his brutish shell.

I dunk my head under water and squeeze my eyes shut. I considered his offer to protect me for a brief moment in his office before I realized I could never take him up on it. For one, I don't trust him enough to reveal my real identity, but more importantly, there is nothing he could do to keep the Garzolos off the island if they ever find out I'm here. Papà and Lazaro are ruthless killers. If they catch wind I'm here, they'll gun down anyone in their way. No one, not even De Rossi, would be able to keep them away.

I need to be careful around him. He's a smart guy. Observant and curious. The latter is a particularly dangerous trait for wealthy, powerful men to have. If he decides he wants to uncover the truth about Ale Romero, he has tools at his disposal to cause some serious damage. Ibiza is starting to work out for me, and I don't want to be forced to leave. I should keep my distance, but instead, I want to see him again. Where has he been all week?

When I get back to the hostel, the receptionist waves me down. "Someone's been calling for you."

My stomach drops. Immediately, I assume it's Papà. "Who?"

"Some guy named Ras. Told me to ask you to call him back as soon as possible."

Oh, thank God. "Sure, can I try now?"

She hands me the phone, and I make a mental note to buy a cell phone now that I should be able to afford it. Ras picks up on the third ring.

"Hello?" I ask uncertainly.

"Romero, I've been calling the number you have on file for hours. Where have you been?"

"I went to the beach."

"Next time, don't disappear like that," he grumbles. "We need help tonight with a big VIP booking. A bunch of our waitstaff went out to this shitty sushi joint on the northern side last night and came down with food poisoning. Can you cover?"

"What's the job exactly?"

"Taking orders and serving drinks. It's not rocket science."

This might be an opportunity to show Ras I'd do well as a server. Vilde has been telling me that the servers in the VIP areas get paid really well because they get huge tips. "What time?"

"Now, Romero. You need to get trained first."

"Jeez, okay. I thought you said it's not rocket science. I'll be there in an hour."

"Find Jessa when you arrive. She'll bring you up to speed. Good luck."

I doubt I'll need much luck. Serving drinks to a bunch of partygoers can't be that hard. Vilde's been working the upstairs terrace bar since she started, and it's been smooth sailing for her.

The first words out of Jessa's mouth when I get to Revolvr make me reconsider. "Brace yourself, sweetheart. You're about to see some bonkers shit go down."

She's a tiny twenty-five-year-old from Canterbury—a small town in England—with a platinum blond bob and expressive dark brows. They move like little caterpillars every time she speaks. "You've got to keep your head on straight, all right? The Werners are renting three of the VIP sections, and those Germans love their orgies."

I must have heard her wrong. "Orgies? *Here?*"

"Gods, no. We don't have the right setup." She waves at the space. "But this is their hunting ground. They invite whoever catches their attention up to the VIP area and then work them for a few hours to see if they'll come to their yacht for the after-party."

"And people go?"

"Course they do. Our job is to serve drinks quickly and keep everyone lubricated. I'll be mixing the drinks, and you and the other two servers will be handing them out. Keep in mind, the Werners drop like a hundred Gs on each of these nights, so we need to make sure everyone's having a good time."

I pull at the neck of my T-shirt. "Sure."

The Werners arrive an hour later with a large entourage, and whatever I imagined them to look like, it's not this. They're a stunning couple in their thirties. The woman's a curvaceous redhead with abundant curly hair, and the man a blond-haired blue-eyed hunk who looks like he starts his days with hours at the gym. There's an air of decadence around them, from the expensive clothes they both wear, to the glittering jewelry that adorns the woman's wrists.

"The wife's name is Esmeralda," Jessa whispers to me. "She's an heiress to a massive fortune from her father's steel empire. Her husband is Tobias. He's half German half Monegasque."

"Mone— What?"

"That's what they call people from Monaco. I don't know what he does. He never talks about it."

"You've had conversations with them?"

Jessa's pale skin turns pink. "Some."

I raise one suspicious brow at her. "You've been to their yacht."

She reddens more. "A few times."

"How was it?"

"Memorable," she says, dragging the back of her hand over her brow. "Definitely memorable. But those memories are for me and me only. Off you go."

I keep my distance from the Werners, allowing the more experienced staff to serve them while I run around getting orders from the other guests that start to trickle in.

Sometime later, De Rossi appears. I realize I'm holding my breath as I watch him cross the VIP area. He's wearing all black today—black suit, black shirt, black tie—like a shadowy god who's come down to walk among his disciples. His presence cuts through the room, drawing eyes to him.

A fluttering sensation explodes low inside my belly. I want to pretend like I'm immune to his pull, but every time I look away, my gaze keeps gravitating back to him. The Werners stand up to greet him with warm smiles and take turns embracing him as if they're old friends.

I wonder how they know each other. Does De Rossi join them on their yacht? Has he slept with Esmeralda?

I shouldn't care, but I do. I register every glance and touch between him and Esmeralda, and each one feels like the sharp prick of a knife. God, it irritates the hell out of me.

De Rossi sits down and looks over his shoulder. His dark gaze settles on my body and sends a shiver down my spine. Esmeralda and Tobias take note. She raises one elegant hand and waves me over with a flick of her wrist.

Crap. I can't ignore her, not when I need to show De Rossi how good of a server I could be.

Clutching my tray to my chest, I make my way to the booth.

"What can I get you?" My tone is affable, but I do my best not to look at De Rossi. Who knows what he might see spelled out across my face?

Esmeralda's lips part in a genuine smile, and she tosses her hair over her shoulder. Beside her, her husband gives me a nod of acknowledgement.

"How are you tonight?" she asks.

I catch a whiff of her perfume—Opium by YSL. Cleo wears the same one. "I'm doing well, thank you."

"What's your name?"

"Ale."

"I don't remember seeing you here before. Are you new at Revolvr?"

"I am. I just started working here last week."

"Well, you picked a great place. I know our friend—" she places her hand on De Rossi's shoulder "—treats his servers very well."

"She's not a server," De Rossi cuts in.

"What is she then?" Tobias says before taking a sip of his drink.

"Ale's on our custodial team. We were short on staff tonight, so she's filling in."

So much for getting a promotion. I do my best not to let my disappointment show and force myself to meet his gaze. "Happy to help however I can."

The coldness in his eyes throws me off. I frown. What's changed since Monday? He accepted my apology and gave me a job. I thought we were past all this.

"You have a good attitude," Esmeralda notes. "You'd be smart to hold on to this one," she says to. "And with a face like that, there's no reason to keep her hidden away. Isn't she beautiful, Tobias?"

"You look just like a young Monica Belluci," her husband comments. "It's uncanny. I'm sure you've gotten that before."

Heat blankets my cheeks. "Thank you, that's a very kind compliment."

A seductive smile appears on his wife's face. "We'd love to invite you to the after-party we're hosting on our ya—"

"I don't pay my staff to stand around and be admired, Esmeralda," De Rossi says in a harsh tone.

The temperature drops. Tobias's eyes narrow and Esmeralda shifts uncomfortably.

"Ale, stop preening and bring us another bottle of champagne with a few glasses."

Preening? My grip tightens around the tray. "Of course." The smile I give De Rossi is deadly.

"It was a pleasure to meet you," Esmeralda says pleasantly, but her expression is perturbed. "Do stop by throughout the night."

Since my hopes for a promotion are firmly in the gutter now, and my presence seems to piss of De Rossi, I think I might. After all, who am I to say no to his important guests? "Gladly."

When I return with the champagne, he watches my every move as I serve him and the Werners. His behavior toward me seems to have warned them off talking to me again, but they thank me as I hand them their glasses. I'm about to leave when De Rossi closes his hand around my wrist and tugs me down until my ear is in line with his lips. An electric current erupts over my skin. "Don't get any ideas." His voice is like a bite of a poisoned whip. "That after-party isn't for the likes of you."

Heat explodes over my cheeks. The likes of me? What exactly does that mean? A spoiled princess? A lazy bimbo? I thought I'd proven to De Rossi he was wrong about me. What else does he want me to do?

I jerk my wrist out of his grip and walk away without a second look. Inside my chest, an angry fire burns.

The likes of me.

Maybe he recognizes exactly the kind of worthless scum you are.

It's an intrusive thought, and it's far from the first time I've had it. I've been Googling how to get rid of these thoughts, because every day they seem to be multiplying. Images of dead, bloodied bodies. Memories of their screams.

No, I won't engage with it. I saved a girl. It took me a long time, but I eventually did the right thing. Doesn't that count for something?

You murdered dozens first.

The voice in my head becomes Lazaro's. *Some days, you were so calm while you did it, I thought maybe you'd finally grown to like it like I did.*

I lean against a pillar and exhale a long breath. I need to get his voice out of my head.

I'll find you. And when I do, you'll pay for your betrayal.

My husband might still be alive. He could be hunting for me this very second. When he finds me…I'm unlikely to survive. And what about Lorna? Did I condemn her to a painful death?

My breathing becomes labored. It's too hot in here, too loud, too packed. I need to get out of here. *Now.*

My feet carry me to the emergency exit, and I push past the door. The small back area is dimly lit and completely empty. I suck in the humid air with the enthusiasm of someone who's drowning and repeatedly pluck my shirt away from my skin.

How long can I function like this, with the past dragging me down? I need a therapist, but that's out of the question. My secrets are coming with me to my grave, which means I just have to suck it up. It's still better than being back in New York. At least I can promise myself I'll never hurt another person again.

I'm taking deep breaths to calm myself when the emergency door is flung open.

When I see who it is, I shrink into myself. "Please, De Rossi. Not now."

My boss stalks over to where I'm leaning against a wall, his face made all the more brutally handsome by his deep frown. He stops a few feet away and adjusts his cufflinks. "I want to make sure nothing was lost in translation. You are not to go onto that yacht."

"That woman didn't even get a chance to get the full invitation out of her mouth," I say.

"I know Tobias and Esmeralda. When they see something they like, they don't give up that easily."

"And why should you care if I go?"

His eyes narrow. "You are not going to that party."

Fury bursts inside of me. "Oh my God, I don't give a crap about the stupid party!"

My shout stuns him. I take the rare opportunity of his mouth being shut to lay it all out. "What is your problem with me? In the beginning, you were testing me. I get it. But I passed the test. You hired me yourself! What else do I have to do to get you to leave me alone?"

His nostrils flare as he takes a step toward me. "That's exactly what I'm trying to do. Leave you alone. Which is why I'm telling you not to go to the same event I'll be going to tonight."

Something in my chest tightens. "Don't want me seeing you having sex? Afraid I'll be unimpressed?"

"That is not what I'm afraid of."

I scowl at him. "Then what is it?"

Frustration contorts his expression. "Goddamn it, Ale. Why can't you just do as I say?"

I push off the wall. "You said the party wasn't 'for the likes of' me. What does that even mean?"

He's staring down at me, his chest rising and falling with rapid breaths. "It means you drive me fucking crazy."

"By doing what?"

"By merely existing."

"I don't understand you."

"Maybe you'll understand this." He presses me against the wall and crashes his lips to mine.

It's like someone pressed the delete key. Everything around me clears, and my awareness zeroes in on the sensation of his kiss. The rough stubble of his chin. The softness of his mouth as he darts out his tongue to lick my bottom lip. His hands are on me—one in my hair, the other on my waist—and they're fiery brands. When he tugs me closer, my hard nipples brush against his powerful chest.

I let out a moan. He takes the opportunity to deepen the kiss, and I think back to all those times I wondered what he'd taste like.

Now I know. Whiskey and sin.

When I drag my nails down his back, he emits a sound I've never heard a man make before. It's half growl half groan, and it travels all the way down to my toes.

He breaks the kiss and hisses through his teeth. "The moment I saw you, I thought you were the most infuriatingly beautiful woman I'd ever laid eyes on," he says against my lips. "One look was enough for me to know I'd lose my mind over you if I wasn't careful. I tried to be. I manufactured reasons for why I should stay away from you, but I can't seem to make any of them stick."

My stomach bursts with butterflies.

"I don't need a distraction right now, but my self-control is hanging on by a fucking thread," he says, dragging his lips over my cheek. "If I see someone else's hands on you, I'll break them. If you come to the party, the only person who'll touch you will be me."

It feels like someone's dripping hot lava into my bloodstream. I'm burning up. "I don't even know your first name," I mumble like an idiot, still in shock at his revelation.

"Damiano," he says. "But don't you dare say it back to me. If I hear my name just once on your lips, I know I'll become addicted."

"You know yourself that well?"

He shakes his head. "I thought I did before I met you."

I let out a ragged breath and push him away from me gently. I can't think with his body practically enveloping me. All of the blood in my brain has travelled elsewhere. "I have to get back."

He lets me pass, but when I'm halfway to the door, he calls out to me.

"Ale, choose wisely."

I know he means it to be a warning. But I think it sounds like a plea.

CHAPTER 12

VALENTINA

WHEN I REENTER THE CLUB, it feels as if my brain has lost some of its key functionality.

Like my ability to think straight.

He said he would lose his mind over me, but it appears I may have beaten him to the punch.

He said if I said his name, he'd become addicted, but I'm *already* hooked after one hit. I'll be replaying that kiss and that ferocious confession in my head until the day I die. When someone says those kinds of words to you, you don't forget a single one.

Damn him.

I walk up to Jessa and ask her to pour me a shot. De Rossi's taste is still in my mouth, and I need to get rid of it before I become too used to it.

Jessa gives me a curious look.

"What?" I ask.

"You made an impression." She extracts something out of her pocket. "Take it."

It's a heavy black card embossed with a gold script.

"It's the official invitation," she says.

"Ibiza Marina, three am," I read.

"It's close to here," she says.

De Rossi was right, the Werners don't give up easily. They also don't seem to particularly care that my boss doesn't want me at their party.

"Are you going?" I ask Jessa.

"No. I'm seeing someone. It's kind of serious."

"You could just come to hang out."

She snorts. "You won't see a lot of people just hanging out at these kinds of parties. If you decide to go, you better be ready to participate."

Images flash inside my head. His big hands on my waist. The weight of his body pressing against mine. That heady male scent enveloping me from every direction. I want to kiss him again so badly it hurts. I want to do a lot more than kiss too.

Thirty minutes later, the Werners rise from their seats. Damiano is with them, and as they're about to walk through the exit, he looks over his shoulder and catches my gaze.

Goosebumps erupt over my skin.

If I see someone else's hands on you, I'll break them.

It's a hyperbole, of course. I have to remind myself that he's not like the men from my old life.

Then I remember how he broke Nelo's nose.

I gnaw on my lip, and he watches me for a second before he finally leaves.

I shouldn't follow. I *really* shouldn't. But then I realize something. Damiano told me not to go, but *he's* going. And according to Jessa, he's not going there to just hang out. Is he going to try to screw me out of his system tonight?

I run my tongue over my bottom row of teeth and shake my head. No, that's not how this is going to work. Damiano said he didn't need a distraction, but that's his own problem. I'm going to do what I want.

I'm getting on that boat.

I wrap up my shift, change out of my uniform, and walk down to the dock. The muffled sound of electronic music follows me. It's just past prime time at most of the clubs. My outfit is as casual as it gets—jean shorts and a T-shirt—but I'm too anxious to get to the party to waste time going home to change.

I still don't know what madness has taken over me, but it feels like it won't let up until whatever this thing is between Damiano and me comes to a head. Either I call his bluff and prove to myself his words were just an exaggeration, or I end up in his bed.

Anticipation curls inside my stomach like velvet ribbon.

As I get closer to the yacht, I get picked up by a group of other partygoers heading the same way.

We get on after showing our invitations to a beefy security guard, and like most things in Ibiza, this yacht is larger than life. I've been on a yacht this size with my family once. Papà had a meeting with one of his distant relatives from Sicily, so he flew the whole family to Palermo to meet Fabio, our cousin thrice removed. His boat was enormous but tacky. Everything was bejeweled and smelled like bad cologne.

This one is nothing like it. It's tasteful and modern. I pass by the main salon where a few couples are making out heavily and take the stairs to the bridge deck.

The sky here is impossibly clear. I'm studying the stars when someone appears by my side. It's a young man who looks to be around my age, thoroughly tanned from long days in the sun.

He catches my eye and gives me an easygoing smile. "Incredible, right?"

"I can't remember the last time I saw a sky this clear," I confess. "I've spent most of my life in big cities."

"Same," he says. "I'm from Chicago."

"You look like you left a long time ago."

"I fell in love with island life. I'm based out of Mallorca now, but I come to Ibiza often for business." His smile turns flirtatious. "And pleasure. My name's Adrian. What's your name?"

"Ale."

"Do you know Tobias and Esmeralda well?"

"Not at all. I met them tonight and somehow got an invitation to this. It's all a bit overwhelming."

"If you want to take the edge off, let me know. I might have something." He pats the pocket of his jacket.

I'm taken aback. Is he offering me drugs?

He laughs slightly at my expression. "You haven't been here long, I gather. I apologize. I shouldn't have assumed."

"Assumed what?"

He lifts one shoulder. "That you're running on chemicals like the rest of us."

I look down at the revelry happening in the salon. Of course, I'm aware people get high here. I just didn't expect him to be so blunt. Back in New York, no one would have dared to offer drugs to the don's daughter. In Ibiza, I'm a nobody, though. I could do whatever I want, and no one would try to stop me.

No one would care.

I have so many things I want to forget. Maybe getting high would help me smudge those memories until I can no longer make out the details.

I chew on the inside of my cheeks. "Well—"

"*Adrian.*" A severe voice slices through the air between us.

The hairs on the nape of my neck stand straight. I don't need to look at De Rossi to know what he looks like right now—gorgeous and powerful and mad.

Adrian's playful expression melts away as soon as he sees who it is. "Señor De Rossi. How are you?"

"Leave us," he orders.

"We're in the middle of a conversation," I say.

Adrian speaks over me, "Of course. I was just saying goodbye."

I whirl around. "Adrian, you don't need to leave. De Rossi, if you want to talk to me, you'll need to wait for your turn."

There's a stunned silence. Adrian is looking at me with wide, bewildered eyes that glint with a hint of fear, and the sight of it annoys me. Is this what I looked like when I meekly obeyed Papà's and Lazaro's orders? Saying no to them always felt impossible. But my life isn't on the line when it comes to De Rossi, and neither is Adrian's. Why does everyone treat him like he's a god? Seriously, is it just the money? If that's all it takes to command this kind of deference, why did Papà even need his enforcers?

Adrian says a rushed *lo siento* and runs off without another glance at me.

"One day, I pray I'll understand why everyone listens to you," I say.

He starts to advance. "He listens to me because he works for me."

"Of course he does," I say, throwing up my hands. "I think next time I talk to someone, I'll need to do a background check first."

"Big words for a woman without a passport."

I frown. Is he just teasing me, or is that a hint that he's been digging?

He halts a few inches away, close enough to blanket me with his heat. Inside his dark eyes, something dangerous is brewing. "You came."

The way he says it makes it clear he thinks I'm here for him. I better set him straight. "We both know what this party is for, De Rossi. You decided you could go, but I couldn't? That's not how it works." I place my hands on his hard chest and try to press him away.

He doesn't budge a single inch. His chin tips downward, his gaze glued to my lips. "I warned you."

"So what? Maybe no one's ever told you this before, but you're not God. Just because you say something, doesn't mean everyone has to listen." I press harder against his chest.

His palms wrap around my wrists. "Why did you come?"

"Because I felt like it."

"Why?" He drags one calloused thumb down the inside of my wrist. I feel that small caress all the way down to my belly. I shouldn't have touched him. When I try to ease myself out of his grip there's zero give. He's not hurting me, but his hold is firm.

I huff a breath. "For the same reason you did. To have fun."

"Do you want to get fucked, Ale?"

My eyes blow wide. A wave of arousal slams into me so hard that I forget how to breathe. "Excuse me?" I choke out.

De Rossi leans in closer to my ear. "You didn't come here to look at the stars," he says in a low, seductive voice.

No, I didn't. The reason I'm here is because I couldn't stand the thought of him screwing some random woman while I spent my entire evening thinking about that kiss.

But I'm not about to tell him that. "I'm not here for you." My voice comes out all breathy.

His lips move against the shell of my ear. "Then who are you here for?"

"For myself."

"And what do *you* want?"

Do you want to get fucked? Heat blooms across my chest. "I don't know."

"Yes, you do," he coaxes. His hand releases my right wrist and trails down the center of my chest before stopping at the waist of my shorts.

I should stop him and put an end to whatever this is pronto, but as he nudges my T-shirt up an inch and starts to caress my midriff with his thumb, my body sings. Sparks come alive beneath my skin and travel all the way down to my clit.

"I think that wet pussy of yours wants to get fucked hard tonight," he whispers. "I think it wants to get ruined by a big cock."

I lose my ability to think. Who talks like that to a woman? Who the hell gave De Rossi permission to use the English language as a method of mind control? "You're wrong," I breathe.

This earns me a decadent chuckle. His fingers dip into my waistband. "Why don't you let me check?"

He wants to feel how wet I am.

My God, Vale. Wake up. Tell him no. Tell his cocky ass to jump off the boat so he can see how wet the ocean is.

I open and close my fist, the one attached to the wrist he's still holding. "De Rossi...this is..."

Just say no.

He lifts my hand to his mouth and gives it a soft kiss. "There's no need to be timid," he says, trailing his lips against my skin. "No need to hide how your body's reacting. Do you want to feel what you're doing to me?"

I nod, because I am weak. The moment he steps closer, presses his groin to my stomach, and lets me feel his hard length, I let out a needy whimper. It's steely and huge and clearly wants to be inside of me. My walls flutter with anticipation. What would it feel like to have De Rossi fuck me with that thing?

"Your turn," he says, pulling his lips away from my hand.

I nod again, keeping eye contact with him. His gaze darkens with triumph, and without any rush, he slides his entire hand past the waistband of my shorts and underwear. We're still standing on the deck. Anyone can see us, although they probably have far more interesting things to watch on this boat.

I'm so damn wet that he can feel it as soon as his middle finger reaches my clit. His expression melts with pleasure as he gently circles the hard nub and makes me squirm in his grip. "That's it." He pushes further in and probes my sopping entrance. "So warm and wet," he mutters. "So perfect."

A moan fights its way out of my throat. "Damiano..."

He shuts his eyes. A tremor runs up the thick column of his throat.

Just then, I remember what he told me about calling him by his name.

"You always remember your first hit," he mutters.

And then he kisses me. The finger that's still inside of me curls in a rhythmic way, setting my nerve endings firing and making my body weak until all I can do is hold on to him for dear life.

We make out on that bridge deck for what feels like hours until I'm dizzy, on the verge of coming, and unbearably hot. Suddenly, he breaks the kiss, pulls his hand out of my shorts, and tugs me into his chest. "Let's go."

"Where?" I ask breathlessly.

"To my bedroom."

"We're on a yacht."

"I own the yacht. I lease it out to the Werners for the season."

Why am I even surprised? The haze of my arousal lifts a tiny bit. "Do you ever get tired of showing off?"

He guides me across the deck, his hand placed firmly on the small of my back. "Never."

By the time we get to the door of what must be his room, I've managed to get some of my bearings back. I can still walk away before this escalates any further. "I don't think we should do this," I say, even though there is zero conviction behind my words. Excitement buzzes under my skin at the thought of what he might do to me in that bedroom.

He unlocks the door with a swipe of a card and holds it open for me with his palm. His gaze melts me from the inside out.

"Get inside, Ale."

This is it. The moment of truth. Once that door closes behind me, I know I won't leave.

His eyes are trained on my face. Warm hazel orbs made nearly black by his enlarged irises. Inside of all that darkness is a spark. A bright candle flame that burns for me.

I latch on to that imagery and convince myself that I'm the one in control here.

And then I step across the threshold.

CHAPTER 13

VALENTINA

DAMIANO FLICKS on the lights and his bedroom comes into focus. There's a wide desk, a king-sized bed, a bar cart in one corner, and two upholstered armchairs placed by a small coffee table. Its sophisticated, tidy, and very male. Nothing is flashy, but it's clear that every piece of furniture and every scrap of textile in here has been meticulously chosen by a professional.

I gravitate to the carved wooden desk. "This is gorgeous," I say as I run my fingers along the glass surface that protects the designs.

Damiano pours two glasses of wine and hands one to me. His eyes drop to the desk. "It's one of my favorite possessions. My sister got this made for me by an artisan outside of Napoli." A rare softness creeps into his expression.

The image of little Damiano holding the toddler in his arms squeezes at my heart. "You're close."

"Yes," he says.

I like that he's fond of his sister. It's a glimpse at a part of his life I haven't seen before, and it makes me feel closer to him. If I told him how much I missed my sisters, I have a suspicion he'd understand.

He clears his throat as if to dispel any lingering thoughts and takes a sip of his wine. Everything about this man is attractive, down to the way his Adam's apple moves as he swallows. Heat blankets my skin again. I down half of my glass in one go and cradle it with both of my palms.

The temperature rises further when he places his glass down on the desk and squares his body toward me. He lifts his hand to my face and traces my jaw with his thumb. "How's the wine?"

"Very good," I say.

"I know you'll taste even better." His voice drags over the place between my legs like a silk tie.

I have a serious weakness, I realize. After Lazaro's disinterest, the idea of a powerful, gorgeous, sane man wanting me is like catnip. I want to believe so badly that Damiano is affected by me, but there's a needy voice in the back of my head that craves more convincing.

"You hated me," I whisper, thinking back to how he wouldn't give me a single break in that first week following us meeting.

Damiano pries the glass out of my hands and places it beside his. "I never hated you." He moves his palm to the back of my neck. "I doubted you. I thought your stubborn strength was an act, but it's not. It's real." The tip of his nose traces my cheek bone. "You are magnificent."

My God, if only he knew who I really was... He's wrong

about me being strong, yet he speaks with such conviction that I almost believe him. It's like he can shape me into someone else by his willpower alone.

He moves closer, pressing the length of his body against mine and enveloping me in his heady scent. When his lips find mine, I moan into his mouth. Everything is languid and hot, like an erotic fever dream.

I'm not wearing a bra. His palms find my bare breasts under my shirt, and the sensation of his calloused thumbs dragging over my nipples turn them into hard points. He twists them lightly, then grunts when I start to buck against him, desperate to ease the pressure building between my legs.

He breaks the kiss, drops his hands to my shorts, and peels them quickly down my legs.

When he kneels in front of me, I press my palms against the desk. Anticipation of what's about to come makes my breasts ache and my pussy quiver. He considers my thong for half a second before he fists one of the straps and tears it off me.

I yelp. "Damiano!"

His wicked gaze lands on my face. "Sit on the edge of the desk," he commands, "and spread your legs."

My heartbeat drums inside my ears. I've only had sex once. *Once.* This is already way more charged than anything that happened between Lazaro and I that one night. I swallow and feel blood rise to my cheeks. I get my butt up but I can't seem to make my legs move.

Damiano notices my hesitation. One of his brows arches up. "Timid?"

"No," I say immediately. He's baiting me because he knows I'll bite.

"Then show me that glistening pussy."

I groan. My face feels like it's sunburned.

He drags his big hands down my bare thighs. "You're shy."

"That's ridiculous."

A hint of a smile appears on his lips. "Then why the hesitation?"

"Give me a moment, okay?"

His eyes fill with a subtle tenderness that nearly unravels me. "You don't need to be shy around me, Ale. There's nothing you can do to make me think your body is anything less than perfect."

He wraps a palm over each knee and starts to move them apart with gentle force. I shut my eyes and breathe. Deeply. I'm probably leaking all over his beautiful desk.

When he's finished spreading me open, he makes a rough sound in his throat. "Fuck."

He shrugs off his suit jacket, and rolls up the sleeves of his shirt, looking like a man possessed. Slowly, he brings his face closer and closer, and then he draws his hot tongue over my seam.

That first lick is so divine that I fall back on my elbows and let out a desperate whine. He twists his tongue over my clit, then drags his teeth over the hood, playing me like a fucking instrument. How does he know how to do this? Do all normal men learn at some point?

When he lifts my thighs and places them over his shoulders, I collapse fully on the desk. Something hard digs into my back. "Ouch."

He peeks up at me, his mouth still sucking on my clit.

"Not you," I pant as I reach under my back and wrap my fingers around the offending object. It's a thick, expensive pen.

He takes it from me.

"What are you doing?"

His eyes darken as he starts fucking me with his tongue. I feel the cold surface of the pen brush against that other hole, and I start to squirm. "Damiano—"

He pushes the end of the pen, wet with my juices, inside just an inch, and I gasp in shock. My thighs shake, it's like my entire body is a live wire, vibrating with electricity. He's still watching me, tracking every reaction he sees on my face, and I'm sure that in this moment, he knows what I'm experiencing better than I do. I'm so overwhelmed with new sensations, I can't think. He replaces his tongue with his thick fingers and does that come hither motion from earlier. It's enough to push me over the edge. I dig my fingers into the carved edge of the desk. Everything dims except for the powerful shocks of pleasure that radiate from my core.

He holds me steady while I ride out the waves, and once they pass, he takes the end of the pen out of me, stands, and presses his body over mine. I'm still panting, my breaths fanning over his wet lips as he says, "You taste so fucking good, Ale."

"Do I?" I've never thought about my taste before.

"Lick it off my lips."

He wants me to taste myself? I'm not sure how I feel about it, but I know I'll do anything he tells me to at the moment. His dark gaze holds me in its grip as I dart out my tongue and drag it over his full bottom lip. Hmm. It's not unpleasant. Earthy and a little salty. I lick him again, and this time he moans and presses his mouth over mine.

I tangle my hands in his hair and wrap my legs around his waist as he devours me. I can feel the desire he has for me, and not just because of the hardness in his pants, but because of the desperate vigor behind his kiss.

This man *wants* me. If I hadn't run, I would have lived my entire life without experiencing this once.

That realization sets off something inside of me. To my utter horror, I begin to cry. Tears trail paths down my cheeks, and I don't want him to see them, so I break the kiss and press my nose into his chest. I want to inhale his skin, to imprint its memory somewhere deep inside my head.

But he's not stupid. Far from it. It takes him only moments to realize something is wrong.

He places his hands on the desk and pushes himself up to put some distance between us. When he sees my face, his expression becomes perplexed. "What happened?"

"Nothing," I say with a watery voice. "I'm okay."

He helps me sit up. "You're crying."

"Unfortunately."

"I don't understand. Talk to me."

God, why does he have to sound so worried? It makes me cry more.

He runs his hand over the back of his head and swears. "This is really not the reaction I was going for." He produces a tissue from somewhere and hands it to me. "Here."

I swipe at my drippy nose and eyes and at last manage to compose myself. "You didn't do anything. It's just..." I glance away. "I'm overwhelmed. You see...I haven't had that done to me before."

His amazement is underscored with a sharp intake of breath. "You haven't had a man go down on you?"

I shake my head. "No."

"I was the first."

"Yes."

He swipes his bottom lip with his thumb and studies me for a long moment. "You don't have much experience with this, do you?"

Embarrassment prickles over my cheeks. "No."

I don't know what I expect him to do, but it sure isn't to sigh and pull me into his chest. "I assumed things. Again."

"It's fine. I—" I clear my throat. "I'm ready to keep going."

"We're done for tonight."

"What? I thought you had other plans."

He rubs his cheek against my temple. "The things I said to you... What did they make you feel?"

"The dirty things?"

"Yes."

"I liked them."

"Did you?"

"God, yes."

He makes a noise of satisfaction. "Good. I have so many more things I want to tell you. To do to you. But not tonight."

He lifts me up by my thighs, making me curl my bare legs around his waist, and carries me to the enormous bed. He's still hard, I can feel him right between my legs, but when I try to grind against him, he moves me so that I can't reach him anymore.

My emotions are all over the place. I'm embarrassed and vulnerable. I really screwed this up, and I don't understand why I couldn't hold my emotions in. It's like my mind isn't working the way it should—the way it did before everything happened with Lazaro.

Damiano pulls the duvet back and places me on the silky sheets.

"I'm a mess," I mumble.

He climbs in beside me and wraps his arms around my waist. The empathy he's displaying at the moment is so unexpected that I start to question my entire perception of him. Who is the real Damiano?

"Get some sleep," he tells me, holding me close to him.

He caresses my back with light strokes until he drifts off. When his breathing slows, I tilt my head up and analyze his face. He looks at peace.

Unfortunately, I can't relate. I won't be able to catch a wink here with him. My heart is bouncing around my chest, and my thoughts race like a herd of wild horses. I think back to him kneeling between my legs, and I can't believe that *that* is what sex can be. Of course, I was aware that what Lazaro and I did could hardly constitute real lovemaking, but even in my most optimistic fantasies, I could never have come close. The way he looked at me the entire time, the way he *saw* me, the pleasure that he made me feel...

I squeeze my eyes shut. For Damiano, this was just one of many hookups. For me, a revelation. This asymmetry is not in my favor, and I can't risk giving him any more power over me.

When I'm confident he's in deep sleep, I climb out of the bed, tug my clothes on, and get off the yacht. As I flag a taxi to take me back to the hostel, I'm sure of one thing and one thing only.

This can't happen again.

CHAPTER 14

DAMIANO

I WAKE up with a dick harder than a steel bar.

Despite the unpleasant heaviness in my balls, a grin unfurls over my lips at memories of last night. I was the first man to taste Ale. The first one to dip my tongue into her hot, needy flesh. Her inexperience is a surprise I hadn't expected, but it awakens something fiercely possessive inside of me. I'm going to really fucking enjoy teaching her all the ways we can get each other off.

Starting now. I extend my hand, searching for a full breast or a firm ass cheek, but all I find is a cold silk sheet.

What the fuck?

I crack my eyes open, and I can't fucking believe it.

She's gone.

With a growl, I shoot out of the bed and check my desk. No message? Not even a text?

Frustration rages inside of me as I text my driver to go check she made it home. I barge into the shower and angrily jerk off.

This is what I get for being soft with her last night, but what the hell was I supposed to do? Have sex with her while she was upset? No. I like my partners willing and enthusiastic.

I scrub the sponge over my back hard enough for it to sting. That dumbass Adrian. It drove me crazy to see him flirting with her. I should have tossed him overboard like I wanted to, but I knew it would cause a scene and put an end to my plans for the night.

Ale came to the party for me. Her weak denials didn't fool me. Even with my warning, she came, and now that we've crossed a threshold, there's no going back.

She's already mine.

My phone is ringing as I step out of the shower. I pick it up. "Speak."

"She made it back to the hostel," my driver says. "The receptionist said she arrived around five am."

"Made it back to *what*?"

"Her hostel."

"*Cazzo*. Where?"

"Sant Antoni."

The cheaper side of Ibiza where a lot of the seasonal workers live. It's been getting more and more dangerous over the last few years, mostly petty crime and robberies, but a few violent assaults too. I don't like the idea of her staying there.

"What does it look like?" I ask.

"The hostel?" The driver blows out a breath. "I mean, it's not great, but it could be worse."

"Take photos and send them to me."

"Yes, boss."

I hang up and watch as the images come through. *Hostel Clandestino*. It's an unkempt property on a street I know isn't well lit at night.

She's not going to be staying there much longer.

Ale has a shift on Saturday, and I make sure she's assigned to clean my office. I can't remember the last time I was here during the day on the weekend, but I don't have the patience to wait until Monday to have the conversation I want to have with her. As I enter Revolvr, I greet the weekend staff and pour myself a *hierbas* from the premium bar before I make my way to the back. I've just gotten settled in behind my desk when the knock comes.

"Come in."

The door cracks open, and there she is, in that plain blue uniform and a cart of cleaning supplies.

How the fuck does she still manage to be the most beautiful woman I've ever seen?

She meets my gaze and sucks in a breath. Does she know I'm imagining her as naked as she was on my boat right now? Good. One look at her, and I'm already worked up. There's no reason why she should be spared.

She shuts the door behind her and parks the cart by the wall. "We need to talk."

What does my *principessa* want to say? It better be an apology for sneaking off in the middle of the night. She doesn't get to walk away after giving me nothing but a little taste. I told her I'd get addicted. I made it clear that once my restraint snaps, she needs to be ready for everything I've been holding back.

Didn't she believe me? I'll remind her of the kind of man I am.

I lean back in my seat. "I have this fantasy where I bend you over my desk, fill you with my cum, and make you spend the rest of the day with me dripping down your thighs."

I can't help but grin when she lets out a helpless groan. She fucking walked out on me. Did she really think she could do that with no repercussions?

It takes her a moment to regain her composure. "You sure you don't want a therapist? He'd have a field day with you. Fantasies like that usually have hidden meanings."

"I know what this one means."

"What?"

I lean forward and place my elbows on the desk. "It means I want to make you mine."

Her eyes widen. There's something really fucking satisfying about making her blush.

"Did you think that after Friday, all you'd need to do is crook your finger at me, and I'll come running?"

"I'm more interested in crooking my finger inside of you," I say. "Maybe you don't know this, but there's a special spot there that makes a woman come."

My allusion to her inexperience makes her turn beet red. "I need to get started on my work," she says in a tight voice.

"We're not done talking."

"Yes, we are," she says, reaching for the mop. "What happened on that boat isn't going to happen again."

Frustration unfurls inside my chest. She's putting up resistance. Why? It's clear as day that she wants to fuck me. What's holding her back?

"Why not?" I demand.

She dips the mop into a bucket of soapy water and flicks her gaze to me.

"I'm not looking to get involved with anyone right now."

"Why?" I repeat.

She brushes a strand of hair off her face, looking nervous. I know whatever comes out of her mouth won't be the whole truth.

"Look, I practically just got here, and I'm not settled in yet. I have a million things on my mind."

A million things I could resolve in a day if she'd let me.

I'll start with one.

"My driver told me where you live," I say.

Confusion mars her features. "Okay. And?"

"You need to move out."

"What for?"

My jaw muscles tense. "That hostel may as well be a halfway house. I don't want you there."

Anger flares inside her eyes. "You don't *want me* there? Where I live is none of your business."

It became my business the moment my lips touched hers. I open a desk drawer, pull out a wad of cash, and slide it toward her. "Use this for a deposit on a nice place."

She's shocked at first, but it doesn't take long for that shock to morph into fury.

"Are you trying to buy me?"

I was about to tell her she can quit her job and I'd pay for all her things, but her outrage makes me backtrack on that idea.

"No. I'm trying to help you," I say. "And I'm also trying to get you into my bed again, but those are separate things. Take it."

She peers at the rubber-banded stack and shakes her head. "I don't want a handout. I know it's not the best place, but I can wait to move until I save up enough."

Clearly, she hasn't spent any time looking at the price of places in Ibiza. "It'll take months for you to earn enough for a deposit at your current pay."

"Then promote me," she says, tipping her chin up. "Make me a server."

"Take the cash, and you can consider it done."

She squeezes her lips together and nods. "I'll pay it all back," she says. "You can take it off my paycheck until I've reimbursed you."

I flick my fingers dismissively. "My payroll team has better things to do than calculating that."

"Then I'll pay you back in cash."

"Sure," I say only to appease her pride. Not a chance I'll take a single euro off her hands. My lips curve into a smirk. "Now, let's get back to that fantasy of mine."

"I don't get it," she says, putting the mop down and crossing her arms over her chest. "Why would you want me after how I reacted last time?"

Is she embarrassed about her crying? *Cazzo,* this woman really has no idea what she does to me. "You cried because you were overwhelmed at how well I made you come with my tongue. You really think that's a turnoff, Ale?"

Her cheeks turn pink again. "So you're turned on by my inexperience."

"And by all the things I can teach you. If you let me."

I rise from my seat and move to stand behind her. She's very still as I brush her hair from her neck and inhale her delicious scent. "I can be gentle, Ale." My lips trail against her skin. "And patient. I can do things to you that will make Thursday night pale in comparison."

Her breath quickens. She tilts her head to give me better access and releases a pent-up sigh. "You said you didn't need a distraction."

"I changed my mind."

A throat clears behind us.

I look over and swallow down a curse word. It's Ras. Can he have any worse timing?

Ale quickly moves away from me, and Ras purses his lips. "Didn't mean to interrupt."

I shoot him a glare. "Knock next time."

"I need to talk to you about something."

"I'll leave you two to it," Ale says as she hurries out. When she passes Ras, he gives her a wary look.

I know he's not going to be shy about sharing his opinions with me.

Just as Ale is about to disappear, I see the money still lying on my desk.

"Wait," I call out.

She halts halfway out the door and turns around.

I lift the cash in my hand. "You forgot this."

Her posture stiffens, and Ras's expression darkens some more. I half expect her to argue, but instead, she plucks the money out of my hand and walks out the door.

It feels like a victory. At this pace, it won't take long for me to wear down her resistance, and then, I can explore that body for all it has to offer.

Ras crosses his arms over his chest.

"What?"

"I looked into her."

"I didn't ask you to do that."

"As far as I can tell, Ale Romero doesn't exist."

I glance away. The news isn't a complete surprise, but I still dislike hearing it. Now that her and I are involved, I can't afford to turn a blind eye to her omissions. It's time to dig up the truth.

"What did you find out?" I ask.

Ras sits down across from me. "There are twenty-four women alive with that name. I checked into all of them, and none of them are her."

"So you know who she's not, but you don't know who she is."

"Not yet. I wanted to talk to you before I spend more time on it." He props his ankle on his knee. "Is this serious?"

"You know I don't do serious."

"What is it then?"

"I want to keep her around for a little while," I say. "She intrigues me."

"Ever since she started here, you've spent more than double your usual time at Revolvr."

I frown. That can't possibly be right. "If I have, it's because I have work to do here."

Ras's gaze is piercing. "Hmm."

I rise. "Look into her, but not at the expense of the other research you're doing."

"Then it'll have to wait a few days."

"Fine."

Like I said, I can be patient, but soon, I'll know her real name.

CHAPTER 15

VALENTINA

IF I WAS SMART, I'd take the money Damiano gave me and run somewhere far. After I get home, I count the cash out again and again. Five thousand euros is enough to start somewhere anew, but for some reason I can't think of a single attractive destination. It's like no matter where I go, I'm risking leaving a piece of me in Ibiza.

The next morning, the front desk attendant at the hostel gives me a letter. Inside is an invitation for a viewing of an apartment on the nice side of the island. There is no mention of Damiano's name on the letter, but it doesn't take a genius to figure out who's behind it. I go to the viewing. The place has a beach view, a private balcony, and looks like an interior designer's wet dream. I pay the deposit on the spot and get my key.

No matter how I fight it, there's only one conclusion that makes sense. There's a part of him that cares about me. Damiano doesn't strike me as the kind of guy who gives up on things that he wants, so I prepare myself for more grand gestures. I can't let him wear my resistance down.

Yes, I want to sleep with him. Who wouldn't? But after my reaction on the boat, I'm not confident I'll be able to keep my head straight when he makes me feel that good over and over again. What if I say something I shouldn't in my vulnerable state? What if I inadvertently allow him to get too close?

I start my first week as a server. Since I work nights now, I have to adjust my sleep schedule, which means I spend the first few days feeling like a total zombie. I manage to break a few glasses and spill a Cosmopolitan onto a VIP, but he turns out to be too high to notice.

"Is everyone here on drugs?" I ask Vilde one night while we're on break.

She laughs. "Took you only a few days to realize, huh? Yeah. That's why our bottles of water are ten euros. High people tend to drink less alcohol, but they need to stay hydrated."

"How do they get all the stuff in here?" I ask. "The bouncers pat everyone down, don't they?"

"They're checking for weapons, not drugs, and there's always someone dealing here, if you know what to look for." She glances around the staff room and lowers her voice. "I'm sure the boss knows about the dealers."

I suspect she's right. I doubt anything happens in this club without Damiano knowing. No one becomes as successful as him without any exposure to the underworld. Still, it's an entirely different thing to be a part of its depths.

The next day, Vilde, Astrid, and I are all scheduled to work in the upper-level VIP area. When we arrive, Ras is there. He doesn't say hello, but even from afar, I can tell he's staring at me with unmistakable suspicion. I have to fight down the urge to squirm. Nerves flare inside of me. Does he know something?

The night starts off without a hitch. Hostesses seat the VIPs as they arrive, and then I or one of the other servers bring over the bottle service. I can't be sure until I count, but I think the tips I manage to collect in three hours might be more than I made during one whole cleaning shift. And that's not including my base salary. My mood lifts with each passing hour. If this is how things keep going, I might be able to pay Damiano back sooner than later.

"We just seated a group of four at Table A," Maria, the floor manager, tells me. "They have a bottle of Chivas Regal. Can you make them a priority?"

"I have another table first."

"Do it later," Maria tells me, looking over her shoulder. "They're the boss's friends."

Damiano's? I glance over at the table, and one look is enough to make my blood still inside my veins.

At the largest booth in the VIP area, the one Astrid was dancing in before she left for her break a few minutes earlier, are three men I don't recognize and one that I do.

Nelo.

I doubt Damiano would refer to Nelo as a friend even if he's his cousin, but the fact that Maria does tells me this can't be his first time at Revolvr. The back of my neck prickles with unease. Does Damiano know Nelo and his entourage are here? There's still a fading green bruise on the man's face where Damiano punched him. At least it doesn't look like Nelo's as drunk as he was the night at the restaurant.

I prep the bottle service, roll my shoulders back, and make my way over.

Nelo registers me when I'm almost at their booth. His thin lips glide into a sneer. "*Bella*," he greets me, his eyes raking down my body.

"Welcome, gentlemen," I say, sticking to my script.

He tracks my movements as I transfer the bottle over to their table. "You work here," he states. "Were you hired before or after the night I met you?"

"Before."

"Wouldn't put it past that son of a bitch to hire you just to spite me."

"I don't think Señor De Rossi spends a second of his time thinking about your feelings."

Nelo's eyes narrow into two lines.

Crap. I shouldn't have said that.

He leans forward, bringing his face closer to mine. "What you know about how De Rossi spends his time?"

Our conversation finally catches the attention of his companions. One by one, their hard gazes land on me. They all look mean, without exception. One of them is sporting a fading black eye. Another has this gaunt look that can only be caused by excessive drug use or a life filled with violence. I've seen his lookalikes back in New York. Foot soldiers, usually. Men who live each day as if it might end with a bullet in their heads.

The last one seems the most normal at first, but then I see his eyes, and nasty déjà vu makes my stomach lurch. His eyes are just like Lazaro's. Cold and utterly empty of any human emotion.

"I know he's very busy," I say, placing the last mixer on the table. "That's all I meant. Would you like me to serve you the first round?"

Nelo flicks his gaze to the bottle and then back to me. "Sure, *bella*."

He's probably used to making people tremble under his stare, but my hand's steady as I pour him and his friends their whisky.

The guy with the black eye says something to him in Italian. There's too much of a local dialect mixed in for me to understand. Nelo snorts an ugly laugh. It's enough warning for me to know I won't like the next words out of his mouth.

He smirks at me. "There are some other ways we'd like you to serve us later."

Placing the bottle back down on the table, I straighten out and pretend I didn't hear him. "I'll be back in a bit to check on you guys. Have fun."

The air grows taut and uncomfortable. It's a game for them. They want to ruffle my feathers and show me just how superior they are to me. Round one is over. I turn on my heel and head back toward the main bar.

I decide I can leave them for at least thirty minutes while I serve my other customers. But not even ten minutes later, they wave me back over.

"We want the thing that table got," Nelo says, pointing to a booth that has a six-liter limited edition bottle of Dom Perignon.

Of course, he does. Men like him are so predictable. They want the biggest, shiniest toy because they think it will make them look good, but in truth, people simply look at the shiny toy and glaze over them. "Great choice. Just so you know, it's ten thousand euros," I tell him while I eye the already-empty bottle on their table. Even with four people, they got through that quick.

"I don't give a fuck. You think I look at the prices here?"

His entourage chuckles.

I resist the urge to roll my eyes. "Great, I'll bring it right over."

"Hurry your pretty ass. And where's the fucking dancer? We've been staring at an empty space since we've sat down."

"She should be back from her break at any moment." I glance around, my jaw tight. I really hate that my friend's going to have to deal with them. I spy Astrid on the other side of the room making her way over here. She'll recognize Nelo even without any warning from me.

The bright smile she wears wavers when she sees my expression. She takes in the men sitting in the booth, and I can see recognition flash over her face. But she's a professional. She gets up on the platform in the center of the booth and greets everyone.

I doubt Nelo noticed her at the restaurant or knows that she's my friend. It's for the best. An association with me is unlikely to do Astrid any favors with this group.

The fancy bottle of Dom is so big that I need the help of another girl to bring everything over. A few people cheer as we walk by them. When we get to Nelo's booth, his friends join in on the cheering.

"I need to get a video of that," the gaunt one says. He pulls out his phone and starts recording as we set the bucket down on the edge of their table.

I'm so distracted by the commotion that I don't notice Astrid isn't dancing until I straighten back up. She's not on the platform anymore. Instead, she's standing directly across from me, by Nelo's side. Her face is paler than normal. It dawns on me Nelo's hand is gripping her wrist.

What the hell.

Guests aren't ever allowed to touch the go-go dancers.

He tugs her to sit on his knee, like she's a toy instead of a fully functioning human being and starts whispering something into her ear. She's trying to pull away from him, but he won't let her. Where are the bouncers?

Nausea appears inside my gut. "Why is she in your lap?" I demand.

Nelo smirks. "You jealous, *bella*? Don't worry, I've got another knee you can bounce on." He releases Astrid's wrist and pats his free knee.

"You're disgusting."

"You didn't seem to think so the other night."

Astrid tries to stand, but he won't let her, pushing her back down with a palm on her bare thigh. She visibly stiffens. Her eyes are wide and scared as she flicks her gaze over Nelo's friends. Astrid isn't a weak girl, but these men are straight-up intimidating, and I can see that she's frozen in fear.

"Let her go," I say. My hand is curled into a fist inside the pocket of my apron, but I'm not De Rossi. I won't be able to break Nelo's nose.

But when his hand trails higher up Astrid's thigh, I realize I'm furious enough to try.

"She's not complaining, is she?" he asks in a low voice, his lips close to her neck but his eyes glued to my face. He's doing this to piss me off.

"She's terrified."

"Terrified? I don't think so. I think this pussy—" he moves his hand to cup Astrid's crotch, "—is nice and wet for me."

My knuckles brush against the ice pick inside my apron. Fury swarms inside of me like a dark cloud of locusts. I curl my palm around the handle. There are no thoughts. I'm not even breathing.

I jerk the ice pick out and sink it through the top of Nelo's hand that's resting on his knee.

Lazaro's lessons with various sharp objects have finally paid off. I know just how hard I need to ram the pick to make it all the way through Nelo's hand.

For a moment that stretches in my imagination, Nelo stares at the handle protruding from his hand. Then he shoves Astrid off him and lets out an astonished shout.

The music around us blares so loud it nearly drowns out the sound. Nelo's men shoot up to their feet and yell in angry Italian. Someone grabs my arm.

"Ale!" It's Astrid. I've never seen her eyes so wide. "Ale, what did you do?"

Nelo pulls out the ice pick with a pained grunt and blood streams out of his hand, dripping all over the floor.

He stands and levels his bloodshot gaze on me. "I'm going to kill you for that, *bella*."

I suck in my first breath in a long while and look down at the blood on the floor. It's like a gruesome piece of art.

My God, what have I done? I promised I'd never do this again.

The guy with the dead eyes pulls a switchblade out of his jacket.

Astrid gasps. "Ale, we have to go." She manages to drag me a few steps before we're stopped by two bouncers. Behind them is Maria. She must have summoned them just now. Where the hell were they moments ago when we needed their help?

"Get the fuck back," Nelo says to them when they move to stand before Astrid and I. "We've got shit we need to sort out."

"Sit down," one of the bouncers says, eyeing the four men wearily. "Señor De Rossi is on his way."

"Fuck you."

Nelo and his companions start slinging insults at the bouncers, but the two men are clearly doing their hardest to deescalate by staying impressively calm. Astrid squeezes my wrist, and I whip my head around to meet her eyes.

What I see inside of them makes me stagger back.

Damiano appears on the other side of the booth and pushes past the seats. "What is going on here?" He does a double take when he sees me behind the bouncers, and then his gaze sweeps over the booth and all the involved parties. If he's shocked at the sight of Nelo's hand, he doesn't show it. His eyes only narrow when he sees the other man's switchblade.

"You brought a weapon into my club?" his voice is deadly.

Nelo's face turns red with rage. "This bitch just cut me." He lifts his hand. It's looking ghastly. "Your rules don't mean shit anymore."

Immediately, Damiano gets in Nelo's face. "Watch your mouth," he warns.

"Or what?"

Around us, other patrons have begun to take note of the commotion, and some are trying to get closer to see what's going on.

"My office. Now," Damiano says.

"No. I think we should do this here, *orphano*. Let everyone see who'll win," Nelo taunts.

I'm close enough to see the muscles in Damiano's back go stiff.

"I'm going to pretend all the blood in your brain is bleeding out of your hand, which is why that sentence just left your mouth. Maybe you're not thinking straight, but I am. Look around. Does this look like a scene *Il becchino* would like to see on the news tomorrow?"

The grave digger. Unease flutters inside my chest. Who is Damiano talking about and why does that sound like the nicknames Papà gave to his men? They always called each other things like that. *Il grasso, il dente, il matematico...* Each name had a story. *Il dente* lost his front tooth in a fight when he was sixteen and walked around like that for a few weeks before my grandfather paid him to get it fixed. *Il grasso* was always snacking on the job. *Il mathematico* wouldn't tell me when I asked, but later I found out from Tito that after every job, he'd always count how many men they'd killed and tally up the numbers in a little notebook he carried in his breast pocket.

Nelo sneers and gives a sharp shake of his head. "Fine. We settle this in your office."

Damiano jostles the bouncers out of the way, takes me by the elbow, and leads me away. I twist my neck to see if the others follow. They do.

Ras runs up to us. "What's happening?"

"The thin one has a knife," Damiano snarls but doesn't stop walking. "Get it from him as soon as we're inside my office and figure out how the fuck he managed to get it past the guys at the door."

"Ale! Wait!" It's Astrid. I see her trying to get to me, but Ras stops her and says something that makes her scowl at him angrily.

Damiano pulls me through a door marked "Private" and the sounds of the club dim.

I notice there's no one behind us anymore.

The full realization of what I've done slams into me right then.

I just...stabbed a man. Spilled his blood like it was nothing. There was no puppet master pulling the strings this time. It was all me.

The edges of my vision blacken. I sway on my feet, and Damiano's grip on me tightens.

He stops moving us and brings his face close to mine. "Are you okay? Did they touch you?"

He's so angry he's shaking. I suck in a desperate breath and force a single word out. "No."

He exhales in relief. "What happened?"

"He grabbed Astrid. He touched her over her clothes. It was sick, he wouldn't let her get away."

"Astrid stabbed him?"

"No. I did."

Something that might be pride flickers in his expression, but that must be my imagination, because there's nothing for me to be proud of in this situation. Yeah, Nelo is sick. But so am I.

Lazaro really did ruin me. And now Astrid knows. I saw it in her eyes when she looked at me moments earlier. She looked terrified of me. Finally, she understands who she's been living with for two weeks.

A monster.

CHAPTER 16

VALENTINA

"Nelo recognized me from the night before," I tell Damiano as we follow the dimly lit service hallway to his office. "He said he'll kill me for what I did tonight."

"He's not going to lay a finger on you," Damiano says in a rough voice. "I'll make sure of it."

I pull at my bottom lip with my teeth. Nelo doesn't play by the rules. I can sense that much. Somehow, I doubt he's going to listen to Damiano's warnings.

"What is he mixed up in?" I ask.

Anger carves his jaw into a sharp line. "Him and his crew are a bunch of shit heads. If they even think about touching a hair on your head again, they won't live long enough to regret it."

It's hyperbole, but he says it with such vicious confidence that I almost believe him. Still, Damiano is only a businessman, and Nelo? Nelo is dangerous, and this is the second time I've caused issues between him and Damiano.

There had to have been another way to help Astrid that didn't involve doing what I did. My instincts immediately turned to violence. Is this how I'm going to solve all of my problems from now on? I can't even convince myself that I won't. I wasn't thinking when I drove that ice pick through Nelo's hand. I just did what felt right.

The panic starts building at the base of my spine. Violence felt right to me. Seriously, what is wrong with me? I can't get close to *anyone* when I'm in this state. I really do need therapy. Years of it. And until then, there is no way out. Nelo may have deserved it, but what if I attack someone who doesn't next time? I need to leave and isolate myself. I won't put more people in danger because I'm out of my goddamn mind.

"Wait here," Damiano says when we stop outside of his office. He points to a chair propped against the wall a few feet away and helps me sit down. "I don't want you in the room with them. We'll talk as soon as I'm done. All right?"

"Sure," I say, meeting his gaze. He's concerned about me, the same way he was when I cried on his boat. He thinks I'm someone who needs protecting, instead of the thing people need protection from.

The sound of footsteps floats from the other end of the hall, and Damiano gives my shoulder a quick squeeze. He opens the door for Nelo and his entourage, blocking me from their sight. I see a flash of Ras before they all disappear inside the room.

As soon as I'm alone, I fold over, and hide my face in my palms. My gut churns. It feels like something rotten has cracked open inside my stomach and filled me with poison.

They're talking in aggressive tones inside the office, but I can't make out a single word through the thick walls.

I can't stay here. I'll explode if I do.

Running to the closest emergency exit, I barrel through the door. The parking lot blurs around me as I sprint past the rows of cars. I don't stop moving until I make it to the beach. My heels sink into the sand. The sky is still dark, but the moon is bright, and it illuminates the waves crashing along the shore. The water is always more restless during the night, flashing with foam that looks like white teeth.

I'm so close to the shore, I can feel the ocean's spittle land on my bare knees. Who would miss me if I walked right into the water and never came back out? My sisters don't need me. My parents probably want me dead. At this point, if they find me alive, I'll be in disgrace for the rest of my life. Papà will probably give Lazaro his blessing to kill me for my betrayal. Was I ever a daughter, or just a tool for them to use? Are any mafia daughters ever more than a thing to barter with?

The water is up to my knees now, and the ocean welcomes me. It pulls on my ankles, wrapping its foamy hands around my flesh and coaxing me deeper.

Tears stream down my face. I need to let it all go and start over, but after tonight, I don't know if I can. Living in fear is the most exhausting thing I've ever had to do. And now it's not just others that I fear. It's me.

The poison Lazaro filled me with hasn't gone away. It has corrupted my mind and erased my character. I don't know who I am.

I gasp when the water reaches the hem of my shorts. It's cold. Cleansing. Maybe it can cleanse my soul. That thought keeps me moving farther and farther. A big wave crashes into me, and I'm suddenly swept off my feet. I fall backwards, and my head dips under the surface.

Wash it off me. My past, my sins, my memories. I want to be reborn.

My feet connect with the seabed. The water's not that deep, I can push off and pop back up if I need to, but I challenge myself to hold my breath. The waves toss my body back and forth, and I relax into them, letting nature do its work.

When I'm completely out of breath, I push my head above the surface of the water and glance up at the sky. There are no stars visible tonight, the moon is too bright. I wish I could see them high above me, to serve as a reminder of how small I am in this big world.

Another wave breaks against me. Some salty water gets washed up my nose, and I start coughing. Another wall of water hits me before I get a chance to take a proper breath.

When the biggest wave yet slams over my head, I think I hear my name, but the sound of the rushing water drowns it out. Then I'm submerged, and this time, when I point my toes, I don't meet any resistance. It doesn't feel like I'm sinking. It feels as if I'm suspended in space and time.

Panic starts creeping in. I swim, but it's too dark, and I don't know which way is up. The water doesn't feel pleasantly cool anymore. It's freezing and heavy and as thick as tar. A pain appears inside my chest and darkness seeps through my thoughts. I can't hold on to any of them.

When I'm finally convinced I'm about to die, two snakes wrap around my waist. They bite into my stomach, digging their dull teeth into my flesh.

"Ale. Ale!"

Not teeth. Fingers. Hands. Two arms.

They squeeze me over and over, until I retch out the salty ocean water. My back slams against packed sand. I'm pushed to my side. I'm coughing harder than I ever have in my entire life.

When I finally blink open my eyes, Damiano is heaving over me, looking irate. He's soaked to the bone, water dripping down his hair and onto my face.

"Holy shit," I choke out.

"Who goes swimming at night when the sea is rough like this? You could have drowned, you *idiot*," he hisses. He looks angry enough to kill me. Darkness clouds his eyes.

"I'm sorry. I just wanted to...cool down."

He's staring at me like he wants to take me apart piece by piece just so he can see exactly where nature went wrong. "There's AC at the club. You would have cooled down if you'd stayed put like I told you to."

I close my eyes and shake my head. "No."

"What do you mean no?"

"You wouldn't understand."

He grips my shoulders and gives me a hard shake. "You don't get to say that to me after I just dragged you out. You nearly *died*."

He's not wrong. I might have died if he hadn't come to my rescue.

Would that really have been so bad?

That would have been one way to keep my violent urges from ever causing havoc again.

Am I really considering suicide? No, I can't give up. Not after everything I did to get away.

A sob works its way up my throat. It sounds awful.

Damiano's grip on my shoulders loosens. "Talk to me."

"I hurt him," I say as tears overflow my eyes and slip down my temples.

"Nelo?" He barks a laughs. "Who gives a fuck about him? He's gone to the medic. They'll give him a Band-Aid and tell him to fuck off."

I move to sit up, and Damiano moves his hand to my lower back to help me.

"You don't get it." The truth wants to spill out. I want to tell him every detail of everything that I've done so that he can see for himself that I'm not worth even a second of his concern.

But when I look at his face, I realize that I'm a liar. I like his concern. I don't want to reject it. I want to burrow deeper inside of it.

"I was violent," I mutter, folding away everything else I was about to tell him. "And I didn't even feel bad about it in the moment. What kind of a person does that make me?"

Damiano exhales an exasperated breath. "You acted on instinct. You wanted to protect Astrid. That makes you a good friend."

"My instinct was to stab him with an ice pick."

"Many would have done worse."

"I doubt it."

"I don't." He tips my chin up. "Look, I know what you're feeling."

"You do?"

"Yeah. What you did feels violent, but it wasn't. By its nature, violence is peak selfishness. What you did wasn't that. You acted with the goal of defending a friend."

"How do you know all that?"

"Violence is a part of my job."

"You mean people getting into fights and stuff at your clubs?"

He looks away and scratches the side of his mouth. "Yeah."

"I thought Ras and his team dealt with all that."

"Most of it. But sometimes, it needs to be dealt with by me. Like tonight. To deal with violence effectively, you need to understand it. A habitually violent person generally isn't very smart. They can't figure out how to deal with a situation. They fail to control their emotions and lash out. When you know what to look for, nearly every act of violence can be preempted. Sometimes all it takes is a few carefully chosen words. Other times, you can only stop it with your own show of force. That's what you did tonight."

"I escalated things instead of stopping them."

"You got Astrid away from him, didn't you? You created a distraction. You made Nelo change his target."

"To me."

"Forget what he said to you," Damiano says. "He's never going to hurt you."

I allow his words to settle over my skin and seep into my blood like a dose of a drug. It's so tempting to believe him. "You won't let him."

"No. I already told you, didn't I?" He reaches for my cheek and drags the tips of his fingers down to my lips. "I'm going to make you mine, Ale. And I always protect what's mine."

A wave crashes, lapping at our toes. I part my mouth and dart out my tongue. He tastes like salt and safety and desire.

I want to be drenched in it. Just for one night, I'll allow myself to believe he'll keep me safe.

He sees my intent before I can voice it, and he pushes his fingers into my wet hair, bringing my lips to his. God, it feels so good to kiss him.

But he cuts the kiss short and glares at me again. "*Cazzo*, I still can't believe you almost drowned."

"I'm sorry," I say. "It was stupid."

"Yeah, it was."

I run my hands up his muscular chest and tangle my fingers into his dress shirt. "Make me feel alive again."

His eyes flash with heat, and then he's all over me, pressing my back into the sand and settling his powerful body over mine. He lets me feel the weight of him, like he knows how badly I need to be anchored to something right now. My fingers dip under his shirt and I draw long lines down his back with my nails. This earns me a pleased grunt and a tug on my bottom lip.

He pushes off me and eyes my drenched clothes. "Take your shirt off, unless you want me to rip it off you."

A rush of heat settles inside my core. Probably best to keep our clothes intact since we still have to get back to the club.

He helps me peel the wet fabric over my head and then reaches around me to unclasp my bra. As soon as my breasts are bare, his hands turn greedy, his mouth hungry for my taste. He takes one nipple into his mouth and pulls on it with his teeth, before doing the same to the other. Electricity prickles all over my skin, and heat coils at the pit of my belly until I'm so desperate for more that I push him away and quickly pull off my underwear and shorts.

Damiano peers down at my naked form. "Fuck," he rasps. "This body was made for me."

Something flutters inside my chest. Why does it sound so right when he says things like that?

He lifts his eyes to meet mine, as if challenging me to protest. When I don't, he gives me a reward.

His mouth between my legs.

I claw at the sand as he licks and sucks on my clit. How is he so good at this?

"Shit," I pant. My vision's blurs as the pressure between my legs builds and builds. He takes me by my thighs and hauls me onto his shoulders, as if I weight nothing. And then he looks up at me, his mouth still glued on my cunt.

Everything bursts and I cry out. No matter how I squirm, he won't let go of me. When I start to come down, he fucks me with his tongue and the hazy pleasure of it all is unreal.

"Damiano," I moan.

At last, he lowers me back to the ground and dips his fingers inside of me, curling them possessively. "I've never tasted a better pussy," he says hoarsely.

I drag the back of my hand over my forehead. *Jesus.*

When he crawls on top of me, I slide my hand into his pants to find his hard cock. He squeezes his eyes shut when I begin to stroke him, then moans when I tighten my grip, but before I can experiment further, he barks, "Enough."

He jerks my hand out of his pants, pins it above my head, and kisses my throat. "I'm going to come inside of you," he says against my skin.

A shiver coasts down my spine when I realize it's his way of asking for permission. I got my last birth control shot on the eve of my wedding, which means I'm still good for a month or so.

"Okay," I breathe.

He makes a satisfied rumble in the back of his throat, lifts off me, and starts to take off his clothes.

When he's fully nude, he kneels between my legs, his powerful body backlit by the moon. It's a visual so striking, it should be captured by a painter, but the beach is completely empty except for us. I drag my fingertips over the defined muscles in his chest and abs and try to capture every detail in my memory.

He grips my chin and drapes his body over mine. The anticipation of what's about to come makes my toes curl. His cock is pressed against my thigh, and I shift my hips and line him up with my entrance. This is the second time a man will be inside of me, and I already know it will be nothing like the first.

He pushes in with one smooth stroke and lets out a harsh breath. My eyes flutter closed at the sensation of being so utterly full. I dig my nails into his ass, and he begins to move, slowly at first, then faster and faster until it's frantic and desperate. I can feel another orgasm building at the edges.

Suddenly, he pulls out, flips me over, and moves me until I'm on all fours, my ass up in the air. He grabs me by the hips, pushes into me again, and quickly finds a relentless rhythm. My arms shake as I struggle to hold myself up.

"This pussy was made for me too," he growls from behind as he keeps thrusting into me. "And this pretty little ass." His thumb brushes against the other hole. "*Mine.*"

I squirm, my breaths coming out in pants now as I get closer and closer to my peak. I'm wild with lust and leftover adrenaline and look over my shoulder to meet his gaze. "It's all yours."

His expression melts with satisfaction, and the sight of it finishes me off. I spasm around him, curling my fingers into the sand and falling down on my forearms. He moves his hands to my hips, pumps two more times, and explodes inside of me.

We fall to our sides, and he wraps his strong arms around me. The sky is lighter now. The sun will rise soon and erase the night.

After some time, he lifts me and takes me back into the water, rinsing the sand off my back and arms, and washing between my legs. I let him. I allow this illusion of being cared for by him to last a few moments longer.

"You will never put yourself in danger again," he murmurs into my ear. "No one hurts what's mine, not even you."

We walk back to the club with sand all over our clothes. It feels weird to walk with his warm palm pressed against my back out in public, but there's no one paying us any mind. At this hour, anyone we encounter on our walk is blissed out on drugs.

"I left my car keys in my office," he says. "We'll get them, and I'll drive you home."

The sun peeks over the horizon. Am I ready to get involved with someone like Damiano? He's no mafioso, but I already know his offer of protection comes with expectations. He wants me to be his.

I like it when he tells me how much he desires me and how he's going to use my body, because I know he'll make sure I'll enjoy it too. But what if he wants more than that? What if he wants to control me in the way Lazaro and Papà did?

No, normal men don't think like that. They don't try to bend people to their will until they're on the verge of snapping. Damiano might think I'm his, but when he says those words,

I know he says them as a promise, not a threat. He wants to take care of me. Is it really so bad to allow him to do exactly that?

What we have won't last forever, but for now, maybe I can enjoy being his.

We stop by his office door, but he blocks me from going in. His brows furrow. "Someone's inside. I left the door locked."

It's open, just a crack.

He puts me behind him. "Stay here. I'm going to check it first."

Is Nelo and his gang waiting for him inside? Fear sparks inside my gut.

He disappears through the door, and I hear muffled voices for a minute or so before he comes back out.

"Who is it?" I ask.

In his gaze, I detect a hint of warmth. "It's my sister. She was worried when she woke up and realized I hadn't come home. She went looking for me. Do you want to meet her?"

"Um." I'm entirely too aware of the fact that we just had sex on the beach and that his cum is still dripping out of me. Heat blankets my cheeks. I must look like a mess.

But I'm curious. The grown-up version of the little girl from that family photo is on the other side of the door. Damiano said they're close, so it feels like a big deal he's willing to introduce me to her.

"Okay," I say.

"Come on." He takes me by the hand and opens the door. "Martina, there's someone I'd like you to meet," he says as he steps inside the room with me on his heels. "This is Ale." He moves aside to reveal someone perched on the edge of his desk.

My greeting comes to a sharp stop inside my throat. My lips part. Everything around me turns blank as my vision narrows on the girl.

The girl.

The one I saw curled up on the floor of my basement through the screen of an iPad.

Her eyes widen in recognition.

Reality feels like a house of cards that's one breath away from crashing down.

She sucks in that breath.

And then, she screams.

CHAPTER 17

DAMIANO

WHEN THE NEWS broke that someone abducted my sister while she was on her trip to New York, I didn't panic or give into the rage I felt. I put my best men on tracking her down, called in every favor I had, and scheduled a flight out to New York. I was in the air when I got the call from Ras that she'd made it back to Spain traumatized but alive and seemingly unharmed. We rerouted the plane. I made it home and held my sister in my arms for a long while.

Then I summoned her bodyguard and put a bullet in his head.

Ras was there when I did it. He can vouch I didn't kill the guard because I was overcome with emotion. No, it was because I run a tight fucking ship, and I can't afford to have 250 pounds of useless flesh on my team. He stopped providing value, so he ended up dead.

It's that same levelheadedness that's allowing me to keep my expression neutral as my little sister screams her head off at the sight of the woman I just claimed as mine.

Mari's a teenager, but even with all those hormones, this isn't a normal reaction.

Something is really fucking wrong.

I slam the office door shut behind me. "Mari."

My sister jumps off my desk and runs to me. Her face is drained of blood, and her eyes are wide. "Dem, I know her," she says in a trembling voice. "She's the wife of the man who took me."

My blood turns to ice.

I knew Ale Romero was lying about her name, but I never could have imagined this. Getting her into my bed had seemed like a more important endeavor than finding out the truth about her. After all, my own secrets were bound to overshadow hers, and I despised being a hypocrite.

Looks like I was wrong.

Looks like I lost my *goddamn mind* over a striking face and a body forged in the depths of my fantasies.

How could I have allowed this?

I pull Mari into my side and inhale her scent to temper the violent anger that jolts through me like a bolt of thunder. My nostrils flare. Even her familiar smell, the smell of home and everything that's good in this wretched world, isn't enough. Slowly, I move my gaze back to Ale.

She's looking at us as if she's seen a ghost.

I clench my fist by my side.

"I can explain," she says, her voice a mere rasp.

I force a smile to twist my lips. "I'm sure this is all just a misunderstanding," I say, squeezing Mari's hip to let her know I'm lying. "Both of you, take a seat. I'll get you some water."

Ale's face softens with relief. She's bought it, which means she must think I'm a gullible idiot. Why wouldn't she? All this time, she played me for a fool.

They sit down, and I head to the bar cart in the corner of my office. While the two of them stare at each other mutely, I type out a text to Ras. *"Office. Urgent."*

Cazzo. The woman who I was inside of less than an hour ago is married—*married*—to the worthless pile of shit who abducted my sister while she was on a graduation trip to New York. Married to the man who murdered Mari's best friend and took my sister to a basement to put her through what I suspect would have been hours of brutal torture. A sour taste floods my mouth. Did Ale follow her to Ibiza to finish the job? And I led her straight to my sister. Guilt wraps around my throat like a noose.

I open a small metal box hidden behind a whiskey bottle and take out a sedative. From experience, I know this one is tasteless when it's dissolved. I fill two glasses with mineral water, crush the pill between my index finger and thumb, and drop the powder in one of the glasses. The bubbles mask any residue.

"I'm so glad you're okay, Martina," Ale says behind me.

I have to stop and take a deep breath so that I don't slap her across the face. How dare she say my sister's name with that lying mouth?

She glances at me. I hand her the drugged water and put on another smile. I swear, each one costs me a year of life. It feels like a gash carved across my face.

I'm worried she'll nurse the glass for longer than I can control myself, but she does me a favor by downing the entire thing in one go. There's a slight tremble in her hands. I imagine tying them together with a rough rope and watching her make herself bleed by fighting against the restraints.

Mari takes a small sip and turns her face up to look at me. She's waiting for my directions. My sweet, gentle sister.

When she got back to me, I vowed to her I'd make the culprits pay for what they did to Imogen and her. She didn't know who took her. They'd knocked her out after they shot Imogen, and when she came to in that basement, the sedative hadn't fully worn off, and her memory of the man was fuzzy. But she remembered the woman. The one who'd seemed like an accomplice until she'd shot the captor and helped her escape.

Mari doesn't know why the woman helped her, but I've lived long enough to know that in our world selfless acts of kindness are as rare as a quiet night in Ibiza. No one does something like that if it's not in their self-interest. Ale must have had an ulterior motive when she freed my sister.

And I'll do whatever I must to figure it out.

Ale slumps against the chair. "I feel strange," she says as her eyelids start to droop.

About fucking time.

I get on my haunches in front of her and curve my palms around the arms of the chair. I don't trust myself to touch her right now. Martina doesn't need to see how her brother deals with good-for-nothing liars. "What's wrong?" I ask.

Her head lolls before she manages to bring it back up. "I can't feel my legs and arms."

For the first time since Mari screamed, I allow the mask to drop. A slow frown spreads over Ale's face as she takes in my expression. "Damiano...what's happening to me?"

"There's a sedative spreading through your blood stream."

Fear flashes in her eyes, and for a moment, she looks so terrified that I feel a faint pang of pity. But then I remember who she is and squash that pity like an annoying fly. "You promised me an explanation."

She tries to nod. Her chin bumps against her chest. I push my fingers into her hair and pull her head back up to look at me. "I don't need your promises," I whisper. "I'll get every last drop of truth out of you."

Her body goes totally limp. Behind me, Mari lets out a strangled sob.

I let go of Ale, but when she starts to slide off the chair, I pick her up before she falls to the ground. Not because I care if she gets hurt, but because I can't risk her banging her head and losing her memory. First, I need to get all of the information hidden in its confines.

Ras appears in the doorway. His gaze scans over Martina and I before halting on the body in my arms. "Should I call a doctor?"

Roughly, I pass Ale to him. "No. Turns out she's the wife of the assassin who took Mari. Take her to my house and put her in the secure room."

Ras's brows shoot up his forehead. "*Merda.*"

"You were right," I say. "I should have been more careful, but now we'll finally figure out who's behind the entire plot."

Ras looks down at her. Suddenly, I want to rip her out of his arms, but I push the ridiculous feeling away. We slept together. Once. There's no way I feel anything for this woman that would jeopardize my ability to interrogate her.

"What do I say to her friends? They're all scheduled tonight."

I move to my desk. "Tell them she left the island."

"They won't believe it."

"Then do your fucking job and make them."

I meet Ras's hard gaze. He's not offended by my tone. It's worse. He's concerned.

I check my watch. "It's nearly eight. Mari, I promised to take you to your dance class," I say roughly. Out of the corner of my eye, I see my sister stand up. She's barely said a word since she saw Ale.

"I can skip it," she says, her eyes trained on the unconscious woman our cousin is holding. "I thought I saw her when I landed in Barcelona, but I was so tired, I was sure I was imagining it."

The memory of the day Mari came back slams into me. I'd never seen my sister so shattered. It terrified me. The thought of her no longer being alive was so hard to stomach that I refused to entertain it, even on that day.

"I want you to go to your class. Señorita Perez is expecting you," I say. My sister is still healing, and her progress has been tepid. I've just managed to convince her to return to her dance classes this week.

Mari tugs on the sleeves of her loose linen top, but I know she won't protest further. My sister is unfailingly obedient to me. "Okay. I'll go."

There's a sad note in her voice that tugs on my heart. "Hey. Come here for a second." I open my arms wide.

She walks into my embrace and puts her cheek against my chest. "I'm sorry I screamed," she mutters. "I couldn't believe it was her. What is she doing here, Dem?"

"She works—worked here."

"Was she looking for me?"

"I don't know, but I'll find out." I kiss the top of her head. "You're safe now. That woman won't bring any harm to you."

My sister steps away. "I don't think she wanted to hurt me. I don't think she and her husband got along."

I stay silent. My sister doesn't need to know how easy it is for a practiced criminal to put on an innocent act. Mari was born to the deadliest family in the *sistema*, but the stories of my father's brutality disappeared with his and my mother's deaths. I have no desire to share those stories with Mari. I've spent all my life protecting my sister from those who'd harm her, and that includes the ghosts of our past.

"We'll take the back door," I tell Ras. He nods and walks through the bookshelf that secretly opens to my private garage. While Mari gets into my car, I watch Ras start to put Ale in the back of his.

"Put her in the trunk," I tell him.

"It's a bumpy ride."

I slam the door shut, so that Mari won't hear. "Good. And string her up for me, just like Mari told us they did to her."

Ras sniffs and purses his lips. "Maybe you should talk to her first."

"Maybe you shouldn't question your capo." I don't wait for his response before I slide into the driver's seat and turn on the ignition.

Before all this, I was thinking I'd take Ale out on a date tonight.

Looks like our date just got a whole lot more interesting.

CHAPTER 18

VALENTINA

WHEN I CRACK open my eyelids, I blink a few times to make sure I'm not dreaming. My thoughts are muddy, my tongue is dry, and my wrists really hurt. There's a weird medicinal taste in my mouth that I want to spit out, but I'm seriously low on saliva. I shake my head to try to get rid of the brain fog and get rewarded with a sharp pain in my shoulder.

Oh, that might be due to the fact that someone tied my wrists together with a rough rope and left me hanging by my arms.

I'm in a square room, about the size of a bedroom. Tiled floor, unfinished walls, and a narrow window near the ceiling that's mostly covered with newspaper, but there's bright light coming through the gaps. It faces somewhere outside. A soft trickle of a bossa nova song makes it past the glass.

Dread swoops in faster than my memory. Where the hell am I, and how did I get here? My toes bump against the ground.

I quickly realize if I stand up straight, I can take my weight off my arms, so I do exactly that.

And then it hits me. Damiano's office. Martina. His strange unnatural smile when he handed me that water.

He *drugged* me.

How long have I been out for? Judging by how sore my arms are, it must have been a while. I whirl in one direction, then the other. There's a door with no handle. I try to kick at it with my foot, but it's way too far for me to even come close to reaching it. Instead, I lose my balance and get rewarded with more agony in my arms.

Anger and fear struggle for dominance inside my chest. Why would he take me to this place and tie me up like some kind of animal? I tip my head back to look at my restraints.

Cold recognition spreads beneath my skin. Ropes suspended off a big fishing hook. It's how Lazaro tied up Martina in our basement.

No, no, no. I fight the dreadful panic and the tears that spring to my eyes. This is payback. He's punishing me.

I don't understand. I helped his sister. Does he think I was working with Lazaro? Why wouldn't he let me explain?

Explain what? a voice in my head asks. *You* were *working with Lazaro.*

My bottom lip wobbles. I'd forgotten the fundamental truth about myself.

I am not a good person.

No amount of explanations will change that.

A single tear trickles down my cheek, and before I can collect myself, I hear the door open.

My gaze immediately connects with his.

Gone is the put-together businessman. Damiano's hair is tousled, and instead of his usual suit, he's wearing a simple black T-shirt and a pair of broken in jeans. He's looking at me like I'm a carcass at a butcher's shop. There's not a flicker of affection in those eyes. My lungs freeze under his icy stare.

What will he do to me? He loves his sister. I've gathered that much. Will he chop me up and put me in a nice big box with a bow for her to open?

I reel my imagination back in. He might be looking at me like he's ready to kill me, but there's only one killer in this room, and it's not him.

Whatever penance he has planned for me, I deserve it. But the need to let him know that I never intended to hurt Martina is so strong that it itches beneath my skin.

"Damiano—"

"Shut up."

Those two words feel like a slap. The sting of them sinks into my cheeks. Fear, heartbreak, and determination are strange emotions to experience together.

His steps carve a slow path around me.

I shift my weight from one foot to the other. "Please, let me explain."

He fists a hand in my hair and jerks my head back, working a frantic gasp out of me. He peers down at me with his dark, turbulent eyes. "No, let me explain something to you. When I tell you to do something, you shut up and do it."

He's so furious, he's not acting like himself. "This isn't you," I say.

"Do you know who I am?" He moves his face closer to mine, searching my eyes for something.

"I don't understand."

He lets go of me and heaves a dry laugh. "Ah. So you know even less about me that I do about you."

I swallow. My eye catches on a tattoo peeking from under the sleeve of his T-shirt. The two times I've seen Damiano without his shirt on it was too dark for me to notice it.

He sees what I'm looking at. "This isn't something I advertise, but since you seem to be confused about what's happening here, I'll make an exception." He turns his arm to me and lifts up his shirtsleeve.

It's some kind of an insignia. Two branches of leaves around a castle with two towers. Above the castle is an intricate crown. I've never seen it before.

"This is the crest of Casal di Principe, the town in Campana where I was born," he says.

Casal di Principe. Something nudges against my memory. Where have I heard that name before?

"It's a town of twenty-one thousand people. Three thousand of them are under near constant police surveillance. Do you know why?"

I have some guesses. The hairs on the back of my neck stand straight. Why did Lazaro take Martina? What did he say—

"It's because that little town is the stronghold of the Casalese clan. One of the most powerful clans in the Camorra. I have a feeling you know what the Camorra is."

The Neapolitan mafia. I tug on my restraints, not because I think they might suddenly break this time, but because something far more primal and afraid awakens within me.

"The police think there's been around one thousand murders carried out by the clan in the past thirty years. They're wrong. I know because my father used to run the Casalese, and he kept an accurate count."

He takes me by the chin and forces me to look him in the eyes. "The real number is ten thousand people," he whispers. "And if you don't tell me who you are, your name on the ledger will bring it to ten thousand and one."

My chest rises and falls with breaths that are too fast. I can't believe this. He's not a businessman. He's just another part of the cruel world I thought I'd managed to escape.

I missed all the signs.

Now, my brain rushes to put it all together. His father used to run the clan—he used past tense, so I assume that means he's dead. Is Damiano the current don? Is that why everyone always seems so afraid of him?

This changes everything. If I tell him who I am, I'll become a bartering chip once again.

"Ah. You understand now," he says as his fingers dig into my chin. "Who are you?"

I squeeze my eyes shut. The song outside changes to another bossa nova tune. What are the chances someone will come help me if I scream? Probably zero. I have no reason to doubt what he's just told me, which means he knows how to hide a person he doesn't want to be found.

I jerk my chin out of his grip and turn my face away from him. "Let me go."

There's a moment of silence, and then he barks out a bitter laugh. "Why would I do that?"

"I helped your sister get away. Please, just let me go."

"I don't think so." He runs his tongue over his top teeth and studies me. "But maybe I'll consider it if you answer my questions. Why did you follow Martina to Ibiza?"

"I didn't follow her. I had no idea she'd end up here. We were on the same flight to Barcelona, but then I came here on my own."

"You expect me to believe it's a coincidence you're here?"

"What else would it be?"

"An assignment."

My heart hammers against my chest. He thinks I'm working for my father? "I'm not working for anyone except you. I've already told you the truth. I'm here because I wanted to get away from my family."

"You didn't know I was Martina's brother?"

"No! I didn't even know her name until you introduced us in your office."

"Why did your husband take her?"

I can't help but notice the inflection in his tone on the word husband. I could tell Damiano what Lazaro said to me

187

about Martina, but it might be the only piece of leverage I have. Until I have a better sense of what he plans to do with me, I can't reveal it to him. "I don't know."

"You're lying."

I glance away from him. "My husband never told me anything."

"Martina told me you shot him."

"I have no idea if he's dead or alive."

He cups my face with his palms and moves my head until I'm looking at him again. "You don't seem to be torn up over it."

"It was an arranged marriage, not a love match."

A tendril of softness creeps into Damiano's gaze. Am I getting through to him? Maybe I can convince him to let me go after all.

"Why did you help Martina?" he asks.

"Because I wanted to. I didn't want her to get hurt."

He drags his thumb over my cheek. "What's your name?"

"Ale Romero."

That softness is gone in a flash.

"You know as well as I do that Ale Romero doesn't exist," he bites out, dropping his hands from me. "What's your name?"

"Why does it matter? I'm not here to cause trouble. I never thought I'd see Martina again. Why won't you let me go?"

"Because I won't rest until everyone responsible for what happened to my sister and her friend is turned into fertilizer. Tell me your name and tell me who your husband worked for."

He wants to get revenge against Papà. He's already halfway there by unknowingly having the don's oldest daughter in his hands. If he knows who I am, he'll kill me, or he'll trade me away for something more valuable.

"I'm not telling you my name."

Darkness clouds his features. "I thought you wanted to explain everything."

"That was before I knew who you really are."

He processes my words for a long second. "Are you really so loyal to whatever outfit you belong to? You'd rather stay here than implicate them?"

A broken laugh escapes past my lips. He's got it all completely wrong. I'd tell him the truth if I thought I could get a promise out of him. A promise not to trade me back to Papà, no matter what. But I know he'll never give that to me in earnest while he's hungry for revenge. At least if Damiano decides to kill me, I might get a quick death.

"Do what you must."

He walks around me until I feel his presence against my back. My heart beats loudly over the distant sound of that hypnotic music. What is he going to do to me?

He steps closer, lining up our bodies. Brushing my hair to the side, he brings his lips to my exposed neck. "Tell me your name, or I swear, I'll make you scream it."

A shiver runs down my spine. "I'm not afraid of pain," I say, but it doesn't sound convincing even to my own ears. In truth, I am afraid of being hurt. After seeing the entire spectrum of pain in Lazaro's basement, I think anyone who says otherwise is a liar.

If Damiano starts cutting into my flesh, I don't know how long I'll be able to keep my mouth shut.

A hand lands on my exposed midriff. I suck in a breath when his fingers start moving in circles over my skin.

His lips touch the shell of my ear. "Was everything you told me a lie?"

"Not everything," I say.

"You're a married woman. Why did you lie to me about being inexperienced in bed?"

My throat tightens. "I- I didn't lie about that."

His movements halt for a moment. "Your husband didn't fuck you?"

"He did his marital duty on our wedding night, that's all. Like I said, it wasn't a love match."

"Why did you decide to get involved with me?"

I exhale. "Because I liked you."

He drags his hand over my shorts until it's over my pubic bone. Heat swirls through my core. It seems my body hasn't caught on to our current situation, and it's still reacting to him in the same needy way. He presses the length of his body against me and lets me feel his hard-on against my lower back. "Did you like it when I made you come?" The words rumble inside his throat.

I drop my head back, resting it against his chest. He looks down at my shirt, and I know he can see the outline of my hard nipples. "Yes."

He unhooks the buttons on my shorts, one by one, like some kind of a count down. It dawns on me that just because I lied to him about many things, doesn't mean he was lying to me. Even made men have their moments of truth. What if despite everything, he still feels some affection for me? What if he doesn't *want* to hurt me?

His fingers dip into my underwear and find my clit. "If you're not afraid of pain," he says in a way that makes it clear he knows I'm lying, "then what are you afraid of?"

I gasp with the first circle he makes. "This is an interesting method of interrogation."

He pinches me with his index finger and thumb, and the pleasure heightens with an undercurrent of pain. I cry out. The multitude of things he's making me feel is making my mind dull with a not-entirely unpleasant haze.

He nuzzles my neck with his nose and sets off a ticklish frisson over my skin. "Tell me your name."

He's trying to confuse me. To break me. I try tugging at the ropes, but my arms have numbed from being strung up for so long. "No."

His other arm wraps around my waist, and he tugs me into him, hard. "I think you're lying to me," he rasps. "You might not be afraid of dying, but you don't want it to hurt. And, Ale." He leaves my clit alone, grabs my shorts with both of his hands, and tugs them down to my knees. "I can make it hurt."

The first hard slap across my ass is so shocking, I'm not able to suppress the yelp that comes out. "Fuck!"

I can't see him behind me, but the long breath he releases makes me think he's enjoying this. My ass burns, and my face feels like it's become liquid fire. Then he does something far worse. He grabs the throbbing flesh and kneads it with his long fingers, as if he's trying to relieve the pain. The physical sensation makes me want to weep—from the pleasure and the pain. I bite down on my lip. This is humiliating, and yet deep inside of me, languid arousal forms.

"You're sick," I whisper.

Another hard slap. I whimper.

"I am," he says, as he kneads my flesh again. "I'm going to enjoy making this ass raw."

When he starts to move his hand lower, I try to move away, but he places one firm hand on my hips and pulls me back into him. His fingers find my entrance, and he makes a noise of satisfaction. "*Cazzo.* Isn't it even sicker that you appear to be enjoying it? Or is that my cum you're still wet with?" He pushes inside my wetness and thrusts his fingers in and out a few times. I squeeze my eyes shut and try to temper the building pleasure.

"I can make you my toy," he says as he keeps his fingers moving. "I can make you feel all kinds of pain. Maybe I'll leave you hanging here for weeks, using you as I see fit, until you're dripping with my cum from every single one of your holes."

A groan works its way out of my throat. He reaches around me and starts to rub my clit with his left hand while his right is thrusting in and out of me in perfect rhythm. Images from the beach flash behind my eyelids. God, it felt so good to be completely filled with him.

The music outside pulls me under its spell. I grind my ass into him and feel how hard he is inside his jeans. How is it possible we went from that tender moment by the ocean to *this* in the span of a few hours?

"Do you like that?" he asks. "Do you want to be my captive whore? I'll make you wear me for days before I let you wash me off your skin."

"Shit." I'm too far gone on my way to the promised land to analyze what he's saying and why it's driving me absolutely insane. The need to come builds until it's the only thing in the entire world that matters.

Then everything stops. "Tell me your name."

"No, no, no," I pant. "*Please.*"

He won't let me grind on his hand. "Name."

I groan in frustration as the orgasm moves further and further out of my reach. But with every second, my brain turns back on. "No."

He makes an angry noise. "I'll let you think on it for the night."

"Please, let me down. My arms hurt."

He stops in front of me. His eyes are ablaze, and I can see he's still hard, but I know better than to think his physical attraction to me is going to make him cave to my request. "No," he says, mocking my consistent response. His gaze travels up my arms, and a flash of anger colors his face, but then it's gone.

I watch his broad back as he leaves and then glance over at the window.

The sun still hasn't set outside.

I'll have an endless night to survive down here alone.

CHAPTER 19

DAMIANO

MARTINA'S DOING something on her laptop in the kitchen when I emerge from the secured room where I left Ale. Her earthy scent is all over my hands, and I resist the urge to take one big inhale before I wash my hands at the sink.

My gut told me she'd make me fucking crazy. Maybe it's time I start listening to that particular organ more.

"What are you working on?" I ask casually, as if there isn't a half-naked woman currently strung up a dozen feet below us.

She's down there, in pain. The thought of it sends a crawling sensation over my skin.

"Nothing," Martina says.

"Have you found a culinary program yet?"

She shakes her head. "No."

I eye her as I dry my hands. She spent four years trying to convince me to let her go abroad for college only for her to scrap that entire plan after her abduction. She was supposed to move to England at the end of the summer. Now, there's no chance of that. Mari didn't even fight me on it. She hasn't been herself since she came back. My sister's got a gentle heart, and the death of her friend traumatized her, so I know she feels safer staying here with me. But I also know college was a dream of hers.

I keep telling her to find a good online program, but each time, she shrugs me off. I'm worried. It's like she's lost her spark. Cooking used to be her favorite thing, but she hasn't made anything since she returned.

I don't know what I can do to help her heal. But making sure that the man who took her is dead feels like a step in the right direction.

I walk over to look at her laptop and steal a piece of cheese off her plate. "Let's look together."

"What about the woman?"

"Mari, forget her, okay?"

She looks down at her hands. "I just... Well, she said she could explain. She *did* help me, Dem."

"I know she did. But that doesn't mean she's guiltless, or that she's not still helping whoever took you." Ale knows who's responsible for what happened, but she won't tell me. If she was innocent and on the run, why would she hold that information back?

Our conversation its interrupted by a knock on the front door. "That's probably Ras," I say.

She nods and folds her laptop under her arm. "I'll be up in my room. Nadia left dinner in the fridge, so I was thinking of warming it up in a bit. Are you going to be here?"

"I don't know. I'll let you know once I talk with Ras."

"Okay," she says. "Maybe we can bring some down to her too. She needs to eat."

"I suppose she does."

My sister nods and heads up the stairs.

I unlock the front door with the fingerprint scanner. One look at Ras's face, and I know he found something.

"Tell me," I say as he steps across the threshold.

He takes a black leather passport case out of the inside pocket of his jacket and hands it to me. "This was in her new apartment, hidden between the sheets and the mattress. It's her passport. The one she said got stolen."

"That was easy," I mutter as I crack open the booklet. It smells brand new, as if it's barely been used. My gaze zeroes in on her name.

"Valentina Conte." That last name doesn't ring any bells.

"Married to Lazaro Conte. Lit up like a Christmas tree when we ran him through the databases."

There's only one man who can get us access to those systems that quickly. "Napoletano is helping you?"

Ras shrugs as we walk in the direction of my office. "I brought in the big guns since I know time is of the essence."

I give him a grateful look. "Who is Conte?"

"The head enforcer of the Garzolo clan of New York. They're one of five families originally from Sicily. She and Lazaro got married a few months ago. Valentina shot him a few days after their two-month wedding anniversary."

I feel a perverse satisfaction at that. "Ouch."

"The whole clan's looking for her."

Ras sits down in an armchair, and I walk over to the mini bar to pour us some whiskey. "Lazaro wants his wife back?"

"I don't know if he's alive or not. No one's seen him since the incident."

"Who's leading the search?" I hand him his glass.

He takes it and meets my gaze. "Stefano Garzolo. The head of the clan. She's his daughter."

Well, fuck.

"You've got yourself a mafia princess."

I down my whiskey in one big gulp. This situation is getting more complicated by the hour. "What are the chances she's here on her father's behest?"

"Zero. He wouldn't send his own daughter here for a job. She's far more valuable to him back home.

There's a bitter tang inside my mouth. She wasn't lying about being here on her own.

"I think she really ran away with only a passport and some cash to her name," Ras says. "There was nothing else of hers in the apartment besides a small amount of clothes. The question is why?"

What made you run, Valentina? "She told me her family weren't good to her."

Ras makes a face. He's not buying it. "She was born and raised into this life. It would take something drastic to make her leave everything and everyone behind."

"Like having an enforcer for a husband? She must have been close to all the dirty work he did."

"I doubt he brought many of his targets home like he did with Mari."

"I don't know about that. Mari said the basement looked like a torture room from the movies." She's never seen the real ones on this side of the world.

"Maybe Valentina couldn't stomach sleeping by a man who murdered people a few meters below their bedroom."

That could explain why she reacted so strongly to the incident with Nelo. It reminded her of what her husband did to people.

"Maybe." I refill my glass and sit down across from Ras. "So where does this leave us? Why would the Garzolos take Mari? They don't have any reason to have it out for me."

Ras looks thoughtful as he swirls his whiskey around. "It could have been a favor for Sal."

Did our don order the abduction of my sister? I've been asking myself this question since the moment I found out she was taken. My gut tells me yes, after all, he had a motive. He wants to keep me in line. But Garzolo's involvement makes me pause. "Why would they grant him this favor? As far as I know, Sal has no relationship with them, business or otherwise."

"We're missing something," Ras says. "Maybe it wasn't Sal after all."

Ras has been warning me all along not to jump to conclusions too quickly. I've made a few enemies during my life, but none that would dare do this to my sister. Sal is the only one who'd have the guts to try.

Ras puts his empty glass on the desk. "You should ask Valentina about what her husband intended to do to Mari. She has to know something that could put our doubts to rest. Is she still downstairs?"

"Yes. I left her tied up there," I say. Shame blazes over my skin.

Ras shoots me an accusatory look and drags a hand over his cheek. "Dem, you can't leave her like that."

"I can do whatever the hell I want," I snap, even as I fight my entire body not to march down there and let her down.

"Sure," Ras says carefully. "But you might get more out of her by treating her well. She's on the run, and over the past month, you've helped her get back on her feet. She has a soft spot for you. Exploit it to get the information we need. Figure out exactly why she ran and offer her protection from whomever she fears," Ras says.

"Offer her protection?" I'd have to forgive her first to do that. Why didn't she give me the truth about herself when I asked her? She had plenty of chances to tell me who she was. I gave her a job, an apartment, my affection, and my trust.

In return, she deceived me.

But she also saved my sister.

I press the heels of my palms against my eyes.

"If you don't want to actually do that, fine. You just need to convince her the offer is real," Ras says. "The moment you get her to believe you is the moment she'll tell you everything."

I drop my hands and look out toward the sea on the other side of the window. I could lie to her, get the information that I need, and then execute my revenge. Now that I know who she is, it would be easy. I could make Stefano Garzolo feel the pain I did by killing his daughter.

Bile rises to my throat. No. I could never do that. I could never kill her.

But I have to do what's right by my sister.

I rise from my seat. "I'm going to go talk to her. See how she reacts when she finds out I know her name."

He gets up. "I'll wait for you."

"Tell Mari you're staying for dinner."

When I get down the steps and see Valentina where I left her, a strange cocktail of emotions drips into my bloodstream.

Self-loathing, mixed with frustration and lust.

She's so absorbed with her task that she doesn't hear me. Her face is angled up, and she's pulling on the ropes at her wrists, her jaw tense with determination.

I grind my teeth. That knot is foolproof. The only thing she's accomplishing is hurting herself.

Her shorts and underwear have slipped down from around her knees and pooled at her feet. Those fucking legs. I want them wrapped around my waist and holding on for dear life as I pound my cock inside of her. She was so wet for me earlier. I don't know how I managed to keep myself from sinking right into her.

I run my hand over my mouth. *Cazzo*. What did I come down here for? I've never met a woman who made me forget about everything but her when she's in front of me.

It's a jarring realization. She made me neglect my responsibility to Mari, which is something that can't happen again. My duty to my sister is the most important thing to me. I can't let anyone distract me from that.

"The only way you're getting out of that is if I let you."

I startle her. She lets out a gasp and then follows it with a hurt look. She's angry with me.

I deserve it for leaving her like this.

"Any idea of when that might be?" she asks.

Instead of answering, I move toward her until I'm invading her space. She glances down at herself and blushes. I follow her gaze. She's embarrassed by her partial nudity. I decide to take pity on her.

When I lower to my haunches, her lips part. She reddens even more as I pull up her shorts and zip them up.

"Can you please let me down?" she asks. "My arms really hurt."

Her wrists are bright red where the rope has rubbed against them. The sight of it makes me feel wretched.

I rise up and start untying the rope, schooling my features to hide all hints of the turmoil I feel at seeing her in pain.

Relief cascades over her expression. "Thank you."

"You're welcome, Valentina."

She makes a choked sound, as if the air she just inhaled suddenly turned dense inside her lungs.

I meet her frightened gaze. "Valentina Conte. I have to say, I prefer Valentina Garzolo. It has a noble ring to it."

The knot comes apart, and as soon as her arms are free, she wraps them around herself. Her chest heaves with a heavy breath. "How?" she whispers.

"Your passport was inside your bed. You didn't try to hide it all that hard."

"I didn't think anyone would search my place," she says weakly. I swear, it's as if she's shrinking in on herself. My threats don't faze her, but me knowing her real name appears to. Why?

"Lazaro... Is he alive?"

"I'm the one asking questions," I say.

"*Please*, Damiano." Her voice cracks. "Is he alive?"

When I nudge her chin up, I see tears pooling inside her eyes. Something squeezes hard around my ribcage. "I don't know."

She searches my face for a long moment and then sniffs when she seems to determine I'm telling the truth. A tear runs down her cheek, and I catch it with my thumb. "Why did Lazaro take Mari? Don't tell me you weren't curious when your husband brought a girl you've never seen to your home. Start talking, Valentina," I say.

I wait while she considers what to do.

She shakes her head.

I let out a loud sigh. "Fine. I'm confident I'll be able to get it out of your father when I tell him I have his precious daughter."

My words hit her way harder than I expect them to, and she starts to weep. Tears roll down her cheek and fall onto her shirt.

Seeing her so upset makes me want to die.

She's breaking me down, and I know I can't show it to her, but in the moment, I can't resist. I tug her into my chest. She bucks against me for a short moment before giving in and crying into my shirt.

"I can't go back. I can't," she says between sobs. "Please, please don't do this."

I'm fucking confused. She's acting like me sending her back is a death sentence, but there's no way that's true. She's the capo's daughter. Runaway or not, she's valuable to him. He's not going to harm her.

I need to figure out what I'm missing.

When I run my hand down her spine, she nuzzles her face into my chest. That makes me feel something... Fuck. It's not a sexual thing. Pity? Concern?

I pull away. "Tell me everything you know about what happened to Mari."

Her teary face makes me hate myself. "Okay. I'll tell you what I know, which isn't much. But you have to promise me you won't send me back to New York."

Can I promise her that? I don't know. I have no idea what I'll need to do after she tells me her secrets, so for now I have no choice but to lie. The lie doesn't come quite as easy as I expect it to. I clear my throat. "If you give me what I need, I won't send you back."

She stares at me, but my face is an unreadable mask. If she's looking for any hints that I'm lying, she won't find them.

Finally, she sniffles and nods. "My husband had your sister in the basement when I got home that day. She was knocked out when I got there, but she came about pretty quickly. I asked him why my father ordered him to take her. He said it was just a job. A favor. He said she was born with the wrong last name."

The light in the room dims as outside the sun sinks past the horizon. I step forward, close enough to peer into her eyes. She's not lying. Goddamn it, she's not lying.

"The wrong last name?" I whisper. There's a buzzing tension in my body, an aggression sparked by her hint and where it leads. "That's what he said?"

"Yes. He called her a little Casalese mouse and said she had the wrong last name."

My eyes widen.

"I swear, I don't know any more," she says.

It doesn't matter. She's given me all the answers I need.

I know who's responsible for my sister's abduction.

CHAPTER 20

VALENTINA

DAMIANO STEPS away from me and looks down to the ground, deep in thought. I thought the meager information I had would hardly be enough for him, but maybe I was wrong. For him, there is a hidden meaning in what I've said.

I wipe the wetness off my face, and my bladder throbs.

"I need to pee," I say.

He sucks in a breath and levels me with a contemplative look. Then he nods.

"Bathroom is through the door behind you," he says. His voice is strangely flat.

My wrists are red. I start to rub them and notice Damiano watching me. He looks away. "Go."

He doesn't need to tell me twice. I duck through the door, lock it behind me, and survey the space as I empty my bladder. Crap. There aren't any windows. I wasn't particularly hopeful there'd be a way to get out of here, but having my suspicions confirmed stings none the less.

He found out my name. I'm so mad at myself I want to scream. Why did I leave my passport in such an obvious place? I could have hidden it better.

No, I'm probably just deluding myself. If I had to guess, he sent Ras to search for it, and if Ras hadn't found it in my mattress, he'd have dug up the entire apartment. I should have gotten rid of it when I could.

It's too late to think of that now. Damiano knows who I am, which means I'm one phone call away from being found. I need to find a way out of here before Damiano makes it.

I finish my business and wash my hands. There's no mirror here, nothing that could be used as a kind of weapon. Maybe I could get creative with the toilet paper. I make a grimace at the thought. I doubt I'd have a chance against the massive man outside even with a shard of glass.

The memory of my little meltdown when he told me he'd call Papà sends a surge of frustration through me. God, why have I lost my ability to keep it together? All of Mamma's training really was for nothing. He found a weak spot when I started to bawl. I need to keep myself in check. The more I show him, the more ammunition he gets.

He's pacing the length of the room when I emerge. I take advantage of his distracted state and glance around for a way out, but the grate on the window looks exceptionally sturdy, and beside the discarded rope, the room is bare.

Suddenly, Damiano stops and turns to me. "Come here," he demands. His expression is thunderous. Clearly, he still hasn't shaken off whatever my information revealed to him.

I move to the furthest corner from him and cross my arms over my midriff. "What are you going to do with me?"

His gaze darkens. "What did I tell you about following my orders?"

"You promised you won't send me back," I remind him.

"Do you think my memory is that bad?" he asks. "You're staying here for now. Now stop arguing and come here."

When I stay frozen in place, he frowns and stalks over to me. In his hands, he still has the rope.

"Please don't string me up again," I beg.

He reaches for my arms, and I put them behind me and back up until my shoulder blades hit the wall.

"I'm serious. My wrists hurt."

"Do you think I care about where you hurt?" His voice is rough, but he refuses to meet my eyes.

I'm not sure I believe him.

"I won't run. I swear," I say.

"We both know that's a lie." He places his palm on my shoulder and turns me around, pressing his hips against mine when I try to resist.

I huff against the wall. "Damn you."

"I'm not going to string you up," he says even as I feel the rough lick of the rope against my forearms. He ties it higher than before, not touching the raw skin. "We're having dinner."

What? My head spins. "This is a bad way to ask someone out on a date."

He finishes tying my arms and moves to my legs. "What can I say? Our courtship is evolving."

"It's not a courtship. It's kidnapping."

When he stands, he brings his lips close to my ear. "And yet you seem to prefer this to being sent home. Want to tell me why?"

Tension blankets my body. "No."

His big hands cover my biceps. "If you tell me, I'll untie you."

I chomp down on my bottom lip. He wants to know all of my secrets, but I can't give him this one. My past with Lazaro has nothing to do with Martina, and if I tell him about the things I've done, I doubt he'll feel any obligation to keep his promise. Whatever affection he might still feel for me will disappear in a heartbeat. "I said no."

He pulls back. "One way or another, I'll get it out of you eventually," he says with dark conviction. Then, he wraps an arm around my waist and tosses me over his shoulder as if I'm a sack of potatoes. "Behave yourself when we get up there."

I don't think twice before starting to buck against him. "Put me down!"

His grip on my waist tightens, and he slaps me hard on the ass. I yelp.

"If you want to be conscious for dinner, stop moving now," he bites out.

"I'm not hungry!"

He carries me over to the stairs and sits me down on the third step. "You're going to pretend like you are and eat whatever my sister's warmed up for us."

That makes me freeze up. "Your sister's having dinner with us?"

"Yes," he says as he digs for something in the back pocket of his jeans.

A vision of her curled up on that cold floor in my old house, so small and fragile, flashes inside my mind, and it sends a chill down my spine. Thank God she managed to get to safety.

"Open wide."

"What the—mphhf!" My words are cut off as he stuffs something in my mouth.

He rolls his eyes at my muffled outrage. "It's a clean handkerchief. Relax." Then he hauls me over his shoulder again and scales the steps.

Does he really plan to present me at dinner like this? Tied up and gagged? As he carries me through the house, I try to take in as much of my new surroundings as I can, but it's a bit tricky when I'm hanging upside down. We pass through what I think is a large living room and enter the dining room. He deposits me in a chair.

I have my answer.

Ras and Martina are sitting across from me, their dinner plates heaped with food. Martina's jaw drops. Ras hikes a brow.

"Valentina is joining us," Damiano announces as he takes his seat at the head of the table.

There's a very long awkward silence as my eyes flit over the three of them.

"We're having roast chicken," Martina says finally.

"Thnkff ouu."

She gulps and shoots a worried look at her brother. "She can't eat like that, Dem."

My captor is already digging into his food, completely unruffled by this scene. Nothing seems to ruin his appetite. "If she promises to keep her tongue in check, the gag comes off."

Martina slowly moves her gaze from her brother to me. "Will you promise?"

I glance at Damiano. He's not even looking at me. He's so absorbed with his damned chicken. "Mhm."

"She said yes...I think," Martina says.

Ras makes a move to get out of his seat. "I'll get that out of your mouth."

"I'll do it," Damiano snaps. He reaches over and jerks the cloth from between my teeth, and Ras sits back down.

I start to cough.

"Give her some water," Martina pleads, and Damiano pours water in a glass in front of me.

My arms are still tied behind my back. "I can't reach it."

He curses under his breath in Italian, picks up the glass, and brings it to my lips. "Drink."

I take a sip. He's staring at me so intensely it makes goosebumps erupt over my skin. "Tilt it more," I say.

When he does, some of the water spills out of the corner of my mouth and drips down my chin. I pull back and lick the water off my lips. He zeroes in on the movement, and a slither of something warm passes through my belly. The moment suddenly feels entirely too intimate.

I turn away and collect myself.

Ras and Martina return to their plates, but every now and then I catch her shooting me curious looks.

It takes her a few minutes to work up the courage, but then she says, "I want to thank you for helping me."

I give her a weak smile. "I'm happy you made it home safe. Even if you have to live with a don for a brother."

The temperature in the room drops, as if someone turned on the AC at full blast. Damiano's lips flatten.

What is it? Is he not the don? He hasn't said it explicitly, but it was a safe assumption to make after what he told me about his father.

It's Ras who deigns me worthy of an explanation. "Damiano isn't the Casalese don. He's the capo of Ibiza."

Maybe here these things don't get tied to one's bloodline like they do with the Garzolos. Still, I can't help but feel there's something Ras has left unsaid.

"You're probably hungry," Martina says.

"I'm all right."

"No need to be shy," Ras says, taking a sip of his wine. "Have a bite. I'd offer you some of this Tempranillo, but it seems like it might be more hassle that its worth." He gestures at the half empty cup of water Damiano left in front of me.

Yeah, I could do without spilling wine all over me.

The chicken does smell heavenly. I eye the half-eaten bird. It looks like it's glazed with honey and there are slices of lemons and fingerling potatoes in the juices on the tray around it.

"I don't think I can eat that without my hands."

"I'm not removing the ropes," Damiano says as he methodically cuts into his meat.

My stomach decides to betray me by emitting a loud growl.

Martina gives me a pitying look. "Dem…"

He looks like he's about to drag me back down to the basement and be done with this whole charade, but instead he plucks the napkin off his lap, drops it on the table, and jerks me from my chair into his lap.

"What on earth are you doing?"

He reaches around me to take a chicken thigh off the tray and starts to cut into it.

I try to get off him. "I don't want to sit on you."

"Stop squirming," he says with a grunt.

I appreciate Martina trying to stick up for me, but I kind of wish she'd just gotten up and fed me the chicken herself, because this is far worse than staying hungry.

"I don't need you to feed me," I hiss at Damiano, but my will to argue leaves me when I smell the chicken up close.

I part my lips, and he puts the fork inside my mouth.

Damn, that's good. I make a hum of appreciation and try to chew in as dignified manner as my current position allows. He's still staring at me when I swallow, so I open my mouth again to let him know I'm ready for more.

Damiano's lips give a hint of a smile. "So it can be trained," he murmurs before feeding me another forkful.

I clamp down on the utensil with my lips and make sure to get everything. Who knows when he's going to feed me next? I might as well get as much as I can while the opportunity has presented itself. That way I'll have enough energy to make a run for it.

He drops his dark gaze to my lips again, and my pulse speeds up. Why is it that one look from him is still enough to get me riled up? Whatever was starting between us is definitely over now, even if he had his fingers inside of me what feels like just moments ago.

I swear he sees that thought reflected in my eyes, and in response, those same fingers tighten around the fork. His nostrils flare with an inhale. His length hardens against the backs of my thighs and sends a burst of warmth through my core.

I'm about to grind against him when I remember where we are.

Jesus. He is my *captor*. I can't indulge in the inexplicable physical attraction I feel for him.

A chair squeaks across the floor and breaks the spell. "I'm done, so I'm going back up to my room," Mari says.

Damiano takes the fork out of my mouth and puts it on his plate with a soft clank. "Take a look at some programs tonight and send me anything you like, all right?"

He went from predator to good older brother in the span of a second, and it's disorienting as hell.

"I will. Good night." She gives me an uncertain smile. "Good night, Valentina."

"Night," I say.

She leaves, and then it's just the three of us.

"What now?" I ask. "Are you going to serve me dessert?"

Damiano's palms wrap around my waist. "Not unless you're offering yourself up as one."

My cheeks redden at his hoarse voice. This man has no shame.

Ras stands, his expression bemused. "I'll wait for you in your office," he says to Damiano.

"Fine." His gaze never leaves my face. The air between us crackles with electricity.

For my own sanity, I need to put an end to this.

"I want off," I say as fiercely as I can manage. "This—" I tilt my chin down toward my body, "—is off-limits to you. Forever."

He lifts me off him with a quiet chuckle. "Toys exist to be played with."

"I'm not your toy," I snap as he puts me back down on my chair. I try to push farther away from him with my feet, but all I accomplish is tipping over my chair. Just when I think I'm about to crack my head on the hardwood floor, Damiano steadies me.

"Time to put you away for the night," he says, lifting me over his shoulder.

I'm about to beg him not to lock me in the basement again when I notice he's taking me upstairs.

"Where are we going?" I ask.

He halts in front of a door on the second floor of the house and nudges it open with his foot. Once we're inside, he deposits me on a bed.

I sit up and look around. It seems to be a guest bedroom that hasn't been used in a while. Besides the bed, there are two nightstands, a console table, and a chair. It's bare of any personal belongings. The most exciting thing about all of this is the large window, until I realize there's a metal grate on the outside of it.

Damiano moves back toward the door. "The alarm will go off if you so much as touch that window. Don't make me take you back below."

"Fine. How long are you going to keep me here?"

He leaves without giving me an answer and locks the door behind him.

I pull my knees to my chest and wrap my arms around them. The air in the room is perfectly still. There isn't a single sound coming through the walls, and I'm left with just my thoughts to keep me company.

It seems the old saying is true. You can never outrun the mafia.

CHAPTER 21

DAMIANO

I LEAVE Valentina and decide I'm not going to think about her for at least the next few days. There's a plan forming inside my head, and I'll have to stay focused to make sure it succeeds. Every single one of my brain circuits needs to be firing at one hundred percent, which means I can't let that woman take an ounce of my attention.

Ras is looking out to the pool when I enter my office.

"Leave your phone here. Let's go for a walk," I tell him. Some conversations are better had outside and without any technology, so there's no chance of anyone listening in.

He does as he's told, and we leave the office, passing by the pool before following the stone path to the garden. It's my favorite part of the massive property I bought a few years back to be a proper home for Martina and I. She fell in love with the light-filled living room as soon as she stepped through the front doors, and I rarely resist opportunities to make her happy.

"What did Valentina tell you?" Ras asks once we reach the olive trees. The gravel crunches softly beneath our feet.

"We have the confirmation we need. Sal was behind it."

Ras's steps slow for a moment. "You sure?"

"Conte told her it was a favor for someone. The reason for it? Martina has the wrong last name."

"That's not definitive—"

"Conte called her a little Casalese mouse. Where do you think he got that from?"

It's Sal's nickname for Martina. As soon as Valentina said it, I knew.

Ras swears. "He's gone out of his mind. Abducting her to keep a leash on you? He must have known the risk he was taking if it ever came to light."

"It was only a matter of time before he did something like this," I say. I should have known that the man who murdered my father to take over the clan would never stop worrying that one day I'd rise up against him.

There's a bench on the edge of the garden that overlooks the calm ocean beyond. We sit down.

"He's taken everything from us once already," I say. "I won't let him do it again."

I remember my mother standing in the kitchen as flames engulf her dress. My sister's frantic bleats. The men yelling in shock. My father's dead body still warm on the floor. It is that moment, so clear in my memory that it feels like it's been set in resin, that's driven most of the decisions I've ever made. Without it, I'd be a completely different man.

A better man.

A weaker man.

I squeeze my eyes shut and take a deep breath. "Martina cries in her room every night since New York. Every time I hear it, I remember how badly I've failed her. She can't go to college like she wanted anymore. She can't even leave this island. We are both prisoners here."

Ras's hand falls on my shoulder. "You know you can count on me."

"There's only one way out of this, Ras."

His heavy exhale tells me he understands.

Water crashes over the rocks below us. I turn to face him. "War."

He steeples his palms, his elbows on his knees, and I can see he's already running through our options. "We need to beef up our security here first to make sure Mari is safe."

"Would it be better to hide her somewhere until the dust settles?"

He shakes his head. "Better to concentrate our defenses on one area where both of you are. Plus, moving her this early would tip Sal off that something's up. He watches all the entry points. I'll call Napoletano."

"Ask him to come as soon as he can."

"How much do you want me to tell him?"

"Keep it vague. Him and Sal have their own ugly history, but I want to talk to him in person first before deciding if we should bring him in. What's your read on the latest sentiments among the families?"

"Hard to say. I'll have to go to Casal and talk to my father. Last time we talked, he alluded to some rumblings from Elio. If it's true, we'll want to meet with him."

"What rumblings?" I ask, thinking back to the last time I saw Uncle Elio. It's been many years.

"Something about marrying off one of his two daughters to Vito Pirozzi."

"Both of the daughters are fucking prepubescent."

"They'll wait until she's eighteen."

The thought of giving one of those innocent girls to the likes of Vito makes me sick. He's smarter than his idiot brother Nelo, but not by much. "That's a match made in hell if I ever heard of one."

"The Pirozzi patriarch wants his boys to settle down, and Sal loves to pick on the remaining De Rossis."

"If we can get both of my father's brothers to back me, along with your parents, it will give us a real chance."

Ras pulls out a cigarette and lights it. "It'll be a start. I'll set up the meetings."

"I should go to Casal with you."

"You can't. It'll set off too many alarms."

I rise from the bench. I want to say to hell with it all. The caution, the levelheadedness, the self-control. I developed all of these traits out of necessity. They were the only way I could ensure me and my sister would survive amidst a collapsing world. But beneath all of those civilized layers lives a barbarian who's hungry for revenge. I feel him inside me now, stretching his arms out and reaching for the bat wrapped in barbed wire. He wants to raise it and slam it into Sal's head until there's nothing left but bloody pulp. "I'll make him pay for everything he did, Ras. Everything."

Ras comes to stand beside me and peers over the edge of the cliff. "What of your prisoner?"

Valentina's frightened eyes flash inside my mind. Can whatever she's running away from be worse than the trouble I'm about to stir? Until she tells me her whole story, I can't know the answer to that question, but at least here, I can keep an eye on her. "I'm keeping her until I figure out how she can best help our cause."

"She's valuable," Ras says.

"I want to know if her husband is dead."

"I'll ask Napoletano to help, but her husband wasn't the one who agreed to take Martina. You know that."

Of course I do. Lazaro's just a soldier, but if he's alive, he better be counting his last breaths. Even if he hadn't terrorized Mari, it's clear Valentina isn't fond of him. That's enough for me to wipe him off the face of the Earth.

"The order had to have come from their don, Valentina's father," I say. "But it's Lazaro who put his hands on my sister. The don will make it up to us in other ways." I rub my palm over my chin. "He was willing enough to grant Sal a favor. The question is why? Garzolo needs something, and when we figure out what, we'll be able to have a real conversation with him. If Valentina knows anything about it, I'll get it out of her."

222

Ras crosses his arms over this chest. "You sure about that? Your foreplay at dinner didn't inspire a lot of confidence in your methods of interrogation."

I scowl. "That wasn't foreplay. You were the one who told me I couldn't leave her down there."

"I said you should exploit the soft spot she may have for you by treating her well, not indulge your BDSM fantasies in front of other people."

My face heats. "Fuck you."

"You made Mari so uncomfortable she ran to hide in her room."

I glare at him. "Fine, no more family dinners with Valentina. I'll deal with her in private."

We return to the house, and Ras leaves for the night. I look at the time. It's nearing midnight, and the house is silent except for the soft buzz of the dishwasher and sounds of the ocean streaming through the open patio doors.

I close them, stop by the kitchen for some water, then head upstairs. American pop music is playing from behind Mari's door, but she's not talking to her friends on FaceTime like she used to before everything happened. She doesn't do much these days besides scrolling on her phone and wandering around the house. Packages arrive from time to time—clothes, bags, fashion accessories—but I've never seen her excited about any of them. She never goes out.

I'm about to knock on her door when I stop myself, fist raised midair. The truth is, I don't know how to help her move on. I've tried talking to her, but it never leads anywhere. There's something inside of her that's tearing her up, and she won't tell me what it is. I wish she had someone else to talk to, but there's no one she trusts enough to share the details of what happened. I've always been her closest confidant, but now that she won't talk to me, I'm at a loss of how to bring her old self back.

Maybe once I've taken care of Sal, she'll be able to attend college in person next year. That would cheer her up.

I move away from her door and continue to the third floor. My bedroom is down the hall from where I put Valentina. When I get closer to her room, I tell myself to keep walking, but then I hear a soft sound, and I halt.

I press my ear to the wood. Sniffling. She's crying.

Cazzo. Now I have not one, but two miserable women under my roof. Pulling away, I pinch the bridge of my nose.

Maybe I should have gone easier on her downstairs. Her wrists looked nearly raw, and she doesn't have anything to clean them up.

I stalk back down to the kitchen and grab the first aid kit. I'll bandage her up and then put her out of my mind like I said I would.

When I walk in, she's curled up like a shrimp on the bed, her long black hair splayed over a pillow. She scrambles to sit up when she hears me enter and pulls her knees to her chest. "Why are you here?"

Her nose is red and puffy. Her eyes are shiny and wet. An ache appears inside my chest.

"I want to take a look at you," I say. I sit down on the edge of the bed and reach for her, but she scoots away from me. It makes me want to punch a fucking wall. Her being afraid of my touch is up there with the worst things that ever happened to me.

I show her the first aid kit. "Let me see your wrists. I'll bandage them up and leave."

She studies the box suspiciously, her brows pinching together. I wait. Finally, she gives a tiny nod and extends her arms.

The angry pink marks look awful on her delicate wrists. I take out an antiseptic wipe and gently dab at the spots where her skin is broken. There aren't many, but she hisses at each one I touch. I bite down on the inside of my cheek so hard I taste blood.

She lets me dress her shallow wounds in silence, leaving me to ruminate on my actions. Ras is right. I don't have it in me to interrogate her this way again.

Why doesn't she want to go back home?

There's something there. A piece I'm missing. A secret she's yet to tell.

I finish tying her bandages and meet her tired gaze.

"All done."

She pulls her hands back, lies down, and turns away from me.

"Do they feel bette—"

"You said you would leave."

The cold ferocity of her words cuts through me like a sharp blade. I've earned it, didn't I?

I made my bed, and now I have to lie in it.

CHAPTER 22

VALENTINA

THE NEXT MORNING, I waste no time before looking for an escape route from my new room. I can't sit around here while Damiano decides what to do with me. His hot-and-cold act has to be some kind of a game. Why else would he treat me like garbage at dinner only to play doctor a few hours later?

I begin with the window. When my thorough examination doesn't reveal any special wires, I conclude Damiano lied to me about it being alarmed, and I try to open it. It doesn't make a peep, but the handle won't move no matter how hard I tug on it. When I exhaust all of my arm strength, I decide to leave it alone for now.

There's a flatscreen TV but no remote, and I can't find any buttons on the screen itself to turn it on. I briefly consider tearing it off the wall and tossing it at the window, but it won't do anything to the steel bars on the outside. Why wouldn't he leave me the remote? Maybe he's hoping to torture me with boredom.

Minutes tick by slowly. At least I assume it's minutes. There is no clock. The room is stylishly designed, but there's literally nothing here. No clothes, no books, not even a pen.

I do my business in the bathroom. At least there's a ton of toilet paper. I pop into the shower and stay there for a long time, trying not to give in to the desperation that's simmering on the edges of my consciousness.

My clothes from yesterday are dirty. I sweated what must be the equivalent of a few buckets, so I really don't want to put those back on. I give them a wash with an available bar of soap and hang them on the towel rack. With some luck, I might be able to put them on later today, but for now, I wrap the towel around me and return to the room.

I spend a long time turning over multiple escape strategies in my mind, but none of them make a ton of sense. If I had a knife or even a spoon, maybe I could start chipping away at the frame of the window. How long would that take? Long enough for Damiano to decide to send me back to my father after all. He said he wouldn't, but I'm not naive enough to believe him. I wish I had something valuable to offer him, something that I could trade for my freedom, but he's got more euros that I have cells in my body, and despite being the don's daughter, I don't have any information that would be valuable for Damiano. I already gave him everything I had.

I played my cards way too soon.

Eventually, my head starts to hurt from all of my fruitless scheming, so I scoot to the top of the bed and stare out the window. The sea glistens in the near distance. Even with that view to keep me company, it's incredible how quickly boredom creeps in. My eyelids drift lower and lower.

Looks like napping is about to become my favorite pastime.

Sometime later, I'm roused by three knocks on the door. I roll off the bed clutching my towel and creep to the door. "Yes?"

"It's Martina. I-I brought you brunch."

Is she going to open the door? She has to. There's no other way to get the food inside. Maybe I can take advantage of it and run. I press my back against the wall and get into a ready stance, putting my weight on the balls of my feet.

"I'm not sure what you like, and Dem told me I can't bring you any cutlery, so I got a croissant, cheese, some fruit, boiled eggs, and coffee."

It sounds like an entire continental breakfast. My stance softens. Martina is trying to take care of me. What if I can get her to help me? And anyway, how far will I get wearing only a towel?

"Thank you," I say as I step away from the wall.

There's a soft click, and the door opens. Martina's on the other side in a cropped T-shirt and a pair of jean shorts, balancing a tray filled with food on her palm.

I take the tray from her and step back. "This is very kind. I wasn't sure if your brother was going to feed me."

She takes in my clothes, or lack thereoff. "Do you want me to bring you something to wear?"

"That would be great."

She nods. Behind her, I spy a huge security guard with a gun strapped to his waist.

Great.

Of course Damiano wouldn't let her come up here on her own. I'm surprised he allowed her even with the backup.

The door shuts, and I eye the food on the tray. Everything looks delicious. I place it on the bed, tear off a corner of the still-warm croissant, and watch a bit of steam come out of the center. It tastes even better than it looks—slightly crunchy on the outside, and buttery soft in the middle. Did Martina bake it herself? It's better than anything I've ever bought, even from my favorite bakery in Lower East Side.

She returns a short while later carrying a small stack of clothes under her arm. "You're taller than me," she says. "But I found a few things that should fit."

"Thank you." I take the stack from her. "I'm not picky."

Her mouth curves into a shy smile. She glances behind her and gently nudges the door to the room to close it, but the security guard clears his throat before she finishes. "Door open, señorita."

A flash of frustration crosses her delicate features, but it only lasts a moment.

"It's okay," I say. "They probably think I'll maul you if we're left alone."

She blinks at me. "Will you?"

"No." As soon as I say the word to her, I know it's true. Unlike her brother, Martina is innocent, and I don't want to pull her into our drama. She's gone through enough already.

I squeeze the clothes closer into my chest. "Do you mind if I change?"

"Go ahead," she says, starting toward the door.

"You don't need to leave. I'll just pop into the bathroom quickly. Then you can tell me who baked that heavenly croissant."

Her face melts into a grin. "You liked it?"

"It's the best I've ever had."

Her bashful laugh follows me into the bathroom where I quickly swap my towel for a pair of underwear and a loose jersey dress that reaches my mid thigh. No bra. Martina is petite, so she probably didn't have anything that would fit me in that department.

When I emerge, she's sitting on the edge of the bed, nibbling on a piece of cheese.

"You remind me of one of my sisters," I tell her.

"Sisters?"

"I have two. They're younger than me, and I miss them. A lot."

"Which one do I remind you of?"

"My younger sister, Cleo. Something about the upper part of your face, like the eyes and the nose. It's hard to describe, but they're similar." I sit down on the opposite corner of the bed and reach for the last bit of that croissant. "She also really loves cheese."

Martina laughs. "Who doesn't love cheese?"

"People who can't taste, clearly. When Cleo and I still lived together, she'd always put together these elaborate cheese boards with all kinds of nuts and jams. Her, my other sister, and I would bring it out to the terrace, sneak a bottle of wine out of my parents' cellar, and watch the sun set over New York." We stopped doing that after I got married. My sisters would invite me, but I made up excuses not to go so that I wouldn't have to spend hours lying to their faces about how my marriage was going.

"I hope you see them again soon." Martina's voice is soft. "I'm sure Dem won't keep you here forever."

Even if he lets me go, chances are I won't see my sisters, but there's no point in telling her that. "Who knows what's going on inside your brother's head."

She grows rigid. I can tell she feels uncomfortable talking about her brother's plans for me. She's probably worried she'll betray his confidence by saying something wrong.

I give her a reassuring smile. "So I gather you like to cook."

She seems momentarily relieved at the change of topic, then her face falls again. "I used to." She traces the embroidered pattern on the comforter with her finger. "I don't do it as much anymore, even though Dem asks me all the time."

"He didn't ask you to bake for me, did he?"

Blood rushes to her cheeks. "No. I just wanted to make something nice for you. I used to cook most of mine and my brother's meals. Now, we've hired someone."

"Why's that?"

Suddenly, she stills her tracing and flattens her hand on the bedspread. "After New York, I lost interest in it."

I see it then in her eyes. A hollowness filled with lingering pain. I'd bet my life it didn't exist until she met Lazaro, and no matter how much I want to look away, I don't allow myself to. This is what my husband does to people if he doesn't end up killing them. He destroys them from within.

Just like he did to me.

Martina doesn't deserve this. She's just a young girl caught up in the cruel games of her brother's world, and she must move past what happened to her.

I want to help her move on. I *owe* it to her.

The security guard is watching us through the crack in the door, so I don't take her hand, but I move my fingers closer to where hers rest. She notes the movement and gives me a questioning look.

"Martina, it will get better," I tell her in a low voice. "Give it time. You must be patient with yourself, but you can't stop fighting."

She squeezes her lips together and takes in a shuddery breath through her nose. For a while, she doesn't say anything, she just shakes her head over and over again. I think she's holding back tears. My heart trembles for her.

Finally, she whispers, "I convinced her to come with me. I —" Her voice cracks, and she scrambles off the bed. Before I even have a chance to utter another word, she's already out the door.

The locks click into place. It sounds like a candle being blown out with a frantic breath.

I spend the rest of the day picking at my food and watching the ocean through the window. When the sun is almost over the horizon, the door opens, and it's that grumpy security guard from earlier. He hands me a tray with my dinner and leaves without saying a word.

When I'm done eating, I decide to take another shower, and that's when my day perks up. I notice that the showerhead is removable with five different settings, just like the one I had back in Lazaro's home. If Damiano wanted to torture me by way of horrible boredom, this is a serious omission on his part.

I take the showerhead out of its holder, lean against the tiled wall, and point the spray between my legs. It takes me a little while to find the right angle, but then I manage to do it, and dear Lord, it's *bliss*. In a moment, I forget where I am and just focus on the soft pulses of pleasure radiating from my core.

It takes me right back to yesterday, when Damiano brought me to the edge and left me there. Damn that man. Being tied up and completely at his mercy shouldn't turn me on, but it does. I remember how he thrust his thick fingers inside of me, how his hot lips brushed against the sensitive spot at the back of my neck. The contrast of him fully clothed and me with my shorts around my knees. He could have come around, lifted me by my thighs, and fucked me right there. I know he wanted to. Maybe be stopped when he did because he was about to lose control. I wish he did. I wish he'd finish me off and then fill me with his cum again. Afterwards, he'd leave me there, and I'd spend the rest of the day with his cum slowly dripping down my thighs.

The pressure explodes, and I bite down on my lip to keep the shout from coming out. Oh God. Waves of pleasure cascade over me, all the way from my head, down to my toes.

My legs shake as I step out of the shower, wrap a towel around me, and sit down on the toilet lid. When my breaths finally slow, I drop my forehead into my palms and allow reality to creep in.

I just masturbated to a fantasy of Damiano—the capo who's keeping me locked up in his house—using me like a doll.

There's something seriously wrong with me.

With that depressing thought, I climb into bed and flick off the lights. Maybe the shower head isn't such a good idea after all. Tomorrow, I'll have to work on finding another way to entertain myself while I wait for Damiano to decide what he's going to do with me.

He never came to see me today. He may have called my father already, and I wouldn't be any wiser. How much stock can I really put into his promises?

I toss and turn in bed until a restless sleep finally claims me.

CHAPTER 23

VALENTINA

UNEXPECTEDLY, Martina delivers me food again the following morning. She slips me the tray, and I manage to utter a thank you before she ducks out of the room.

The next day, she isn't in such a rush to leave. When I invite her in, she gives me a shy smile and steps through the door.

"I tried something new today," she tells me.

I take the tray from her hands. It's another pastry, square and flaky, with raspberries piled into the middle, and covered with a layer of powdered sugar.

My mouth waters. "Your future husband, whoever that is, will be a very lucky man."

Leaving a crack in the doorway, she perches on the edge of the bed. "I think I might be asexual."

I nearly choke on my first bite. Does her brother know this?

When she sees my expression, she laughs. "I mean, I'm not sure. I've just never met a guy I was attracted to."

"What about girls?" I ask with my mouth still half full.

She wrinkles her nose. "Nah."

"My youngest sister wasn't attracted to anyone for a long time," I offer. "She's your age, but she only had her first crush when she turned seventeen."

"Who was it?"

"Some new boy at her school who organized Free Britney marches in downtown New York." I can see my statement confuses her. "My sister is a bit obsessed with Britney Spears," I explain. "She was very active in the Free Britney movement."

"I'm glad Britney got out," Martina says. "What her father did to her was horrible. What happened with the boy?"

"Turns out he already had a boyfriend."

"Oh." Martina shrugs. "The dating scene can be tough, I guess."

"Especially for women like us."

I don't need to explain what I mean. For all of his faults, Damiano seems to love Martina. Based on what I've seen so far, he seems to be more like her father than a sibling. Will he barter her away for power? Give her away as a reward?

She adjusts herself to sit cross-legged. "Your husband... You didn't choose him?"

The thought is so ludicrous, I can't help but laugh. "I didn't have a choice. My father handled the matchmaking, and I didn't even think to question his judgement. I thought he'd make sure to find me a good fit."

"He didn't though."

"No, he didn't."

Martina grows quiet, and I finish the rest of my pastry in silence.

"Was it good?" she asks.

"Delicious."

She smiles. "I'll make you another tomorrow."

Why is she being so kind to me? I meet her gaze. It radiates melancholy. If she opens up to me, maybe I can help her.

"Last time, you said you convinced your friend to come to New York," I say gently.

Her smile falls immediately. "Yeah. She wouldn't have been there if I hadn't insisted on it."

I wait for her to continue, sensing that she needs to talk about this with someone.

She rubs her biceps with her palms and looks over her shoulder toward where the guard stands just beyond the crack in the door. When she speaks next, it's a whisper. "I wanted to go to Eleven Madison Park. It's a restaurant."

"Yeah, it's incredible. I've been there before." Papà took the entire family one year for Mamma's birthday.

"I dreamt about it ever since I got interested in cooking. Imogen was nervous, her parents didn't want her to go, but she managed to convince them after I kept pressuring her. Dem booked us a special private lunch with the chef. We were leaving the hotel on our way there when it happened." Her voice quivers like a plucked string. "She died because of a *meal*."

I'm about to tell her it's not her fault, that many people travel to New York on their own and return home completely unharmed, but it's as if a jar full of words has been knocked over inside of her, and now all of them are spilling out.

"It was raining awfully that day," she says hoarsely. "When the three men first ambushed us, I was struggling with my umbrella, and I was so disoriented, I told them our names the moment they asked. It didn't even occur to me to question why someone was asking for our names just outside our hotel. That's all the confirmation they needed before they stuffed us into their van. They shot Imogen while she was sitting beside me. Right in the center of her forehead. It didn't bleed at first, I thought it was a joke, a bad prank someone was playing on us. I shook her. I shouted, *Imogen, stop it! It's not funny.* Then the blood started to drip, and she became so still. It wasn't a prank. It was real."

I clamp my hand over my mouth. This is so, *so* horrible.

Martina rakes her nails down her cheeks. "It was hideously selfish for me to force her to go. There's no one to blame for her death but me. When Dem and I went to her funeral, her parents wouldn't even look at me, Valentina. They hate me now. And why shouldn't they? Being my friend was the worst thing that ever happened to their daughter. It's the worst thing that can happen to anyone who's not a part of our world. The friends I had before New York? We don't talk anymore. I deleted their phone numbers, shut down my social media. No one will ever be safe around me, so what's the point of getting close to anyone? I'd rather be alone than love people and watch them die."

Silent tears drip from her eyes, and my own throat twists until it's too tight for me to choke out any words. I want to give her a hug, this poor girl who's carrying far too heavy a burden on her shoulders, but I can't. If the security guard sees me touching her, he'll take her away. I reach for her hand and grasp it in mine, hoping the angle of our bodies won't allow him to see.

"Martina."

She's staring down at her lap, and her tears falling on her gray leggings, leaving dark round spots.

"Martina, look at me." I squeeze her hand.

Her glistening eyes flicker up.

"I understand what you're feeling." I really do. I force myself to breathe through the tightness in my throat. "The rage and the guilt and the utter disbelief that your life could take such a horrifying turn. I've felt those things too after...I witnessed what my husband did to people." I can't tell her the full truth. If she knew what I've done to people, she wouldn't be here talking to me.

"But you were brave," she whispers. "You helped me. I didn't help my friend."

"You couldn't. And yes, I did help you, but there were others before, and I didn't help them." *I murdered them because my husband told me to.* "I was a coward up until the moment I met you."

"Do you regret not helping them?"

"Every day."

"How do you live with it? Some days I wake up and think there's no point in getting out of bed. There's no point in anything."

I glance at the floor. "I used to have those thoughts too. It will take time, but eventually, they'll disappear."

Letting go of her hand, I scoop my knees to my chest. "I knew my husband and his men well, Martina. They're professional killers. It didn't matter what you did once they had you. There was nothing you could have done for your friend."

She wraps her arms around her midsection. "I'm scared it will happen again. Something bad."

"I get that. I'm not going to pretend any relationships are easy in this world. Most of my friends were related to me or they were sons and daughters of men who worked for my father. It made them more compatible for friendships."

"Here, we're on our own. It's Dem and Ras and all of his hired guards. There aren't any other big families on the island." She sniffs. "It's on purpose, so that—" Her mouth slams shut, and she shoots me a cautious look. She was about to say something she shouldn't.

She's vulnerable enough to probably tell me more if I press her, but my conscience holds me back. Instead, I give her a smile. "I can be your friend. Trust me, our friendship can hardly put me in a situation worse than the one I'm already in."

She lets out a watery laugh. "I suppose that's true." Sighing, she looks out toward the water. "I should go back to my room. Dem told me I can't spend more than thirty minutes here with you."

I roll my eyes. "He wants me to die of boredom."

"I won't let that happen," she says as she climbs off the bed. "In fact, I have an idea."

"Hmm?"

She wraps her hand around the door handle and looks back at me. "I don't want to get your hopes up. Let me talk to him first. I'll be back tomorrow."

CHAPTER 24

VALENTINA

THE FOLLOWING MORNING, Martina comes with a pile of clothing instead of her usual food. She hands it to me. "We're going to spend the day by the pool," she announces as an excited smile lights up her face.

In my shock, I manage to utter a single word. "How?"

"Dem agreed to let you out of your room with the condition that we'll have two of his scariest guards keeping watch over us. Abbott is an ex-MMA fighter who bit an ear off his opponent, and Clyde kind of looks like that guy in Game of Thrones who played the Mountain."

I place the clothes on the bed. "Haven't seen it, but that name alone paints a clear picture." Scary guards or not, the prospect of finally seeing something other than four cream-colored walls around me sounds like heaven. Not to mention it's an opportunity for me to look for possible escape routes. The longer Damiano avoids me, the more I worry about my fate. Why hasn't he come to see me in the past three days?

"I'll wait outside while you change," Martina says.

I dig through the bathing suits. They're all bikinis that look too small for me. I decide to pair a black bottom with a neon-green triangle top that covers a bit more than the other two options. There's no mirror for me to check my reflection, but I suspect it all looks a bit vulgar. With a sigh, I remove the old bandages from my wrists, tie a thin white cover-up around my waist, and walk up to the door. "Ready."

Martina takes a peek at me and gives me an encouraging smile. "You look great."

Tugging my top in place, I shoot a glare at the two guards standing just outside the door. They really are enormous, like two flesh-covered grizzly bears with scowls to match.

"Not getting into your bathing trunks?" I ask them.

Quickly, their expressions grow even more grim. The one with the shaved head addresses Martina. "Why is she wearing that?"

Martina purses her lips and adjusts her posture. "We're going to the pool."

It appears the guards weren't informed of that detail.

"That's not what Señor De Rossi approved," one of them says.

"He said she can come out of her room if the two of you are around us at all times."

"As long as she stays inside the house."

"The pool is a part of the house, isn't it?" Martina challenges, displaying a backbone I didn't realize she had. "It's completely walled off."

"That is not what your brother had in mind. You can't go there."

"My brother will be very upset to learn you prevented me from getting some sunshine," Martina says.

The guards look at each other. The quiet one's nostril's flare with an exhale. He turns to me. "You do anything sketchy, and we're taking you back here. One strike, and you're out."

"I take it you won't be joining us for a swim?" I ask, feigning innocence.

They ignore me and wave us forward.

On the first floor, past the living room's floor-to-ceiling windows is the pool. Martina slides one of them open, and I step over the threshold, immediately feeling the warmth of the sun on my skin. It's a glorious Ibizan day.

A few loungers are scattered just ahead of us, and Martina plops down on one of them. I'm too eager to enjoy my tiny slice of freedom to stay still, so I walk up to the edge of the pool and peer down. The bottom is covered in colorful patterned tiles. Balancing on one leg, I dip my right toe into the water. It's not cold, but cool enough to be refreshing.

I turn around at the sound of another person's voice. Martina is talking to an older woman wearing a white uniform with an apron tied around her waist.

"Do you like rosé, or would you prefer champagne?" Martina asks me.

An incredulous laugh bubbles up my throat. I'm a prisoner here, but apparently, I get a choice of which wine I'd like to drink. "Rosé is great."

I face the pool again and notice a gate that might be a way out of the compound, but to be honest, it doesn't fill me with hope. The guards won't let me get away. I'll probably just hurt myself if I try running, and that will be the end of any future outings with Martina. Maybe I should just enjoy the rosé and try to talk to Damiano. He has to check on his sister at some point during the day, right?

"Is your brother around?" I ask Martina when the other woman leaves.

She pulls her loose summer dress over her head and tosses it to another lounger. Beneath, she's wearing a shimmery yellow bikini. "He's at Revolvr, but he should be back in the afternoon."

"What time is it now?"

She glances down at her phone. "Eleven am."

I sit down on the lounger next to her and eye the device. If I managed to steal it, who would I call for help? The only phone number I know off the top of my head is Gemma's, and I can't risk calling her when Papà is likely tracking all of her calls. He knows if I call anyone, it will be her.

The rosé arrives and with it, a spread of sliced fruits and veggies. Martina and I snack on the food and drink the wine, all the while talking about what TV shows we like. When we've thoroughly exhausted that topic, we start discussing books. She shows me the copy of Jane Eyre she brought with her. Then we move to her favorite topic of all

—food. Hours fly by, and by the time we're finished with our bottle, I'm tipsy, sweaty, and ready to go for a swim.

I dive into the pool and try to see how far I can make it without popping back out. I get about halfway. Not bad. My thoughts are sluggish from all the sun and alcohol, and the water's not cool enough to sober me up as quickly as I hoped. I'm on my tenth lap when a soft breeze carries over a familiar voice. I whip around.

Damiano steps out of the house, dressed in a crisp white dress shirt, black slacks, and his usual Italian-leather shoes. His gaze finds me immediately, and he looks at me as if I'm a clump of hair his pool boy forgot to fish out of the water the night before. I guess we're back to him being cold. There should be nothing happening inside of me under that scrutinizing gaze, but instead, something hot and languid curls in the pit of my belly. I swim to the edge of the pool, place my palms on the deck, and lift myself out of the water. I can feel his eyes following my every move as I skip over the burning hot stones that sting the soles of my feet as I make my way to the loungers.

There's a suited man behind Damiano that comes into my view. One good look at him is enough to make some blood rise to my cheeks. Wow, he's attractive. Razor-sharp bone structure, thick dark brows that appear to be permanently knit together and piercing blue eyes. You make that kind of a man smile, and it's game over—say goodbye to your heart.

I stop by Martina and grab a towel to dry myself off. She's also a little pink in the face, and her furtive glances in the direction of the tall newcomer tell me maybe she isn't asexual after all.

"How's your impromptu pool day going?" Damiano asks his sister.

"Fun," she says and gives him a smile.

His expression softens for a split second before he notices what's on the side table.

He plucks our empty wine bottle out of the bucket filled with water. The ice melted a long time ago. "I can see that. How are you feeling? Headache coming on already?"

Martina bristles at his tone. I sense she doesn't like that he's treating her like a child in front of his handsome guest. "Of course not. This isn't the first time I've had wine."

His lips thin. "Not the first time, but it's been a while."

"Everything is fine."

He drops the bottle back into the water and pokes Martina on her shoulder. "You got a lot of sun," Damiano says. "Your skin is about to be burned. Maybe it's time to call it a day."

The man behind him zeroes in on the fading fingerprint before slowly tearing his gaze away. When he realizes I noticed, he narrows his eyes at me as if to say I should wipe my memory clean. A wave of frost runs through me, but I hold his eye contact and arch a brow.

"I said everything is fine," Martina snaps.

Her tone takes Damiano aback. He frowns at her and then me. "One day with my sister, and your attitude's already rubbing off on her."

"Better mine than yours."

A muscle in his jaw ticks. "We need to have a word."

"I'm not done drying myself," I say, rubbing the towel over my midriff.

He crosses the distance between us with two long steps, grasps the towel, and tosses it away. "You are now. Mari, maybe you remember Giorgio? You met a long time ago. He'll keep you company while Valentina and I talk." He wraps his warm palm around my elbow. We leave a panicked-looking Martina with Damiano's dark-haired guest and return to the house.

"If I think the time you're spending with my sister is doing more harm than good, I'll put an end to it," he says.

I huff a laugh. "You can't blame me for your sister not wanting to be treated like a child. She's eighteen, not eight."

"Her age is irrelevant. Mari always listens to me."

Irritation flickers inside of me. "I can't believe I didn't see it earlier."

"See what?"

"That you're just like the rest of them. All that talk of wanting to make me yours... It's that insufferable machismo all mafia men seem to possess. Here's some news for you: the women in your life don't exist solely for you to boss them around. That includes your sister."

His grip on my elbow tightens. "My relationship with my sister is none of your business. And from what I can remember, you liked it when I bossed *you* around."

"I'm dripping all over your floor," I inform him as we cross the living room, while I try my best to ignore how good he smells and how his hand burns against my skin.

"That's the least of your problems."

"It's not a problem for me at all. I'm simply pointing out a safety hazard in your home."

When we get to the kitchen, he shoos the cook away and corners me against a wall. His eyes blaze as he takes in my nearly naked body. The tips of his leather shoes brush against my bare toes. "Are you worried about me?" he asks. "And here I was thinking you're probably spending your nights scheming how to kill me."

"You wish I spent my nights thinking about you," I say. My voice comes out too breathy.

A drop of water runs down the valley between my breasts, and he tracks it with his gaze. My skin still tingles from the sun, but the electric charge running through my veins is all him.

He works his jaw, trying to tame something that wants to burst out of him. He seems conflicted.

Then his palm lands to the side of my head, and he leans in, lifting his gaze off my body. I think he might kiss me, but instead he takes my hand and raises it to study the scabs around my wrists. The fire in his eyes dims.

"You took off the bandages."

"They would have gotten wet during my swim."

Turbulent emotions skate over his face. Very slowly, he laces our fingers together and I stop breathing. Outside, a bird chirps.

I'm torn between wanting to kiss him and wanting to push him away for how he's treated me. Hurt blooms inside my chest. I've told him everything. He knows I had nothing to do with capturing Martina. Why won't he let me go?

"Please let me leave," I whisper.

He sucks in a breath and drops my hand. "No."

I place my palms on his chest and try to shove him away, but his body behaves as if it's made of granite. He doesn't budge.

He takes my chin and tilts my face toward him. A powerful shiver runs through me.

"Cold?" He flicks his gaze down to my bathing suit where I know he'll find the sharp outline of my nipples.

I can't allow him to know the effect he's having on me. "As I've been trying to tell you, I'm dripping wet, and the AC is on."

He leans forward and presses his warm body flush against mine. I gasp when my breasts connect with his hard chest.

"Better?"

"No."

He snakes one arm around my waist and places his other hand at the nape of my neck. "How's this?"

It feels like Pop Rocks are popping over the entire expanse of my body. "Awful," I breathe.

"Liar," he says with a smirk. His eyes flare with desire and the fact that he's not even bothering to hide it this time tells me he thinks he's winning this game.

He's wrong.

"Get off me," I say.

"As soon as I do, I'm taking you back to your room. Is that what you want?"

I bite my lip.

"Ah, so you don't want to go back upstairs?"

"No," I admit.

"You don't like your room?" He traces circles over the small of my back.

"It's a cage. There are literal bars on the window."

"Think of them as being for your own safety."

"What are you going to do with me?" I ask.

At this, he pulls back and stares down at me. "I don't know yet."

"How much longer do I have to wait?"

"I don't know."

My eyes narrow, and the haze induced by the rosé and his close proximity fades. I'm so damn tired of being in this limbo. The uncertainty weighs on me heavier with each passing day. "I'm ready to go up."

This time, when I push my palms against him, he moves away.

There's a twinge in my chest. I tell myself it's just my body missing his physical warmth.

When I'm inside of my room and he locks the door behind me, I nearly manage to convince myself it's the truth.

CHAPTER 25

DAMIANO

AFTER I LEAVE Valentina to stew in her room, I make my way back to the pool and try to forget the visceral sensation of her curves pressed against my chest.

It's worse that I've touched her everywhere already, because I know exactly how soft her skin is, and how perfectly her tits fit in my palms. I even know the little sound she'd make if I tugged the tiny triangle of her bathing suit a few inches over and put her nipple in my mouth.

Why did I go to her and Mari? One moment Napoletano and I were walking to my office, and the next I was standing on the pool deck, trying not to audibly groan at the sight of that insane body emerging out of the water.

I think it must have been the glimpse of her silky black hair through the glass that made me change course. I barked something to Napoletano about needing to check on Mari, and he probably saw right through it, the smug bastard. Nothing ever flies past him.

To my utter amazement, my sister has started to bake again. When I walked in on her kneading dough in the kitchen a few days ago, I couldn't believe my eyes. For weeks, I've tried to get her to do something. *Anything*. She always had an excuse ready. But one day with our prisoner, and everything's changed.

I step back outside and note that Napoletano and Mari haven't moved a single inch since Valentina and I left. My sister's sitting with her arms wrapped around her knees, a book hanging from one hand. When she notices I've returned, she shoots me a guilty look. She must feel bad about talking back to me earlier.

Standing beside her lounger, Napoletano is as stoic as always, his hands in his pockets, the sun glinting off the face of his watch. Did they exchange a single word while I was gone? Unlikely. My old friend isn't much of a conversationalist unless it's about business.

"I'm finished," I say to him. "Ras is waiting for us in my office."

Napoletano nods. I move inside, expecting him to follow me, but to my surprise, he hangs back and says something to Mari.

My sister's brows shoot up before she buries her face in her book.

"What was that?" I ask once he joins me in the house.

"We were talking about the book she's reading," he says in his deep voice.

"What book?"

"You haven't read it."

"How do you know what I have and haven't read?"

His response is a subtle twitch in his lips, and it makes me square my shoulders.

"Don't answer that," I say. He probably got bored one Sunday and hacked the camera in my library just for the fun of it. I've yet to hear of a security system that's impervious to Napoletano. He's the best of the best. That's why he's tasked with storing so much of the loot the clan has collected over the last few decades—jewelry, fine art, and priceless historical artifacts. They're spread all over Italy in hyper-secure storage facilities designed by him. If I ever had something valuable I needed to hide, I wouldn't doubt for a second it would be safe with him.

We enter the office and move to take our seats. I sink into a chair across from Ras. "Do you have the research I asked for?"

Ras picks up a brown folder from the coffee table beside him. "Here." He tosses the folder at me.

"You shouldn't leave a paper trail," Napoletano says. "That's how plans get exposed."

I open the folder and scan the two sheets of paper within. "What plans?"

"Your plan for overthrowing the don."

How could he possibly know that? I raise a brow at Ras. "You told him when you picked him up from the airport?"

"I didn't tell him anything," Ras says, looking uncharacteristically perplexed.

Napoletano extends his legs out in front of him and crosses them at the ankles. "You told me you need to make this compound breach proof. Unless you've managed to piss off all the tourists enough to try storming this place en masse, there's only one other thing you can be worried about."

Ras and I exchange a look.

"How are you and Sal getting along these days?" I ask.

Our guest takes out a small metal cigarette case from inside his suit jacket and lights one up. "We haven't talked in months. I much prefer it that way."

Interesting. If Sal is growing paranoid like Ras and I are suspecting, why wouldn't he ask the sharpest security guy in the clan for some reinforcements?

"And your father? Is he still walking the streets of Naples every Sunday?"

Smoke billows out of his mouth. "My father will do his Sunday walk until the day he dies."

Such is the fate of the clan's submarines, the men tasked with delivering stipends to the lower-level members of the *sistema*. Napoletano's father has been in that job for nearly twenty years, which makes him one of the longest standing submarines in the clan. They don't have much power, but they usually have the best pulse on any rumors swirling around. "What has he heard?"

Napoletano takes another drag of his cigarette and looks out the window. "The capos are getting nervous. Rumor is, Sal had ordered the hit on the Forgione funeral procession last week."

"The bombing that killed the dead guy's kid?" Ras's tone is incredulous. "Why would he do that? The Forgiones haven't been a problem for years."

"A few possible explanations, but none of them are reasonable. It is not the behavior of a rational man. He doesn't trust anyone these days."

"Not even you?" I ask, even though I already know the answer.

"He's never trusted me. He tends to dislike men who's mothers he's killed." Our eyes meet and an understanding solidifies in the air between us. He wants to get his revenge on Sal as much as I do, and just like me, he's been biding his time.

I wipe a speck of dust off my desk. "Do you know why I haven't tried to get off Ibiza all this time?"

Napoletano nods. "Your sister."

"I thought being capo here and staying far away from Casal would keep her safe. Turns out, that's not the case. He ordered a hit on Martina."

A dark cloud passes over his expression. "When?" he bites out.

"Last month. She managed to get away with the help of that woman you saw by the pool."

Napoletano flicks his gaze to Ras. "The one you asked me to run through the system a few days ago. Valentina Garzolo."

"Yes," I say. "She gave us enough information to confirm Sal was the one behind it." I summarize our knowledge of what happened, and by the time I'm done, a thoughtful silence blankets the room.

"Staying on the sidelines is no longer an option after this escalation," I say. "I'm ready to take back what should have always belonged to me."

Napoletano reaches for the ashtray on my desk and puts out his cigarette. "You've decided to trust me then."

"We know you're not a forgiving man," Ras says.

We wait for him to voice his commitment. Without Napoletano, this will be much harder.

"I'm thirty-two this year," he says finally, flicking a piece of lint of his leg. "My mother died when I was fifteen. Sometimes I tell myself it's time to move on. I can't even remember what it felt like to be loved by her. But I remember the burning rage when I saw her body and the vow I made to make him pay."

"I know the feeling well," I say.

He holds my gaze and nods. "It's time for a change. I'll help you."

The tension in the room eases.

I pass him the folder containing details about our security at the compound. He flips through it. "I'll audit your set up here and give Ras a list of suggestions," he says before slipping the folder under his arm. "When I return to Naples, I can start planting seeds. You'll need to give them time to grow."

"Not just time. We need to give them fertilizer," I say. "I need to demonstrate to the families that I can lead us better than Sal."

"You can't do that when you're his work horse," Napoletano says. "The flow of money from Ibiza needs to stop."

"If we stop paying, he'll tell his suppliers to stop delivering the goods," Ras says. "Our revenue will be cut in half overnight."

We'll still have the legitimate businesses—restaurants, hotels, clubs—but they need customers. And those will dry up as soon as word gets around that drugs on Ibiza are suddenly hard to come by.

There's only one thing we can do. "We need to find a new supplier. Cut Sal out completely."

"That would spell the beginning of his end," Napoletano says. "If his suppliers find out he can't control his wealthiest capo, they'll lose confidence. It's only a matter of time before they abandon him and agree to work directly with you."

"We have to find the right partner," I mutter. "Sal is too well connected with the Moroccans and the Algerians. They won't turn on him until I prove my power. I have to go further. The Colombians? But why would they take a bet on me, especially when I only need their supply until Sal's suppliers turn on him? No, I need a temporary solution."

"You have one sitting by your pool," Napoletano says. "The Garzolo's primary business is cocaine."

Foreboding slithers down my spine.

"You can go through the Americans," he says while my pulse grows louder in my ears. "Ask them for a few shipments to tide you over. They'll agree because you have something they want."

"Valentina," Ras says.

Her name feels all wrong coming out of his mouth. How am I supposed to trade the entirety of her away when I don't even like hearing anyone but me utter her name?

But I can't find a flaw in Napoletano's suggestion. It works, and it's clean. Sending her to her father will get me what I need to checkmate Sal, and once I'm don, I'll have a multitude of ways to make Garzolo pay for what he did to Martina.

It's a clear path to everything I've ever wanted.

Nearly everything.

I rise from my seat. "If her father wants her back, he'll find a way to get us everything we need."

From the moment I discovered who Ale Romero really was, I knew there was a good chance I'd have to use her as leverage, and yet that knowledge does nothing to ease the weight I feel as I leave my office.

It's the perfect plan. So simple that on paper it seems nearly too easy, but somehow, it feels like the hardest thing I've ever done.

My feet carry me to Valentina's room. I don't know why I'm going to her. I doubt that sharing the news I intend to break my promise is going to soften the blow, but for some reason, I want to anyway. We've spent the entire time we've known each other lying to one another. The truth won't be sweet, but at least it'll be real.

I take the key to her room out of my pocket and insert it into the lock. She'll cry when I tell her what I plan to do to her. *Cazzo*. Her tears make me feel like the world's most wretched man.

When I step inside, she's not there. The shower is running in the bathroom, and steam is slowly seeping from beneath the door. I walk over to the window she hates so much. There are a few sailboats on the water, but there's barely any wind, and they're moving slowly. I watch them sail for a long while, and still, the shower runs. What is she doing in there?

Another few minutes pass, and I decide to check on her. For all I know, she's trying to drown herself. The thought propels me into the bathroom.

I see her silhouette through the matted glass and move closer.

Ah, there she is.

My mouth goes dry when I realize what she's doing.

She's pressed against one of the shower's walls, her legs spread wide, one hand on the safety bar, and the other holding the showerhead to her pussy. Her eyes are squeezed shut. I watch as her lips part on a moan that gets swallowed up by the sound of the running water.

Every drop of blood inside my body rushes to my cock. I feel light-headed. It has nothing to do with the oppressive heat inside this tiny room, and everything to do with her. Her abdomen contracts, and she claws at the wall as her orgasm nears.

When her mouth moves, I can't hear her, but I read her lips.

It's my name she moans.

An inhuman growl tears its way up my throat. I've never wanted a woman more in my entire godforsaken life.

She hears it. Her eyes spring open, and she registers me standing right there. I try to breathe, but I can't. It's like the last bit of oxygen inside the room has disappeared.

Instead of stopping, she drops her head back and finishes herself off before me, her hooded gaze steady on me.

"*Merda*," I breathe.

She trembles against the wall while I try to get my fingers to properly work. I've never hated button-up shirts before, but I do right now.

My eyes are greedy. They trail over her heavy breasts, the dip of her waist, the thickness of her thighs... *Fuck me.*

"Why are you here?" she mouths.

I drop my shirt on the floor and unbuckle my belt.

"I came to talk," I say hoarsely. "You were taking too long."

Her fingers tighten on the safety bar. "You should leave."

My pants come off. "If you think I'm capable of walking out that door right now, you've got me all wrong."

She drags her teeth over her bottom lip and drops her lazy gaze to my boxer briefs.

"What did you want to talk about?" she rasps.

Fuck all that. I am not thinking about that right now. I step into the shower, take the showerhead out of her hand, and press a button to reroute the water. It cascades over us, drenching my hair and leaving drops on her thick dark lashes.

She stares at me, want and doubt playing across her face. I want her so badly, I'll happily fall down to my knees and beg if that's what it takes.

But she doesn't make me beg. She sucks in a breath and runs her fingertips over my wet boxers, touching the underside of my cock. I nearly keel over. Slamming my palms against the wall to the sides of her head, I lean into her space.

"You said my name," I say as I drag my nose against the shell of her ear. "Did you imagine it was me licking your sweet cunt?"

She lets out a slow, steadying exhale. "I imagined suffocating you with it." Her other hand wraps around my waist, and she drags her nails down the curve of my ass. It makes white spots appear in my eyes.

"That's not a bad way to go," I say breathlessly as I grind my cock into her abdomen.

She pushes me away and starts pulling down my boxers. "Then I'll need to make sure to leave you with a bad case of blue balls first."

"You're still mad about that?"

"Not at all. It gave me all the inspiration I needed to thoroughly enjoy my showers."

"You're telling me you've been doing this to yourself all week?" I grab a handful of her hair.

"Yes. Next time you decide to leave me in isolation, think about that."

Every molecule of air leaves my lungs. I'm never leaving her on her own again. What's the point? I won't be able to get anything else done with that image playing in my head.

When I'm fully bare, I skim my palms down the backs of her thighs and lift her up against the wall. She's so fucking soft, it doesn't seem real. I catch one nipple between my teeth and suck on it until she starts to squirm against me, her breaths coming faster and less even.

"Fuck. Damiano."

I pull away and capture her lips.

She doesn't let me deepen the kiss. "I want your cock, not your mouth." She pants as she tries to grind against me.

"Too bad," I say as I push inside of her. "You're getting both."

I take advantage of her gasp to steal the kiss she says she won't give. She changes her mind on that fast enough. Our tongues tangle, and I begin to thrust into her. She clenches around me like she's afraid I'll disappear and digs her nails into my shoulder blades. God, I hope she leaves marks.

The water rains over us, and the steam is so thick I can barely see her. I press her harder against the wall and adjust the temperature with one hand. She moans as the temperature drops and air clears.

Her eyes find mine. "I hate you," she whispers without any conviction.

Pleasure starts to pool at the base of my spine as I sink my cock inside of her again and again.

"You tied me up and told me you'd use me however you wanted," she says.

I nip at her lips. "Uh-huh."

"You spanked me."

"Yeah, I did."

"Fed me like a wild animal."

A smile pulls at my lips. "My little beast."

"Left me alone until I was so bored out of my mind I started anger-fucking myself to fantasies of you."

"I'm really never going to get that out of my head," I mutter as I change my angle.

Her eyes roll back. "I hate you so much," she pants. "Why did you do all those things to me?"

"Is that really why you hate me?" I move my hand between her thighs and find her clit.

She makes a tortured noise and blinks her eyes open at me. "No."

My movements become more frantic. I bite at the place where her neck and shoulder connect. "Then why?"

She squeezes me so hard I'm sure I'm about to pass out. She's so fucking close, I can feel it. I won't let myself fall over the edge until she's spent herself all over my cock.

Her heels dig into the backs of my thighs, and she lets out a gasp. "Because I still want you, and I hate it. I hate it so much."

My chest feels like it's just fractured. But then I feel her start to come, and I let go of my control. My seed spills inside of her, and I'm fucking levitating.

In that post-orgasm moment of clarity, I realize a very inconvenient thing.

I've claimed her as mine.

And I'm never letting her go.

CHAPTER 26

VALENTINA

I KNOW I've done a very bad thing. I've allowed myself to become confused. The Damiano I want is a man that doesn't exist. He's not the smart businessman who seduced me with his dirty words and clever wit.

I reach over and turn off the water. As the last drops fall, it's as if reality has restarted itself once again.

The mafioso standing in front of me runs a thick towel over my skin. He does it gently, as if he's afraid I might shatter from too much pressure. He had no qualms about my break-ability when he was thrusting into me moments earlier, but maybe his own reality is setting in as well.

His dark eyes meet mine, and I know I'm right. This was a goodbye. He's going to send me home, and he knows I'll never forgive him for it. This is all over.

It's a bitter, painful end to something that was never destined to be a love story.

I dry the soles of my feet on the rug by the shower and walk into the bedroom with him right on my heels. When I climb onto the bed, he follows. Hasn't he had enough? I don't think I could have another orgasm. He's wrung every bit of pleasure out of me, and now I feel empty. I don't have anything left to give.

When I lie down on my side, he wraps his palm around my shoulder and turns me to my back. He's propped up on his elbow, peering down at me with furrowed brows.

Here it is. He's about to tell me I'm going back to New York.

"I'm sorry."

I shut my eyes. Why should I look at him while he breaks my heart for the second time?

"I shouldn't have hurt you like I did." His lips brush lightly against my wrists. "Every time I see these marks on you, I want to throw myself off a cliff."

An ache appears in the back of my throat. He's about to hurt me way worse than that.

He leaves my wrists alone and brushes a rough thumb over my lips. Then he sighs. "What would you do if I let you go?"

It takes a moment for me to process his words. When I do, a weird feeling fills my chest. It reminds me of when I opened the cage of a bird I kept as a child and watched it fly away.

I blink at him. He waits for my answer, his gaze steady on my face.

"I'd go somewhere far," I say. "Somewhere there's no risk of running into the mafia."

The corners of his lips turn up in bitter smile. "That place doesn't exist. The underworld's reach stretches to every corner of the world."

I refuse to believe that. "There has to be *some* place."

"And if there isn't? What will you do if your father finds you?"

My mouth goes dry. "I can't go back."

"So you keep saying, but you still won't tell me why," he says in a thoughtful tone.

It might feel cathartic to tell someone about what happened down in the basement of the house that never felt like home. Who would I become if I confessed my biggest secret and my biggest shame? Would it help me sleep at night? Would it allow me to heal?

It's so tempting to find out. But at the last moment, I chicken out. "You're asking me to share something very personal," I say softly. "I know barely anything about you."

"You know me better than most," he says as he traces a circle around my belly button.

An acerbic laugh escapes me. "Is that because you don't let anyone in? You forget I've spent my life surrounded by made men. I know how you relate to other people."

"How's that?"

"With a gun hidden behind your back."

He takes a deep breath and gives a shake of his head. "What would you like to know?"

An offering. He's asking what it'll take for me to feel on even ground with him.

A dozen questions spring to mind, but I distill them down to the few that'll reveal the real Damiano to me. "What's your real business on Ibiza?"

He dips his finger inside my belly button. "Real estate, restaurants, clubs, and...drugs."

"The drug dealers at the clubs are yours?"

"They all work for me," he says, moving his fingertips to graze the underside of my breast.

"*All* of them?"

"Yes. Even in the clubs I don't own. Ibiza is my territory, and I have a mandate to keep it that way, no matter what it takes. Competition is dealt with quietly and swiftly."

He speaks softly, as if the mere act of touching my body is hypnotizing. A subtle ache appears between my legs when he reaches my right nipple. So much for being drained. I guess he knows just how to fill me back up.

I need to stay focused. Who knows how many questions of mine he'll entertain? "Your father was the don," I say.

"Mhm."

"Why aren't you?"

His movements halt, and the temperature in the room drops a couple of degrees. In his eyes, I see a shuttering, a door being closed, but in the last moment, something inside of him forces it back open. He gives me a heavy, heavy look and flattens his palm on my abdomen. "My father's power was taken from him in the proper Casalese way. To usurp a sitting don you must strangle him to death. Sal Gallo, a distant uncle, murdered my father and began his rule when I was eleven years old. For me to become don, I'll have to do the same."

My heart picks up speed, and I know he's close enough to notice it. This isn't a fairytale, and Damiano is no prince. He's a made man, and it's not the thought of committing murder that's keeping him from making his bid. "Why haven't you?"

He tips his head back. "That is a very loaded question, Vale."

This is the first time he's called me Vale instead of Valentina or Ale, and the familiarity sends warmth spreading through my chest. It's what my sisters call me.

He removes his hand from me and drags his palm over his mouth. I can tell he's trying to decide what he should tell me. "There's a story that's become a relatively recent legend among the Casalese. They present it to children as a story of love and betrayal, but in my opinion, it's a cautionary tale. The story is as follows. A Casalese woman loved her husband so much she couldn't bear to live without him. One day, he was murdered. When five men tried to return his still-warm body to her as a sign of respect, she saw them through the window of her bedroom and let out a blood curdling scream. As they made their way through the front door, she ran to the kitchen, tore open the pantry, and grabbed the spare can of gasoline. She doused herself with it. When the first of the men burst into the room, she lit a match and set herself on fire. The fire killed all the men and burned the body of her husband to a crisp. It's said they found the remains of the man and his wife beside each other, even though no one could explain how they ended up like that. Perhaps she used her last conscious moments to

270

get as close to his body as she could. So they could stay together even in death."

The air around us stills.

I swallow past the tightness in my throat. "The woman was..."

"My mother." He sits up on the bed, and in the dimming late afternoon light, he looks older than his age. "The version I just told you omits what I consider to be an important part. It's a shame, really. I think it makes the story far more interesting. What they don't tell very often is that in that house with the woman were her two children. A boy of eleven, and a toddler of two."

Horror thickens the air inside my lungs until I can't breathe. My hand reaches for Damiano's, but he won't let me take it. Men like him don't know how to accept comfort, and maybe this isn't the time to teach him. I give him space.

"The boy watched his mother pour the gasoline from the shadows of the living room. Her screams woke him, and he ran downstairs to check on her. What he saw in the kitchen... He thought he was still asleep, having a nightmare. When the fire started to spread, he ran to get his sister out of her room, and they managed to escape the house before the entire thing went up in flames. They watched their whole life burn. It's an image one can't ever forget."

I suck in a harsh breath. "Damiano, I'm so sorry."

He shakes his head as if he can shake off the sorrow of the memory. "I barely remember the weeks that followed, but a few images stand out. Sal inviting me to his new office—my father's old one—and making it clear that the only way my sister and I would stay alive is if I confirm my father's body had marks of strangulation on it so as to legitimize Sal's takeover. You see, the code specifies there must be a living witness otherwise the claim is contested. A photo isn't enough. His five witnesses all perished in the fire and Mari was too young to talk. I had to stand in front of all the capos —men who had given me gifts and played cards with me— and describe to them what my dead father's body looked like. I couldn't really remember, so I made a bunch of stuff up.

"Ras's parents took us in—his mother is my mother's sister. They convinced Sal to keep his word and let Mari and me live. They told him over and over again that I was too young to hold on to any anger. But Sal's always been too paranoid to ever fully believe that. When my business acumen started to earn me a reputation, he decided to send me here, where I'd be isolated and unable to forge any strong connections with the other capos. I agreed, because protecting Mari has always been more important to me than getting my revenge."

My God, he's nothing like Papà. He put his family first, even if it meant he had to sacrifice any real chance at gaining more power. No matter how hard I try, I can't imagine Papà ever doing something like that for me or any of my siblings.

"Is Sal the one behind Martina's abduction?" I ask.

"Yes."

"You knew it after we spoke."

He nods. "You said Lazaro called her a little Casalese mouse. Little mouse is what Sal has always called Martina. He must have said it to Lazaro at some point."

"Why would Sal do this?"

"To have something to keep me in line. He's been making more and more bad calls in the past few years, and I've started to call him out on it. He needs me to keep making him money, but he wants me to do it with my mouth shut."

I reach for his hand again, and this time, he lets me take it. Our fingers twine together.

"What are you going to do?" I ask.

"Take back what should have always belonged to me." The look he gives me makes me feel as if I'm standing on a precipice. "And I want you to help me do it."

CHAPTER 27

VALENTINA

My head spins. "Help you how?" I don't even feel like I can help myself at the moment.

He leaves my question hanging, swings his legs off the bed, and walks to the bathroom, giving me a view of his sculpted ass. I wish I was in the right state of mind to properly appreciate it, but I'm too rattled by our conversation.

I can't stop thinking back to that photograph of Damiano and Martina I saw in his office. He told me back then their parents had died, but now that I know how it happened, the bond he has with his sister makes a lot more sense. He saved Martina from what would have been certain death for someone her age, and he's spent his entire life protecting her. She's lucky in that way, more than she probably knows. In my experience, it's rare for people who are supposed to protect us to actually deliver. My father condemned me, my mother abandoned me, my husband ruined me.

He disappears behind the door, and I collapse back down on the bed, rubbing my eyes with the heels of my palms. I can't believe what he just told me. His mother *set herself on fire* in front of him. How could she do that to her kids? I'm torn between empathizing with her over the pain of losing the love of her life and blaming her for not being strong enough to push through it.

Then I remember I left family behind as well when I ran. My sisters needed me. Do they still need me now?

Damiano comes out of the bathroom zipping up his slacks, his shirt tossed over his shoulder. "Here's my proposal," he says, running his fingers through his wet hair. "I need your father to agree to be my temporary supplier. My initial idea was to use you as a bargaining chip, but after further reflection, I've identified some flaws with that plan."

"What a relief," I mutter as I sit up and pull the blanket up to my bare chest.

"If your father knows I have you, I suspect he'll go straight to Sal and demand he returns you. Sal will be tipped off that I know he's behind Mari's kidnapping, and he'll make an offensive move before I'm ready to respond."

"At least you weren't planning on telling my father you'd kill me if he contacted Sal."

"He would know it was a bluff. You're useless to me dead."

"You continue to demonstrate to me that you are a romantic."

He slips his arms through the sleeves of his shirt and arches a brow. "I prefer to keep you alive. What's not romantic about that?"

I huff a laugh. "So what's your new plan?"

"My new plan is to approach your father with carrots, rather than sticks. Tell me, does your father do a lot of hits for other people?"

The fact that he thinks I'm someone who'd be in the know on that makes me roll my eyes. "How on earth would I know? That's a topic reserved for my father's office, not the family dinner table."

"You were married to his top enforcer. Did you talk to your husband about his work?"

Crap. I *did* his work for him. I look down at my hands. "A bit."

"Who were his targets?"

Lazaro didn't bring everyone to the basement. I didn't know what his criteria was. I never asked. My guess was it was based on his mood and whether he thought they deserved it. But out of the people I saw...

"Mostly clan associates who stole or went against the clan. A few contacts outside of the clan that caused problems or defaulted on their obligations. Probably members of other New York clans when there was some kind of a dispute."

"But never random hits," Damiano says.

"I wouldn't say never. I mean, I have no clue. But based on what...Lazaro told me, no. He was an enforcer, not a hitman for hire."

"Then there had to be a good reason your father agreed to Sal's request. What do you think that might be, Vale?"

"I don't know," I say.

Damiano shakes his head. "Think."

I narrow my eyes at him. "What do you think I'm doing?"

"Did you hear or see anything that seemed out of the ordinary? Anything at all that seemed...off?"

A memory clicks into place. The bridal shower. That day feels like forever ago, even if it's only been a little more than a month.

I get out of the bed and pull on my clothes while Damiano watches me intently. "I didn't see anything, but my sister..." Gemma said Papà had upped their security detail. What else did she say?

"What about your sister?" he asks once I'm dressed.

Instead of answering him, I walk over to the window. Yes, there were certain strange comments made that day. Comments that didn't mean much to me, but maybe they'd mean something to Damiano, like how what Lazaro said to me about Martina meant something to him.

I have something to bargain with. He's decided not to tell my father he has me, but where does that leave me?

I turn around and flatten my expression. "If I tell you what I know, will you give me my freedom back?"

His eyes flash with an irritated kind of amusement. "Ah, we're back to this game again."

"Will I be able to walk out of here?"

"I'd be willing to let you roam the house."

"That's not what I meant. Will you let me leave?"

"Not yet," he says bluntly.

"Why not?"

"Because you don't have a plan. The chances of you getting caught by Sal's men when you try to leave this island are exceptionally high."

"Your don didn't catch me when I got here."

"Probably because your father hadn't ramped up his search by that time and called in reinforcements. You wouldn't have been so lucky if you'd waited a day longer."

"I'll take my chances."

"Vale, you won't last a *day*."

"What else am I supposed to do?"

"Stay here."

"As your prisoner? No thank you."

"Not as my prisoner. As my guest. When I'm the new Casalese don, you'll be under my protection."

His words infuriate me so quickly I don't stop to pick my words carefully. "Not this again. I've lived my entire life under the protection of a powerful don. Guess what? It protected me from *nothing*. I've learned many important lessons from my father, my favorite being that men like you make promises you have zero intention of keeping. They're lies. All of them, without exception. I won't ever put my life in the hands of a don again."

I can see my outburst is unexpected. His skin loses some of its color, and his expression dims. "I am not your father. You won't tell me what he did to you, but I know I'd never go back on a promise I made to my daughter."

"That's because you don't have a daughter yet," I counter.

"No, but Martina is practically a daughter to me, and I've done everything I can to keep her safe."

What can I say to that? Damiano put his ambitions on hold for well over a decade to protect his sister. Papà would never make a sacrifice like that for me.

But Martina is his blood, and I'm not.

"What if I want to leave when you become the don? Will you let me?"

His shoulders drop, and there's a grim twist to his mouth. I can see he hates the idea, and this realization makes something warm settle inside my chest.

"I won't keep you here against your will," he says finally.

It would be easy for him to lie to me, but somehow, I know he's telling the truth.

He finishes buttoning up his shirt. "Think on it tonight and give me your answer tomorrow."

One night isn't nearly enough time, but I nod, and he takes his leave.

The room suddenly feels too empty. *I* feel too empty.

My elbows connect with the bed, and I toss my head back to stare at the ceiling. There's a lot for me to think about.

The details about that day with Gemma slowly start coming back to me. There was also that conversation with Tito in the car. Papà had Tito, Lazaro, and Vince doing work for someone else—Sal? Must be. But how is that connected to him increasing the family's security? What was he afraid of?

Gemma always took more of an interest in Papà's business matters. When she was younger, she'd eavesdrop outside his office door, but she'd never tell me what she heard when I asked. Back then, I thought she liked keeping secrets. Now, I wonder if she was able to sense even at that age that I didn't *really* want to know. I preferred to think of Papà as a valiant protector, rather than the boogeyman, even if the latter was far closer to the truth.

When the evening comes, a guard brings me dinner. I discover I'm exceptionally hungry, and when I consider why that is, images of Damiano dripping wet in the shower make heat rise to my chest. I down the cold gazpacho and devour the Spanish tortilla. By the time I finish dessert—a slice of incredibly creamy cheesecake—I'm finally full.

What if Damiano protected me with the same devotion he has to Martina? Would I stay then? Of course, that's not a realistic scenario. He might want me physically, but he doesn't love me. There's no way I'd ever be someone truly important to him. Even if he intends to keep his promises now, there are always sacrifices to be made for power in our world. There's no guarantee that one day I wouldn't be one of them.

Still, what options do I have? If I don't cooperate with him like he wants, then what? He might still change his mind about the carrots and go back to sticks.

No, refusing isn't an option.

I'll tell him what I know, and then when he's the don, I'll leave.

CHAPTER 28

DAMIANO

I TELL Ras I've decided not to trade Valentina back to her father when we sit down for lunch on the terrace the next morning.

When I finish my explanation, he places his cutlery down and crosses his arms over his chest. "This isn't going to work."

"Why?" I ask. It makes perfect sense to me.

"Because she doesn't know anything. The line about the sister was just a ploy to buy herself more time."

"It wasn't."

He rolls his eyes. "*Mio Dio*, you've lost your head over her. When will you admit it?"

"Admit what, exactly?"

"That you're in love with her."

My mouth goes dry, and something sparks inside my chest. "That's absurd."

"When she was still working at Revolvr, you started spending a lot more time there. All so that you could be around her."

"I had work to do."

"You were either talking to her or daydreaming about her in your office."

"How would you know what I daydream about?" I retort, not wanting to pause and reflect on the truth in his words.

Ras shakes his head. "I thought you'd move on after we realized who she was, but you've just dug in deeper and deeper. And now this. You want to bring her into our plan. A plan that requires me, Napoletano, and many other men to put their lives on the line. You know I'll follow you to the ends of the earth, but you're not going to win a lot of respect from the other capos if they see your strategy for taking over as don has your dick as a compass."

His words light the fuse of my anger, but I take a breath and put it out before it explodes. "I did realize who she was. The woman who *saved my sister*. That makes her someone worthy of respect, mine and yours."

He chuckles. "Oh, I respect her. Very much. She's done the impossible. She's brought you to your knees."

My hand tightens around the fork. "Then maybe it's respect for me that you're missing."

"You know that's bullshit." He heaves a sigh. "Goddamn it, Dem. You know I want you to be don. And not just because you're a brother to me, but because unlike Sal, you're a real leader."

"Then have a little faith. She wasn't lying. She knows something." A flicker on the security monitor attached to the wall pulls my attention to it. "The guards just let in a car. Are you expecting someone?"

Ras's brows pull together. "No. Is it Mari?"

I walk over to the screen and zoom in on the car as apprehension coils inside my gut. "She's in the Mercedes with her driver. She shouldn't be back from her shopping trip for another few hours. This is a white BMW. Why would the guards let someone through without checking with you?"

He comes to stand by my side just as the car parks in front of the house. We watch as the door opens.

Ras swears. "It's the Pirozzis. Nelo and Vito."

"What the fuck."

"They have to be here on Sal's orders. It's the only reason the guard would let them pass." Ras's phone rings, and he picks it up. "Speak."

Not two seconds later, Ras hangs up. "The guard just confirmed it."

"Tell Martina's driver not to come back until we tell him it's clear," I say as I grab my gun from the nearest cabinet and check to make sure it's loaded. "I'm going to go greet them. Stay here unless you think I need backup."

As I walk to the front door, the bell rings. It's a good sign they used it instead of barging in. I tuck the gun in the front of my slacks and button up my jacket. I don't know what they're here for, but I'd prefer not to start a war today. We're not ready for it yet. I need to buy us time, which means appeasing whatever this is.

They're standing on the other side of the door wearing two shit-eating grins.

"*Ciao, cugino.* We were afraid you might not be here today," Vito says.

"My car's right there," I say, pointing to the Mercedes they parked beside. "Did you think I went for a long walk to contemplate the scenery or something?"

Nelo steps over the threshold. His cologne is layered on so thick my eyes nearly start to water.

"You've got plenty to contemplate these days," Vito says as he runs a hand over his gelled hair.

"Same as always. The business doesn't run itself."

"Is Martina here?" he asks as he passes me.

Ice drips into my bloodstream. Why the fuck are they asking about my sister? "No."

We enter the living room, where Nelo immediately goes to the bar to pour himself a drink, and Vito follows the smells coming from the kitchen. The cook is making our lunch in there.

"Is that *spezzatino di manzo*?" Vito exclaims with exaggerated glee. "Smells better than the one my mamma makes."

I stop behind him and gesture to the cook she should leave. Her eyes turn to saucers, but she manages to give Vito a tight smile. "It is. Almost ready. Just need to let it simmer for another five minutes."

"Take a break, Angela," I tell her, and she doesn't hesitate to take off her apron and disappear through the back door.

"I think we'll stay for lunch," Vito says, slapping me on the chest as he walks back into the living room. My fists clench. I force them open.

They make themselves comfortable on the couch. Nelo is nursing what looks like a double shot of whiskey while he studies the chandelier above his head. "That's a gorgeous piece."

I take a seat in the armchair. "It's from Murano."

"Stunning work. My glassware is from there. The don recommended me the same workshop he got all of his own glassware from."

Vito props his ankle on his knee and grins. "The don's a real generous guy."

"He really is. Isn't he, Damiano? Look at all of this." Nelo spreads his arms. "He gave all of this to you."

I don't bother correcting him. Sal didn't give me anything. I grew the initial investment Ras's father gave me into a fortune, and it was only after I proved myself that Sal insisted on giving me more capital to deploy. I did him a favor taking his money and growing it year after year.

"Why are you here?" I ask. Even my patience isn't infinite.

Nelo takes a sip of his drink. "Remember what happened to me at Revolvr? You know, it really wasn't that big a deal." He lifts his hand up and shows me the scab. "It's nearly healed. I was ready to move on and forget about it, but somehow it got back to the don—"

"I wonder how that happened."

"No idea. I suppose he's got eyes everywhere."

There's no doubt in my mind Nelo told him himself. These two *are* the don's eyes on Ibiza.

"He wasn't happy," Vito says with a shrug. "He said when someone insults us, it's the same as if they were insulting him."

"And Sal doesn't like to be disrespected," Nelo adds.

They're taking their sweet time spitting it out. "What do you want?"

The preemptively triumphant glint in Nelo's eyes puts me on high alert. "I've had some time to reflect on all the fun I've had, and I think I've had enough for a few lifetimes," he says. "I'm ready to settle down. The don approved of the idea. He suggested Martina might make me a good wife."

My fingers dig so hard into the wooden armrests, I feel my fingernails splint. Red fills my vision. How *dare* he suggest such a vile thing?

Sal's still trying to get my sister under his thumb. Does he think I'll just hand her to them after their kidnapping attempt failed? He's living in fantasy land. Martina will never be Nelo's wife. I'll rip his throat out before I let this asshole have her.

Whatever the two of them see play out across my face makes them sit up straighter. Vito makes a subtle movement of his hand, bringing it closer to the gun tucked behind his back. My own gun burns against my abdomen.

"She's your cousin," I grit out. "Even for you, that's sick."

"We're related by our great-great-grandmother," he says as he places his empty glass on the coffee table. "C'mon. You know that barely counts."

"Martina's not looking for a husband."

"Why not? She's almost nineteen."

"Single," Vito says.

"And beautiful," Nelo adds. "I could see her warming my—"

If he finishes that sentence, I'll rip out his tongue.

CRASH.

Vito jerks in his seat. "What was that?" he asks, looking toward the stairs.

Nelo arches a brow at me. "Is there someone else here?"

It must have come from Vale's room. I grit my teeth. What the hell is she doing in there?

"I thought you said Martina wasn't home," Nelo says, looking at me as he moves toward the stairs.

I stand up and block his way. "It's not Martina."

"Who is it then?"

Cazzo.

"Give me a moment," I bite out. "I have a guest staying with me."

Without giving Nelo a chance to ask me more questions, I scale the stairs and duck into Valentina's room.

She's standing by the bed, her breakfast tray broken at her feet. She's wearing Martina's clothes—a pair of spandex shorts and a white T-shirt. Her eyes shoot up to me. "It slipped off the bed."

I lock the door behind me. "Listen to me. Nelo and Vito are here sniffing around. The don sent them. You're going to come downstairs with me. You don't know anything about who I really am, got it? You're only an employee who's sleeping with me."

Her lips part in shock. "The guy I *stabbed* is here?"

I pick up one of my sister's sweaters off the floor and toss it to her. "Put this on. Yes. Did you hear what I said?"

"We're sleeping with each other, I got it. Why do I have to go down there?"

"Because they heard the crash." I grab her by the elbows. "We don't have time for explanations. Just follow my lead."

She nods, and we exit the room.

Nelo is waiting at the foot of the steps, just where I left him, and the stunned surprise on his face when he sees Valentina with me is unmissable.

"You." The word is an accusation.

"Me," Valentina responds.

When he won't move to let us pass, I give him an annoyed look. "You were so curious to know who was in my room, I thought I'd show you."

A prominent vein appears in his neck. "Vito, you know who this is?"

"Who?" his brother calls out from where he's still sitting on the couch.

"The bottle-service girl who stabbed me," he says. "Apparently, she's also Damiano's new girl." His expression darkens even as he steps aside.

"Let me see her," Vito says, coming up to us. "Ah, what a beauty. No wonder you seem so impatient to get rid of us, *cugino*," he says. "I would be too if I had her in my bed."

Valentina keeps her head high as Vito rakes his gaze over her. An urge to cut his eyes out solidifies in my stomach. I step between them.

For a moment, everyone is silent. Then Vito makes a loud sniff. "The *spezzatino* smells like it's ready." He tips his head at Vale. "Why don't we go check on it."

"Let's all go," Nelo says, his gaze flicking between Valentina and I. "I'd like to get to know Damiano's new flame a little better. Our previous two meetings were cut short, wouldn't you say?"

Valentina stays quiet, but when Vito starts making his way to the kitchen, I nudge her to follow. I don't want either of them out of my sight.

The three of us take our seats on the wooden stools around the kitchen island while Valentina makes her way to the pot.

I do *not* like how Nelo is looking at her. It's clear he's far from getting over his embarrassing injury, and men like him deal with embarrassment in one way.

Violence.

"Ale, was it?" he asks the back of Vale's head.

"Yes," she says without turning around. She takes a wooden spoon the cook left on the counter and mixes the stew with it.

He directs his next question to me. "Is she living with you?"

I know what he's trying to get at. He wants to know if Vale is important to me, which means I have to show him she's anything but that.

"She stayed the night."

"You don't bring many women back here, do you? You must really like this one."

"Just because you can't convince any women to go back with you to your place, doesn't mean others have that problem."

Vito snickers a laugh but shuts up quickly when Nelo glares at him.

Vale opens a bunch of cupboards before finding the one that contains the bowls. She takes out four and starts pouring the stew inside of them with a ladle.

"You're quieter than before," Nelo notes. His gaze dips to her ass, and it makes me want to strangle him. "Was Damiano's lovemaking so depressing?"

Her shoulders square. She turns around and brings the first bowl to me.

"Thank you," I say.

"You're welcome."

Nelo's face turns red. "You're ignoring me."

I send Vale a cautious look. There's no worse insult to a man with an ego like Nelo's than being ignored.

She serves the next bowl to Vito. "Be careful, it's very hot."

"Sure," he says.

A vein in Nelo's temple twitches as he watches Valentina go back to the stove. I hope he's decided to stay quiet to save himself from further humiliation, but I know that's wishful thinking.

When she comes over to him, the tension in the room reaches a fever pitch. The bowl lands on the wooden island with a soft clank. She places a spoon beside it.

Nelo peers down at the stew and hums loudly. "It looks juicy. Just like your fat ass, *bella*," he says as he places his hand on Vale's behind and squeezes it.

Hard.

Hard enough to make her flinch.

Hard enough to make her gasp in pain.

The room around me starts to tremble.

There's no holding it in this time.

Flinch. Gasp.

It sets off an inferno of rage.

I move as fast as lightning. My bowl and the entirety of its steaming hot contents end up in Vito's face. He shrieks from the burn. Good. I hope he goes blind.

Nelo jumps, reaching for his gun. Suddenly, Ras is there, pushing Vale out of the way and knocking Nelo's gun out of his grasp.

I jerk Nelo by his wrist and slam the hand that touched Vale on the island. The dark scab stares up at me for a moment before I cover it with the barrel of my gun.

"I really thought you'd learned your lesson the first time you insulted her."

His wild eyes meet mine. "You're fucking crazy. What the fuck—"

Flinch. Gasp.

I pull the trigger.

CHAPTER 29

VALENTINA

THE LAST TIME I heard a gun go off was when I shot my husband. I remember the silence that followed as Martina and I stared at his unconscious body and the growing pool of blood.

This time, the silence is replaced by screams.

Screams that trigger a host of other memories. Nelo, in particular, sounds just like this one older man Lazaro bought to me. My fourth. He was so loud. It was like he thought the louder he was, the less it would hurt.

When my gaze drifts over the hole in Nelo's hand, I start to retch.

Damiano's got his gun pressed to Nelo's head. "Get her out of here," he snaps at Ras.

Ras makes a move toward me, but I shake my head. He needs to stay here. Vito is still curled in fetal position, whimpering on the floor with remnants of the stew stuck to his face, but the pain will fade eventually. Damiano shouldn't be here alone with the two of them.

"I'm fine," I say to Ras and get the hell out of the kitchen.

I don't stop moving until I'm back in my room. For once, I wish I could lock the door from the inside. The broken plates from earlier are still scattered all over the floor, and when I step on a shard, a sharp pain shoots through my foot. Crap.

I sink down to the floor and cradle my foot in my lap. The piece of glass is lodged inside, but I can tell it's just a shallow cut.

The same can't be said about Nelo.

What is Damiano going to do?

He said they were here sniffing around on behalf of the don, and if their clan is anything like the Garzolos, shooting one of the don's men is a big no-no. Given what I now know about the relationship between Damiano and Sal, this could be all the excuse Sal needs to deal with his Damiano problem once and for all. So much for avoiding an escalation.

He just jeopardized his entire plan for...me.

He stood up for me.

It might be the first time anyone in the mafia has actually given a shit about my discomfort. Shouldn't it feel good that he cared enough about me to do what he did?

But it doesn't feel good. My stomach roils.

I'm starting to believe Damiano really could offer me protection, but that protection would be wasted on me, wouldn't it?

Noises of a commotion break out below. It sounds like Damiano is kicking his guests out. I consider going down there for a moment but quickly decide to stay put. I'd only get in their way.

I should take the glass out, but I don't want to see more red. If someone ever wrote the story of my life, it would be written in blood. Sometimes when I close my eyes, all I can see is me bathed in it. Did I feel empathy for Nelo when he screamed just now? Or did I do that thing again? The one I'd gotten so good at down in that damp basement...

The noises cease, only to be replaced with rapid footsteps. My fingers tense around my foot just as the bedroom door swings open and Damiano barges inside.

He finds me sitting on the floor and releases a heaving breath. "Vale."

"Hi." My voice is a whisper.

He kneels beside me and lets his gaze fall to the sole of my foot. His heavy breaths make his shoulders fall up and down as his brows pinch together. "You hurt yourself. Let's get you cleaned up."

"No." I hunch over, hiding my injury from him.

He frowns at the movement and then sighs. "I wish you didn't have to see that. It must have been a shock. There was a lot of blood."

My body jerks.

I turn away from Damiano, but he won't let me move far from him. A hand curls around my shoulder. "Talk to me."

"It wasn't a lot."

It takes him a heartbeat to catch on. "Of blood?"

"It wasn't a lot. You must've missed the radial artery. If you'd hit it, he would have bled out all over your kitchen floor. Then again, if you went through it completely, the body may have sucked it up and stopped the flow."

The air in the room compresses to a point. "How do you know all this?" he asks slowly.

I look at my right hand, the one that would always hold the knife. Keeping a secret doesn't become easier over time. The weight of it accumulates, until you're faced with a choice— crumble beneath it or let it go.

I don't want to crumble.

"I learned a bunch of anatomy after it started," I say. "I thought maybe I could find ways to kill them quickly, so that they wouldn't feel so much pain. It worked for a few. I learned all the arteries, and I'd nick the closest one in whatever area he told me to cut. He caught on and told me the next time they died too early, he'd do to me what I was meant to do to them."

"Lazaro?" Damiano asks, his voice so low it feels like a tremor inside my heart.

"I often thought the thing he got off on the most was watching me decide. Would I follow his commands? Would I abandon my empathy for other people? No, not even abandon, just push it aside, turn it down to zero. It was interesting to him, I think, because he always gave me the illusion of a choice. I could tell him no. But it was just that, an illusion. If I didn't kill whoever he brought to me, he'd kill someone I loved, like Lorna, our housekeeper. At the end of the day, blood would be spilled."

"He made you kill people?"

"First he made me torture them. Cut off their fingers and toes. Mark their flesh with words. Skin them alive. He liked doing it himself but for some reason he liked watching me do it more."

Damiano's skin loses all its color.

My memories of those nights are blurry. I know what I did, but my brain has tried to hide the details away.

I run my hand down the side of my neck. "To do such a thing to a person, you have to stop viewing them as a person. You have to dehumanize them so that they become a bag of bones and meat. Not real. Not people with lives and families, flawed as they may be. You have to pretend they're just a physical object that can't feel real pain. To be capable of that kind of disassociation is an awful thing. It makes you disassociate from yourself as well.

"Very quickly, I stopped feeling like I was human. I stopped seeing my family. It felt really important to me *not* to see them, even if I couldn't really explain why at the time. In retrospect, it was because I was afraid of a few things. I was afraid I'd hurt them. I didn't know how or why I'd do it, but it felt like a real possibility. And I was afraid they'd see the truth about me. They'd look me in the eye and see I had no soul left. I didn't want them to know that, even if it was the truth."

He drags his hand from my shoulder to my wrist. "Vale..."

I meet his shattered gaze. "He made me do awful things. He sat the very first man he brought to me down on a chair the wrong way around. He tied his wrists to his ankles so that he was immobile. The man had this fleshy back covered with marks and tattoos. Lazaro said he liked one of the tattoos and wanted me to give it to him. I didn't understand. He explained he wanted me to cut it out for him.

"It didn't really compute. I stared at him while the man in the chair started to beg. This big, burly guy you wouldn't want to get into a fist fight with begged Lazaro—and me— not to cut out his tattoo. I said to Lazaro I couldn't do that. I thought maybe my new husband had a dark sense of humor that I really didn't understand, but he gave me a knife and very calmly told me to be careful, that he liked the tattoo, and he wanted to admire it while holding it in his hand."

It's hard to force the words out, but I have to. I have to tell Damiano everything, because if I stop, I know I won't ever find the strength to do it again. "I went into shock. I think I laughed. I told him I wouldn't do it, but he wouldn't take no for an answer. 'Do it, or I'll hurt you, Valentina,' he said. I told him he was my husband. He couldn't hurt me. He laughed at that and said he was the *only* one who could hurt me. I started to cry, and he took me by the hand and pulled me into an embrace, comforting me. When I calmed down, he said I was a good person, that he could see I'd protect someone at my own expense, so he'd make the choice easier for me. He said if I didn't do as he asked, he'd do the same thing to Lorna. And as he said it, he pressed the cold blade of the knife to my back, to the same spot where this man had his tattoo. I took the knife. It felt like it was the only option at that point. In my wildest nightmares, I hadn't expected anything like that. We'd just gotten married."

I'm shaking so hard I start stumbling over my words. Damiano moves so that he's crouching on the floor right in front of me, and the glass crunches beneath his dress shoes. "He was a mad man," he concludes. "He put you in an impossible position. This is difficult for you. You don't need to tell me mo—"

"I need to tell you everything," I say. If I don't get all of this poison out, I'll choke on it. "I asked Lazaro who the man with the tattoo was. Lazaro said he was someone who stole one of my father's shipments and killed three of our men. That made me feel a little better, but as soon as I got close to him and he started to scream again, it wasn't enough. That's when I told myself he wasn't a real person. He was just meat. I cut out the tattoo. Lazaro took the piece of flesh and admired it for a long time. After a while, he praised me. Said I did well for my first time.

"The next man came a week or more later, I can't remember. Time lost meaning after that first night. I didn't get out of bed for anything other than to use the bathroom and to get food from the kitchen when Lorna wasn't around to bring it to me. I told myself I wanted to die, but I was lying. If I'd wanted to die, I wouldn't have obeyed him for two months. I wanted to live, and I wanted Lorna to live too. Before she came with me to Lazaro's, she'd worked for my family for over a decade. She was fifty-five, with two grandchildren she talked about all the time, and she was good person who took care of me while I was nearly catatonic." I wonder where she is now. I pray she's okay.

"The longer I stayed with Lazaro, the more resigned I became to my fate. It took..." I take a deep breath. "It took Martina showing up to finally make me snap."

The truth feels like a hideous sculpture made of gore, flesh, and blood. It holds our attention for a while. I can tell Damiano's thinking. He's probably coming up with appropriate ways to make me pay for my sins. He's not like Lazaro. He doesn't worship violence, but for me, he might make an exception now that he knows what I might have done to Martina.

When his arms wrap around me, I go completely still. He tucks one arm under my knees, the other around my back, and lifts me off the ground.

"Let's get you cleaned up," he says gruffly. "I have a first aid kit in my bathroom."

He carries me out of my room and down the hall until we reach what must be his room. Inside, it's cool and dark. The blinds have been drawn. His bed is unmade and messy, the blue sheet tangled as if he wrestled with it all night. The housekeeper obviously hasn't been in here this morning. Maybe he doesn't like having people in his space, and yet he's brought me in here.

The bathroom lights flick on, and Damiano lowers me to the cold marble counter by the sink. His black hair falls over his forehead as he bends down to look for something in the drawers, and when he straightens back up with a plastic white box in his hand, he won't look me in the eyes. He can no longer even stand the sight of me. That's the reaction I expected, but for some reason, it still wounds me. His inability to look at me is somehow more awful than any murderous intent he might have.

I wring my hands while he washes his in the sink.

"Lift your foot," he says and opens up his palm to take it.

His touch is gentle as he cleans my injury. When he removes the shard, I pretend I don't feel the sharp sting, but the alcohol-soaked cotton ball he presses to it afterward drags a hiss out of me.

"It's not deep," he murmurs. "You won't need stitches. That was the worst of it."

He doesn't sound like someone who's preparing to commit murder, but he won't ever want me under his roof with his sister now that he knows what I'm capable of.

When he puts a bandage over the cut, I can't take it anymore. "I know who I am. I'm a monster. The worst of the worst. I should have told you all this earlier. What Nelo did was nothing. I deserve far worse."

The growl that tears out of his throat stills my heartbeat. His hand wraps around the back of my neck, and he pulls my face to his, his gaze finally pinning my own. "You are never going to say that again, all right? You're not a monster. You're a fucking survivor. You survived something that most hardened made men wouldn't be able to come back from, and you put your neck on the line to save my sister. There's only one monster in the story you told me—your husband. He will pay for what he did to you, Valentina. My God, he will pay a *high* price."

He presses his face into my neck, and I stop breathing.

"And so will everyone who failed to be there for you," he whispers against my skin. "Where the fuck was your father when Lazaro was forcing you to do all those things? Did he know?"

"He did," I say. "My father and mother both know Lazaro was not normal. I was raised to obey my husband and to go along with his will. When I begged them for help, they told me it wouldn't be right for them to interfere in my marriage."

"And your siblings?"

"They had no idea. I couldn't tell them. You're the only person that knows the full extent of it."

He takes a deep inhale and pulls back to meet my gaze. "This is why you don't want to go home."

Tears flood my eyes. I try to blink them away, but they spill down my cheeks instead. "I still don't know if Lazaro is alive. If he is, Papà will hand me right back to him. I got away from him once, but I know I won't be able to twice. And if Lazaro is dead, there's a good chance I'll be forced to get remarried to someone who might be a different kind of monster. I can't do that, Damiano. You might have me locked up here, but being back in New York would put me in a much worse prison."

His rough hand cups my cheek. He's looking at me with the kind of sympathy I thought men like him weren't capable of feeling. "I won't keep you here anymore. You're free to leave if you want."

I bow my head as a strange emptiness appears in my chest. He's letting me go. Isn't that what I wanted? I should be relieved at getting my freedom back.

But when I lift my gaze to his, I realize that freedom doesn't live beyond the walls of this house. It lives in the under-standing reflected in his eyes.

He reaches for my hand. "But I don't want you to leave. Stay with me, Vale. Stay with me, and you'll never have to fight another battle again. I'll fight them for you. I'll protect you. I'll avenge you."

I lean into his touch. Forgiveness is a tricky thing. I've tried to forgive myself many times after I got to Ibiza, but my attempts always seemed like throwing a bunch of seeds over dry, infertile soil and expecting them to sprout. They never did.

Damiano's words feel like rain.

They soak the dusty earth and reach all the way down to the place where my soul has been hiding.

One day, we may have a flower yet.

CHAPTER 30

DAMIANO

SHE PRESSES her face into my chest, and I cup the back of her head with my palm. In the bathroom mirror behind her, my reflection stares back at me. It simmers with heartbreak and rage.

I can't erase the image of her shaking on the floor of her room.

When I found her like that, I thought it was because she saw me shoot a hole in a man's hand. I hated myself for putting her through that. I've lost control around her more times than I can count. It's like she turns the dial up on all my feelings until they burst. It's terrifying how alive she makes me feel.

I rake my fingers through her hair and pull her closer. There's a dull pain in my chest. The back of my throat stings. I want to burn everyone who's hurt her to the ground, starting with her husband.

If he's alive, he won't stay that way for long.

My blood turns ice cold. Just when I'm about to lose myself in fantasies of violence, she slides her hands around my waist and presses her lips to mine.

Everything melts away. I fist her hair and dip my tongue into her mouth. She makes a gentle sound in response, a little moan so sweet it hurts. The need to protect her is so overwhelming in this moment. It feels like I'm falling into an abyss. I'm not a romantic. I refuse to believe in love. In my experience, it's toxic and makes people do stupid, unforgivable things.

But no matter how I search, I can't find another word to describe what I'm feeling.

Cazzo. I've gone so soft for this woman I'm surprised I'm still able to stand.

She wraps her legs around my waist, and my thoughts turn to baser things. Blood rushes to my groin. I tug on her bottom lip with my teeth. I want to fuck her so badly.

She seems to get the same idea. Her fingers pull down my zipper, and she takes me into her trembling palm.

Why is she trembling?

I pull away and see that her eyes are glassy and wet. "Vale, you're upset."

She doesn't answer. She just starts stroking me. It should be enough confirmation she wants this. It would be in any other situation, but not this time. I stop her. It physically hurts, but I stop her. "Not now."

She sighs and drops her forehead to rest against my chest. Then when I'm about to ask her if she's okay, she starts to cry.

Yeah, this is going to have to wait. I tuck myself back in, lift her from the vanity, and bring her back out to my bedroom to place her down on the bed.

She downs the glass of water I give her, which I take as a good sign, and eventually, she goes quiet. I can tell she's processing something, so I give her time. Ras is probably downstairs wondering what the hell I'm doing up here. He can wait for a bit longer.

She places the empty glass on the nightstand. "You shooting Nelo is a problem, isn't it?"

"I'll need to call Sal to try to smooth it out. Whether I'm able to or not is another question."

"What does it mean for your plan with my father?"

"We need to move quickly." I've lost the luxury of taking my time with this. Sal will be on high alert as soon as Nelo gets into his ear about what happened. He might get curious about the woman I have with me, and if he discovers it's Valentina Garzolo, he'll know I'm aware of what he's done. He won't wait for me to make my move before he sends his army here to eliminate me. He values the money I make him, but not enough to risk me starting an uprising that can only end in his death.

Valentina nods and wipes her cheeks dry. When she looks at me, there's unmistakable conviction in her eyes. "I'll tell you everything I know. It's not much."

Hope floods me. "It might be everything we need."

She looks less convinced, but she gives me a soft smile. "Let me clean up a bit first."

"Go. I need to check on Ras," I say, as we rise off the bed. When she starts toward the door, I curl my hand around her wrist. "I want you in my bed."

Her skin pebbles with goosebumps. "Do you?"

"Bring your things here."

"They're Martina's things."

"I'll buy you a new wardrobe tomorrow."

She laughs softly. "What about my imprisonment?"

"Like I said, it's over."

Her gaze falls to my lips. She swallows. "I'll tell you what I know about my father's business, but I don't know if I'll stay."

She will, she just doesn't know it yet. She's mine, and I'll do whatever I need for her to realize it.

I go against my instincts and let go of her hand. "Understood. You'll be more comfortable here while you decide."

The relief I feel when she acquiesces with a small smile is palpable.

Downstairs, Ras is pacing the living room. He looks up when he hears me approach and swears. "Dem, you need to get on the phone with Sal. There's still a small chance Nelo hasn't been able to reach him since he's likely getting stitched up."

He's angry at me. He thinks I'm fucking everything up because of my feelings for Vale.

But shooting Nelo doesn't feel like a mistake to me, even now that I've cooled down. It feels like justice.

"You think I shouldn't have done it," I say.

"Doesn't matter what I think. What matters is that we do everything we can to cool the situation down."

"He shouldn't have touched her," I say as I take my phone out of my pocket. "Is the kitchen clean? Everything needs to be in order before Mari gets home."

Ras lets out a long breath. "They're cleaning it now. I told the driver to bring her back in two hours."

"Vale is going to share what she knows about her father," I say. That should be enough to ease Ras's concerns about me not thinking clearly at this point because of Vale. I know that's what he's worried about, I can see it in his face. As much as I want to tell him off for doubting me, I can't deny that in my family, there's a history of people making rash and destructive decisions because of love.

But I'm not in love with Valentina. I can't be. Attraction isn't love. Need isn't love. This wordless thing I feel for her... It can't be love.

As I dial Sal's number, my skin crawls at the thought of hearing his voice and pretending I have no idea what he tried to do to my sister. I can't let my emotions show. He has to think I'm clueless.

After a few rings, he picks up. "Damiano, *ragazzo mio*. You caught me just as I was about to start my late lunch," he rasps in a gravelly voice, courtesy of his pack-a-day smoking habit. "Chiara spent all day on *risotto alla piscatora*."

He likes to pretend we're the best of friends, even if everyone knows it's a charade. "Lucky you. I won't keep you hungry for long."

"I like to hear that. How is my favorite *topolina* doing? Has she recovered from her New York trip?"

This fucking asshole. "She's feeling much better."

"We'll find whoever is responsible for what happened," he says. "These things can take time, but justice always gets delivered."

Don't I know it.

"There's been a small misunderstanding with Nelo and Vito," I say.

"Oh? Did they visit you today like I asked them to?"

"They did."

"Did Nelo tell you the good news? I think him and Mari will make a beautiful couple."

I remind myself their marriage is as likely to happen as Sal choking to death on his risotto, but his words still light a flame of fury inside of me. "He mentioned it," I say curtly.

"What do you think?"

"I'm afraid Nelo's behavior today disqualified him as a potential husband for my sister."

There's a prolonged silence before Sal responds with a humorless laugh. "What did my nephew do this time?"

"I had a woman in my home when he stopped by. He got handsy."

"Hardly a big offense."

"She wasn't his to touch."

There's a rustling sound, and I imagine Sal is leaning forward in his seat. "Whose is she?"

"Mine."

This time, he ejects a gleeful laugh. A new weak spot for him to probe at. "You mustn't have been happy about that."

"I shot his hand. He'll be fine."

"*Mio Dio*. I'd like to see this woman who has made you so possessive. Well, I'll tell Nelo that wasn't done well. He was a guest in your home after all."

"I would appreciate that," I force out.

"The business with Mari... Let's not write it off so quickly. Nelo will act the perfect gentleman next time he's around. You have my word on that."

By now, Nelo is well aware the next time he comes around, he's not leaving this house alive, but I don't bother getting into it with Sal. "If you say so. I'll let you get back to your dinner."

"Say hello to your new friend from me. What's her name by the way?"

"Ale Romero," I say without hesitation. "She's just a seasonal worker."

"Maybe I'll have to stop by before the season's up," he muses. "Goodbye, Damiano."

I hang up and head back upstairs to get Valentina.

I find her in my bedroom, folding her clothes on my bed. The sight of her in my space is like a warm caress. It pleases me more than I care to admit.

She hears me enter and turns, holding the clothes in her hands. "I wasn't sure where to put these."

"The maid will clear space in the closet for you," I say. "Leave it for now. Ras is waiting for us downstairs."

Her posture stiffens. "Did you tell him about Lazaro and me?"

Does she really think I'd share her secret as soon as I left her? "No, and I won't if you don't want me to."

She relaxes. "Thank you."

I can tell she's still ashamed. She blames herself for what her husband forced her to do, that sick fucking waste of—

No, enough. I'll wait to know if he's alive or not before I contemplate all the brutal ways I'll make him pay.

We descend to the living room and make our way to my office. Ras is standing by the bookshelf, his arms crossed over his chest. He cocks his head to the side when he sees me helping Vale walk, so that she doesn't need to put much pressure on her injured foot. She eases down into a chair and looks at him. "I won't waste your time. Here's what I know."

A smile tugs at my lips at her directness.

"The morning of the day Martina and I got away, there was a bridal shower with all the inner-circle women."

"Your sisters were there?" Ras asks.

"Only Gemma came. Cleo didn't make it. She and Mamma had a huge fight, so she wasn't allowed to go. Mamma said it was important for me to show up."

"Did you hear anything of interest?"

"To be honest, I wasn't listening all that deeply. I was..." She rubs her hands up and down her thighs. "I was just trying to keep it together in front of everyone."

Ras's frowns. "Why?"

"Things were bad with my husband, and I didn't want anyone to pick up on it," she says. "The specifics aren't relevant to this story." She shoots me a look. "Anyway, Gemma was worried about our father. She said something about him seeming off. He'd added additional security detail to the entire family."

"He was scared of something," I conclude.

"Papà's always been cautious when it comes to security, but Gemma wouldn't have exaggerated something that wasn't real. She always paid a lot more attention to his dealings than me."

"What else?" Ras presses.

"I left the party early. Lazaro wanted me home. My cousin Tito drove me, and we started talking. We've always been friendly. He alluded to being frustrated he's had to put in long hours working for some asshole. He didn't specify who the asshole was. He said he, his father, Lazaro, and my brother, Vince, were all involved."

"Brother?" I ask.

"He lives in Switzerland."

Ras scratches his chin. "He's your father's money guy?"

"Yes. My impression was that they were all essentially on loan to someone outside of the clan and doing their bidding."

"That has to be Sal," Ras muses. "We know Lazaro was tracking down Martina."

"Does your father have a habit of doing favors?"

Valentina pulls her top lip between her teeth. "Not as far as I know, but that doesn't mean much. I preferred to stay away from his business."

Ras pushes off the wall and makes his way closer. "But your sister is more involved?"

"I wouldn't say she's involved. Just curious. When we were kids, she'd eavesdrop outside of father's office. She liked hearing his secrets." Vale crosses her legs. "I didn't."

Ras and I exchange a look. It's not much, just like Vale had warned me. We're closer to confirming Garzolo was in some kind of an arrangement with Sal, but we need more specifics.

"You sure you don't have any idea why your father would have agreed to work with the Casalese don?"

She shakes her head, her expression sullen, then her eyes widen. "Oh! Gemma also said Papà was hinting at giving her to one of the Messeros. They're another family in New York, but as far as I know, we've always kept our distance from them. It surprised me that there was talk of marriage. I have no idea why Papà was looking for an alliance with them."

"What if you could talk to your sister?" Ras asks. "See what else she knows. If she's nosy by nature, I can't imagine your mysterious disappearance would make her less curious."

Valentina pales. "Talk to Gemma? But…how? I can't just call her cell phone. Papà always monitored our phones."

"If we figure out the logistics, would you talk to her?" I ask. "Do you trust her to keep your whereabouts a secret?"

She chews on her lip before answering. "Yes, I think so. She's always been loyal to our family, but she wouldn't betray me. I have to hope that hasn't changed."

I turn to Ras. "It's our best bet at getting more information. Can we get a burner into her hands?"

"I can see what contacts we have in New Y—"

"Contacts can be bought," Valentina interrupts. "I don't want to risk pulling my sister into this only for Papà to get word of it before we talk to her."

Ras considers her for a moment and then looks at me. "I can go."

Sending my right-hand man to do the job will ensure it'll get done properly, even if it feels like overkill for what should be a fairly simple task. But Vale's visible relief at hearing his offer makes me acquiesce. "Take the fastest route, I want you back in forty-eight hours."

"What does your sister do outside the house?" Ras asks, pulling out his phone to start making the arrangements. "Is there a place she goes where her security detail gives her space?"

"Yes. Her pilates studio. She's there four days a week." Vale hobbles up and finds a pen and paper on my desk. "I'll write down the address and her private class schedule. Because it's just her, the instructor, and the receptionist, the guards stay in the car. If you can find a way in, you should be able to get her alone in the changing room."

Ras takes the paper from her and shakes his head. "New York. I hate that goddamn city."

I slap his back. "It's a short trip. Try to appreciate the sights."

And if Gemma has what we need, it might be the first of many times we pay the Garzolos a visit.

CHAPTER 31

VALENTINA

DAMIANO TRIES to help me walk back upstairs to his room, but I tell him I'm fine and leave him alone with Ras. They've got logistics to work out, and I've got some thinking to do now that there's a real chance I'll be talking to my sister sometime in the next two days.

There's a weird combination of longing and nerves tangling inside my stomach. Of course, I'll be thrilled to hear Gemma's voice. But how will she react to hearing from me after so many weeks of being missing? For all I know, she thinks I'm dead.

She might also think I'm a traitor.

I shut the door to Damiano's bedroom and press my back against it. Will I have to tell her the truth about my marriage for her to forgive me for running away? I've spent so long trying to shield her from the horror of my life that everything inside of me rebels at the idea. But she won't betray Papà's secrets unless I explain everything to her. I have to convince her I'm not being coerced. Otherwise, she may well run to Papà and tell him I'm alive as soon as we hang up. She might even think she's doing me a favor.

It isn't fair of me to keep her in the dark. She's going to be engaged soon, if she hasn't been in the time I've been gone, and if she knows what happened to me, she might fight harder against an ill-chosen match. If I was there, I could fight on her behalf. I could make sure she wasn't given to a monster.

There's an urge to run back down to Damiano's office and demand Ras take me with him, but it's a fantasy. Even if I return to New York—the thought makes me shiver—there's nothing I can do for my sister when I'm labeled a pariah. I'll probably be barred from seeing my siblings and be placed under house arrest.

No, it's time to just admit that when it comes to my duty as an older sister, I majorly fucked up. Add that to the list of many. There's nothing I can do besides tell Gemma the truth and beg for her help.

Sinking down into a chair, I turn to the window and see my reflection. Damiano called me a survivor.

Yeah, I guess I am. Unlike Lazaro's victims, I'm still alive, but at what cost?

It would be easy to stay. To accept Damiano's protection and wait to see if he's able to take back his throne. I could be his kept woman. I could share his bed until he grows bored of me, which he inevitably would. Afterward, he'd probably set me up someplace. It would be a comfortable life.

And one where I'd spend my days wallowing in guilt and regret.

My stomach dips.

I'm far too early on my long road to redemption to take the easy path.

A knock on the door snaps me out of my thoughts.

"Yes?" I call out tentatively.

"It's Mari."

I rise from my seat. "Come in."

Damiano's sister enters the room with a few shopping bags in tow. "I thought I'd get you some things your size," she says, handing them to me.

Damiano's guys must have managed to clean all evidence of what happened with Nelo earlier, otherwise I doubt Martina would look so unbothered.

"Thank you," I say as I accept the bags and peek inside. "Wow, Mari. This is a lot. You really didn't have to."

"I did if I want my clothes back," she retorts with a teasing grin.

"Ah, right."

"I'm just kidding," she says. "I don't mind sharing with you, but I thought it might be weird for my brother to see you in my clothes." She glances around. "Especially now that you've...moved in here."

I laugh awkwardly. Is there a playbook on how to talk to the sister of your ex-captor about the fact that you're sleeping with him?

No?

Better change the topic.

"I never thanked you for the pool day," I say.

Mari climbs onto the bed and folds her legs under her. "Don't worry, I know Dem didn't really give you a chance. I had a fun time." She looks like she wants to say more but hesitates.

"What?" I ask.

She averts her eyes as I pull off my T-shirt and tug a new one on. "That man that came with him…"

I'm not surprised he stayed on her mind. "Giorgio, right?"

Martina's cheeks tinge pink. "Do you think he's…"

I venture a guess, "Handsome?"

"No. I mean, of course he is," she says in a rush. "But that's not my question. Do you think he's a bad person?"

Alarm bells go off inside my head. "Why would you ask that? Did he do something?"

Her eyes widen. "He didn't. It was just something he said. You know what? Forget it."

"What did he say?" I press. Giorgio appears to be Damiano's friend, but I'm not about to put blind faith into a friendship I know nothing about. If he overstepped with Martina, I need to know so that I can tell Damiano to pick his friends more carefully.

Martina picks up one of my new shirts and starts examining the label. "My brother said he and I met, and I felt awkward because I couldn't remember it. I told Giorgio I wasn't sure how he slipped my mind. He didn't say anything at first. I thought he was offended, but then he said it's for the best I didn't remember him. He said he isn't someone girls like me should know. What did he mean by that?"

I resist the urge to roll my eyes. Mafia men. Sometimes I think it makes them feel good to intimidate women for no reason, even women who have no interest in them. Martina's probably never going to see him again. "I wouldn't worry about it," I tell her. "Truly bad men don't waste their time warning you about how bad they are."

She lifts her gaze off the label, considering what I said. "Hmm. You're probably right."

We play dress up for another hour, and it turns out Martina has quite an eye for estimating sizes. Nearly everything she bought me fits perfectly. When the sun sets, we head down for dinner and discover Damiano left earlier and isn't back yet, so we eat without him. I try to stay up until he returns, if only to get an update on Ras's mission, but before long, my eyes have trouble staying open, and I climb into bed. His scent wraps around me and lulls me to sleep.

A warm body sliding in beside me wakes me some time later. Outside the big window, it's nearly pitch black, with clouds obscuring the moon, and only a few stars glimmering in the sky.

A hand curls around my hip. "Did I wake you?" His voice glides over my neck and chest and settles somewhere between my legs.

"Yes, but I'm glad you did." I turn onto my back and look at him. In the darkness, all I see is the straight line of his nose and the glint of his eyes. "Where's Ras?"

"He just texted me he landed in New York."

"That was quick."

"He took a flight to Valencia and jumped on a chartered flight from there."

"Won't Sal wonder where he went?"

"Ras lost his tail at the airport in Valencia."

"But won't Sal be suspiciou—"

He places his index finger on my lips. "Vale. Take a deep breath. It's a calculated risk, just like everything I do. Ras could have had many reasons to go to New York for a short stint and going to talk to your sister is not one that's on Sal's radar."

I exhale and force myself to relax. "You must be tired."

"Yeah," he says quietly, "but I'm never too tired for you." He slides his hand from my hip to cup my right breast. A satisfied rumble leaves his throat. "God, you feel good, Vale. I fucking love these tits."

He dips his head to my chest and licks one nipple before moving to the next one. I bury my fingers in his hair and tug him closer.

Damiano presses his nose against the valley between my breasts and inhales. "I've been wanting to fuck you all day."

"Just today?" I tease.

He rises on his arms above me and huffs a chuckle. "Every day since I first laid eyes on you. You somehow made even that blue uniform look good, your little ass sticking up while you cleaned my office."

I smile. "I knew you were looking."

He glides down my body until his face is in line with my new panties. He licks me over them, teasing my clit just a tiny bit. "I was always looking at you," he says against my pussy, and it feels deliciously dirty. "Now, let me see."

I lift my hips so that he can slide my underwear down and then widen my legs. He sucks in a breath, mutters approvingly in Italian, and buries his head between my legs.

The scratch of his short beard against my thighs drives me nearly as mad as the sensation of his tongue lapping at my clit. I coil his hair around my fingers and tug on the strands, but no matter how I pull him toward me, he doesn't relent. A coil tightens more and more inside my lower belly, until I'm thrashing in his enormous bed, desperate for a release.

He wraps his big hands around my thighs and lifts me up, never allowing his mouth to leave my pussy. Just when I think I might die if I don't come right fucking now, he takes my clit into his mouth and sucks. *Hard.*

I burst. My entire body is flooded with pleasure. He lowers me down on the bed, pushes two fingers inside of me while I'm still pulsing with my release, and somehow, inexplicably fucks me with them until I'm back on the edge again.

"Oh my God," I sputter.

He smirks. "He's not here. I am."

A shiver runs down my spine. "I think I might come again."

"Good girl," he says hoarsely. "Show me what you've got."

He's relentless, hitting this spot inside of me over and over again, and then suddenly, it happens. I think I see my entire life flash in front of me. I arch my back, cry out his name, and feel myself fall over that cliff again.

He groans. "Fuck me. Baby, you just squirted."

Despite the mind-numbing euphoria, his words are so shocking I get my wits about me quick. "*What?*" I can't see anything, but when I sit up and press my hands against the sheets, they're wet. "No way." I'm absolutely mortified.

"Fuck, I can't believe I didn't see it." Damiano reaches over me to flick on the light on the nightstand and then moves back to where he was.

I thought he'd look disturbed.

Instead, he looks like someone proudly admiring their work as he stares at the ruined sheets. He looks so pleased, and it immediately eases my embarrassment. Then he lifts his eyes to me and gives me a spirited look. "We're going to do that again with the lights on."

I laugh and fall back on the bed. "Later, please. I don't think I'll survive another one."

He's there above me seconds later. His mouth finds mine, and he kisses me for ages. I'm desperate to return the favor, even if I'm sure I won't be nearly as adept at it as he was with me. When I ask him to sit up on the edge of the bed, and he understands my intention, his gaze grows hooded.

I push my nervousness aside and wet my lips. I can't believe what I'm about to say. "You told me you'd fill every one of my holes with your cum. So far, you've been under delivering."

A lazy grin spreads over his lips. "You're fucking filthy, Vale."

I rub one cheek against his hard length, then the other. His fingers tangle with my hair, but he allows me to control my movements. I lick the underside of his cock and swirl my tongue around the top.

He groans. "Put it in your mouth."

I do, and I take it as far as I can manage, which isn't all that far. He's thick and long, and when my mouth doesn't reach more than halfway down, I wrap my hand around the base.

He seems to like it. His breathing grows harsher the more I stroke him, and his grip on me tightens.

"Relax your throat," he says. "You can take me farther, baby."

He's right. I push my butt harder against my heels, and he angles his hips forward so that it's a straight line between his cock and my mouth. It hits the back of my throat, and my eyes water, but somehow, I manage not to gag.

"You're doing so well," he whispers. "Fuck, Vale. You're fucking perfect."

The next time he pulls out, I remember how amazing it felt to have him suck on my clit, so I try the same on him. He makes a tortured moan. "I'm going to fill your pretty little mouth with my cum," he pants. "That's what you want, isn't it?"

I can't speak, but I increase my speed to show him that's exactly what I want, and moments later, I feel him stiffen even more and explode on my tongue.

This is the first time I've tasted a man. The taste isn't entirely pleasant, but God, the act of making him lose control is delicious enough on its own. I fall back on my hands and watch him try to gather himself. He's barely holding himself up.

His elbows rest on his knees, and he looks so spent, so *shattered*, it fills me with pride. I *made* him look like this.

He props his forehead into his palm and peeks up at me. "I'm afraid of what you'll do to me after you get more practice."

"Maybe I'll tie you up and have my way with you," I say. "They say payback is a bitch."

He barks a laugh and pulls me to his lap. "I think I'll enjoy that kind of payback."

I nuzzle my face into his neck and smile against his skin.

A sense of peace washes over me.

I wish the sun wouldn't rise.

I wish I could forget everything and stay like this with him forever.

CHAPTER 32

VALENTINA

I WAKE up late to find Damiano already gone. After we stripped the bed and changed the sheets in the middle of the night, it took me a while to get back to sleep, and now I'm groggy.

I blink at the clock hanging on his wall. It reads...half past noon.

Gemma's class is at ten a.m., and accounting for the time difference, I might be speaking to my sister in just a few hours. Suddenly, I'm very awake. What am I going to say to her?

I hop out of bed, get myself dressed, and hurry downstairs. Martina is in the kitchen, cooking, and when she sees my harried appearance, she gives me a questioning look. "You look like you're late for an exam. What's going on?"

"Is your brother around?"

She shakes her head. "He left a few hours ago. I'm not sure where he went."

Damiano should be here when I talk to Gemma. I *need* him to be here. How quickly he went from the man I was trying to get away from to the man who's support I crave.

Martina frowns at my anxious expression. "Sit down, Vale. I'll get you some coffee." She slides a plate of potato medallions topped with eggs and ham across the island. "*Huevos rotos.* Eat."

I climb up on one of the stools—the one Vito sat on when him and Nelo came by—and grab a fork. The food is delicious, as always, and when Martina hands me an espresso, I drink it in one gulp. "Thank you," I say.

She sits on the stool across from me. "What's bothering you?"

I move the potatoes around the yolk. "I'm going to talk to my sister Gemma today."

Martina sips on her own espresso. "Isn't that a good thing? I thought you said you miss your sisters."

"I do, I just...don't really know what to say to her." I meet Martina's clear hazel gaze. "I feel guilty for leaving her in New York."

"You didn't have a choice," she says. "There was no time for you to get her when we were running away. If we'd stopped, we may have been caught."

I cross my feet at my ankles. "I know. There's no way I could have gotten her out at that time, but maybe once I got you to the airport, I could have gone back for her." The moment I say it, I realize it's just a childish fantasy. I sigh. "To be honest, I'm not sure she would have even gone with me. I would have had to explain everything to her. You, Lazaro, and everything leading up to that moment." My stomach twists. "My husband was a bad man, Martina."

"I know," she says quietly, looking down at her cup. She's remembering things. Things she shouldn't need to remember for my sake.

"The real kind, not the kind that warns you of how bad they are," I say, alluding to yesterday's conversation and giving her a soft smile.

She lifts her hand to hide her giggle and shakes her head. "Don't tease me. I feel so stupid for how I reacted. I probably turned as red as a tomato."

I laugh. "Don't worry about it. How likely are you to see him again?"

Her expression dims. "Not likely, I suppose."

We eat for a while before Martina clears her throat. "Well, it doesn't sound to me like you could have done anything differently about Gemma. You did the best you could in that moment. I'm sure she'll understand."

"Maybe. I just don't know how to stop feeling guilty."

"Is she happy in New York?"

The truth is, I don't know. I don't know what my sister wants, and she probably doesn't either, because just like me, she's been a puppet of Papà's for as long as we've been alive, and she's been fed lies about our family for equally as many years. I can't let Papà marry her off to some monster like Lazaro.

"I guess I'll find out soon enough," I mutter and finish my breakfast.

We lounge around the living room and put on a movie, but I hardly pay any attention. When Damiano walks through the door, I jump to my feet. "Anything from Ras?"

His eyes grow soft when he sees Martina and I. "He texted me that he managed to get into the studio, and he's waiting for her to arrive," he says. "Let's go to my office so that we're ready for when he calls."

It's really happening. If Ras made it inside, there should be no reason for him not to find Gemma.

We leave Martina on the couch and close the door to his office behind us. He places his cell phone face up so that we can see the caller ID when someone calls and tugs me into his chest. I sink into him. It's shocking how easy it is to accept his comfort, how natural it feels to yield to his touch. Can I really walk away from this when the time comes?

He nudges my chin up with his index finger and gives me a kiss. When he pulls away, his eyes narrow. "You're tense."

"It's been a long time since she and I talked."

He slides his hand down my arm. "She's still your sister."

When the phone starts buzzing, we both look at it. Damiano lets it ring once and then puts it on speaker.

"Ras?"

Why isn't he answering? Did he get caught? Is that one of Gemma's guards calling us?

"Yes."

I suck in a breath. My God, that was the longest second of my life.

"Ras! Is Gemma with you?"

There's a laugh as dry as the Sahara on the other end of the line. "She's here, all right. Valentina, what *the fuck* is wrong with your sister?"

Damiano and I exchange a look. "What do you mean? What ha—"

"Give me the phone, you maniac!"

That's Gemma's voice. My chest soars with relief. "Let me talk to her."

Ras swears. "She's got a few screws loose. She *bit* me."

"You groped me."

"I didn't fucking grope you, you tiny psycho. Here, talk to your sister so I can get the hell away from you."

"You're the one who locked us in this dusty closet." There's a rustling sound.

"Gemma," I call out.

"Vale, is that really you?"

I can't believe I'm talking to my sister. A ball gets lodged inside my throat, but I force the words past it. "Yes. Gem, it's me."

She makes a strangled sound. "Oh, Vale, you're alive. We were so worried. I haven't slept a full night since you left, and neither has Cleo. Are you okay? Where are you?"

"I'm fine. How much time do you have until your class starts?"

"Forget the class. I can skip it."

Damiano places his hand on the small of my back and whispers, "No, she can't."

"You can't skip your class," I say. "No one can know we talked."

"You have five minutes," Ras says, his voice coming out slightly muffled.

"How are you?" I need to know she's okay before I can talk about anything else.

"Miserable since you left. Mamma's gotten even more strict, and Cleo's constantly at war with her. We're only allowed to leave the house on prearranged outings, and nothing that would put us around a lot of people. Where are you?"

"I'm somewhere safe," I tell her. "What about the Messeros? Are they still talking about marrying you off to them?"

"I'm engaged."

My stomach drops. "No."

"To Rafaele. The contract is already signed, but no date has been set."

Despair feels like a cold trickle down my back. "How is he?"

"I don't really know. We met once at that dinner I told you about. He was cold and uninterested. I didn't think he wanted me, but after you ran, Papà made it happen somehow."

I bring the heel of my palm to my forehead. "I'm so sorry, Gem."

"Don't be. I'm fine. It's what Mamma always said would happen. Of course, Cleo's already declared that if she doesn't like her future husband, she'll shoot him like you did."

I huff an amused breath. "She would, wouldn't she?"

"I told her she'd better have a sharper aim."

Pinpricks travel up my arms. "What do you mean?"

"Lazaro survived. You know that, right?"

Suddenly, I feel light-headed. I sway for a moment before two hands steady me by my waist.

"Sit down," Damiano says, leading me to a chair.

"I didn't know," I whisper into the phone.

"Why did you do it, Vale?"

There's no time for lengthy explanations. I shut my eyes. "Lazaro was ordered by Papà to capture and harm an inno- cent girl, so I helped her get away. Her and I ran together. I'm safe now, but I can't tell you where I am."

"I don't understand," Gemma says. "Papà wouldn't ask Lazaro to hurt some random girl. It doesn't make sense."

"He would, and he did. I swear on my life that he ordered it. I couldn't let Lazaro do it."

There's a long silence on the other end. "You're sure? Is someone making you say this?"

I can hear the skepticism in her voice. She's loyal to our father and has her guard up, but I need her to believe me.

"Lazaro was abusing me," I force out. "He made me do awful, horrible things. He's evil, and Papà knows, but he married me off to him anyway. That saying we have about Papà always prioritizing our safety? It's a lie. The only thing Papà prioritizes is power."

Damiano's hand curls into my shirt. "Three minutes, Vale," he whispers.

"Why didn't you say anything?" Gemma asks. Her voice trembles, and I think she's crying.

"I couldn't. Listen to me, one day, I'll tell you everything, but we don't have time now. I need your help."

Come on, Gem. Please give me a lifeline.

"Okay. What do you need?"

There's no time to feel relieved. "That day at Belinda's bridal shower, you told me something was going on with Papà. He increased everyone's security detail. Has anything else happened since? Do you know what he was worried about?"

She takes in a deep breath. "After we found out from Lazaro you were gone, Papà lost it. He said you made a terrible mistake that the whole family would end up paying for. He called Lazaro an amateur for failing to accomplish a simple task that was given to him. Papà said he won't be able to close the big deal he's been working on, which means the truce is going to end. Mamma yelled at him to watch his tongue in front of me and Cleo, and he left. Since that night, he's barely spoken to any of us. He spends all day in his office. I don't even think he leaves it to sleep."

"What deal?"

"I don't know, but it had something to do with whatever Lazaro was supposed to do for him."

"A deal with Sal," Damiano mutters. "We already knew they were working on something."

"Who is that?" Gemma asks.

"There's no time to explain," I say. "You said there's a truce? With who?"

"With one of the other clans—the Riccis—but there's no truce anymore. The week after you left, they killed Tito."

Pain stabs through my gut. "My God, poor Tito..."

"They're retaliating for something, but Mamma won't give us any details. Still, she can't hide the death of our cousin. We know something dangerous is going on. I think that's why my engagement was so rushed. Papà needs allies."

"One minute," Damiano says.

"Gem, do you have any way to find out more?" I ask.

I can imagine her nibbling on her bottom lip as she considers my question. "Papà's got a guard outside his office all the time now, so I haven't been able to eavesdrop. But maybe I can try something to get the guard to leave his post tomorrow. It's a long shot, but I might get something."

"That's good. Take the burner, hide it well, and call the number on it if you get anything. No one can know we talked, okay?"

"I won't tell anyone."

"Time's almost up," Ras says.

Tears well up in my eyes again. "I love you. I miss you more than you can imagine."

"I love you too. When I call you next, we'll talk longer, okay?"

"Okay. Please, be careful."

Damiano hangs up the call.

I place my palms on his desk and lean forward. My heart races like a pack of wild horses. I thought talking to my sister would make me feel better, but I was desperately wrong. It feels like my chest is about to split open.

Lazaro is still alive.

My husband—my tormentor—is somewhere right now, scheming how to find me. Fear wraps around me and squeezes all the air out of my lungs.

Damiano places his palm on my shoulder. "Vale, breathe."

"He won't stop until he gets me back," I say.

Damiano kneels beside me and puts his hands on my thighs. His eyes glint with sharp conviction. "I promise you on my life he'll never touch you again."

I compel myself to believe him. Maybe with the entire Casalese arsenal at his disposal, I'll be safe.

But first, he has to get that arsenal.

"We still don't have enough information," I say, dragging my hands down my face.

"No, you did well. We know your father is at war with another New York clan. It means he's vulnerable. We can work with that."

I suppose he's right. "What could Papà possibly want badly enough to agree to execute a hit on Martina?"

Damiano's expression grows tight. "In our business, it usually comes down to money or power."

Even knowing what I now know, it's hard for me to accept this truth. "How much money is enough to kill an innocent girl?"

Damiano purses his lips. "Probably less than you think."

CHAPTER 33

DAMIANO

I SPEND the rest of the day ensuring all of the new security measures Napoletano recommended are put in place. Since Ras is gone, Jax—one of his tech guys—has taken over getting all of the extra cameras and software set up, and he tells me he should be finished with everything within the next twenty-four hours.

"There's a connection problem by the pool," he says. "We need to get an extender for the signal, but it should be an easy fix."

"Get it first thing you can."

"You got it, boss."

The night that follows is restless. Vale twists and turns in my arms, and I wish she'd talk to me, but I get the sense she wants to be alone with her thoughts.

I wonder what she's thinking about right now—Lazaro being alive? Her sister's engagement? Or maybe she's coming to terms with who her father really is and the things he's willing to do.

It seems like she was far more sheltered from his dealings than a typical Casalese woman. For nearly a decade, my mother managed the finances of the clan. As far as I could tell, there wasn't much my father kept from her. He'd come home for dinner, we'd sit down at the table, and he'd talk about his day to all of us, even the children. Mari was too young to understand, but I ate up every word out of his mouth. I loved hearing about the feuds and the scuffles, all of which ended in him victorious.

I like to think I inherited my steady temperament from him. In his stories, my father was always calm and calculated, even when he was dealing with traitors. My father was a brutal don, feared by his enemies, but he wouldn't have done what Sal and Garzolo tried to do to Martina.

I notice Vale's breathing has grown deeper. She's finally asleep. I pull her closer, inhale the scent of her hair, and soon, my own consciousness begins to slip.

A loud ping makes my eyes snap open. It takes me a moment to push past the veil of sleep. How long was I out for?

My palm curls around the phone, and I lift it up to my face. It's a text message from Gemma. I open it and find two words.

Luxury counterfeits.

I frown at the letters.

Even though I loathe to do it, I nudge Vale awake and show her the message. Maybe she can help interpret what the fuck it's supposed to mean.

She squints at the screen. "That's all she sent?"

"Yes. Does your father deal in counterfeits?"

"Not as far as I know..." She moves her jaw in thought. "Wait, the Riccis do."

The family Garzolo is at war with? How do counterfeits connect to the deal with Sal?

I sit up and run my hand through my hair. The Casalese clan controls a massive amount of counterfeit factories in the area around Naples. We supply the entirety of Europe with goods that are impossible to distinguish from the real thing, and that's because the luxury houses use our factories for the production of their authentic merchandise as well. The only difference between what they sell in their glittering stores and what we sell on the black market is the price. It's the dark underside of the fashion industry few people know about.

What's Garzolo's angle? Was he trying to undercut his rival's business by flooding the New York market with his own merchandise? Was he trying to get his supply from Sal?

Shit, that could be it.

The phone begins to ring.

Valentina sits up and pulls the sheet up to her chest. "Who is it?"

I eye the caller ID and hand her the phone. "It's Gemma."

Her eyes grow wide. She picks up and puts it on speaker. "Gem? How did it go?"

"Hello, Valentina."

Vale's jaw slams shut. I don't need to ask to know who the gravelly voice belongs to.

"What possessed you to do this, daughter?"

Stefano Garzolo has caught on to what we were trying to do, which means I need to calibrate my approach.

"Papà," Vale breathes. "Where's Gemma?"

"Your sister is in her room, under guard. She's unlikely to be leaving it any time soon after the trick you two pulled."

Vale brings her hand to her mouth.

I make a gesture at her to stay quiet. "Garzolo, I suppose we might as well jump to introductions. My name is Damiano De Rossi, and I have your daughter in my possession."

There's a pause on the other end of the line, and I can tell whatever Stefano Garzolo was expecting, it wasn't this.

"Your don told me that when your sister returned to you, she returned alone."

"He lies, especially to people who fail to do his bidding." I need to sow doubt and do it fast. Garzolo is in trouble on his home turf. That's his main problem. If I can position myself as his chance to solve it, I'll get what I want out of him.

"I presume it's all in the open now," he says.

"It wasn't hard to figure out who hired you once Valentina told me her side of the story."

He huffs a laugh laced with disappointment. "Of course she did. I bet it didn't even take much. Do you have children, De Rossi?"

"No."

"You will one day. I pray yours don't disappoint you like mine do."

His words send a spike of anger through me. No wonder Vale didn't want to go back to this. She pulls the sheet to her chest, her knuckles turning white while her cheeks redden. I steady her by placing my palm on her thigh.

"So what now, De Rossi? I take it you're not a forgiving man."

He wants to know if I'm going to make a move on Sal. Once I confirm it, this conversation will only have two possible outcomes. Garzolo will come to my side, or he will rat me out as soon as we hang up the phone.

What's life if not a series of calculated risks?

"I'm not," I tell him.

The man on the other end of the line lets out a sigh. "And what do you plan to do with my daughter?"

"That depends on how this conversation goes." I look at Vale. When she mouths *Gemma*, I nod and ask, "What are you going to do with Gemma?"

"That's none of your business."

"Papà, please don't punish her," Vale begs.

"Enough of that Papà crap," he snaps. "You've lost your right to call me that after you abandoned your family. Now, let's cut right to it. What do you want, De Rossi?"

My eyes beg Vale to trust me. I can see she's on the verge of freaking out. Once I have a deal with Garzolo, we'll be able to do more for Gemma. Finally, she gives a barely perceptible nod.

"I want to give you an opportunity to right the wrongs leveled against my family," I say. "Sal will never work with you again after your failure, but I might."

"You're a capo on an island. Rich but isolated. You don't have anything I want besides my daughter," Garzolo says, his voice harsher than before.

"I won't be on this island for much longer," I tell him. This is where I need to bluff. "Everything's already in motion."

"You want to take over."

"I *will* take over. It's my birthright, and my duty. Sal's running the clan into the ground, and people are noticing. They see me as the natural contender, which is why he wanted to take Martina to keep me in line. The money I make on Ibiza makes up more than fifty percent of the clan's revenue. Without me, he's nothing."

The implication is clear. Once I'm the don, I'll be able to make whatever counterfeit deal he was interested in from Sal.

"How do I know this isn't just some fantasy?" he demands. "What makes you think you'll succeed?"

I'll succeed if Garzolo agrees to give me his cocaine, but I can't tell him that. He can't know how much leverage he has. "Sal's made a lot of enemies in the last few years. The families are unhappy and ready for a change. You know as well as me that all great empires fall from within. Let me be clear, I don't need you, Garzolo. Once I become the don, I'll be even less forgiving. We have a debt between us. One way or another, it will be paid."

He exhales a sigh. "What kind of payment are you looking for?"

I brace my elbows on my knees. "A short-term supply of cocaine. I'll pay you a fifteen percent markup if you can get the product to Ibiza."

There's a lengthy pause. Vale places her hand on my back while her father thinks.

Come on.

"Done, but under the condition that we sign the deal the Messeros and I were negotiating with Sal."

Relief cascades through me. "I'll have to look at it, unless you want to bring me up to speed now."

"The Riccis have grown too powerful here in New York. The Messeros and I have partnered together to take them down a notch and reestablish our dominance. The Riccis' main supplier of counterfeits in China is no longer operational. It's been taken over by the Triad. So they went to Sal."

Ah, it's all starting to become clear. "And you tried to get Sal to agree to work with you instead."

"We almost had our deal signed. Sal's last condition was the business with your sister. When we didn't deliver, he was furious. He exposed our plans to the Riccis. The tensions are high. It's urgent we get it done."

"Understood. It will be my top priority after the dust settles."

"Good. When are you sending back my daughter?"

I meet Vale's gaze. "She's staying with me."

"Excuse me?"

"You heard me. Valentina is mine."

"She's a married woman. Her husband wants her back."

"Her husband is never going to see her again."

The silence stretches.

"Lazaro left for Spain a few days after she disappeared," Garzolo says finally. "We tracked her to Spain. He's been searching ever since. When you told me your name earlier on the call, I messaged him to tell him Valentina is in Ibiza. He's on his way."

Valentina lets out a gasp.

"Call him off," I grind out.

Her father sighs. "That's not going to be possible. In our clan, not even the don can interfere within a marriage."

I squeeze the phone harder with my hand. "Good. I've been wanting to have a few words with him."

"The business with your sister was ill conceived," Garzolo says. "I understand if you want to get your revenge."

As if I need his permission to kill Lazaro. He makes no mention of what that scumbag did to Valentina. He hasn't even asked how she is the entire time we've been speaking.

"You're fine with him dead?" Valentina suddenly asks. "I thought he was your loyal soldier."

"He was."

"You gave me to him."

"As a reward for his prior good work, not his recent failure."

She scoffs and gives a shake of her head. "He's no longer useful to you."

"No."

A tear travels down her cheek, and I wish I were able to reach into the phone and shake some fucking sense into the man. He still hasn't attempted an apology.

Sadly, I doubt he ever will.

"Goodbye, Father." Valentina hangs up the phone. "Lazaro's coming here," she says.

I meet her worried gaze. "He won't leave alive, Vale."

That's a promise I intend to keep.

CHAPTER 34

VALENTINA

FOR THE SECOND time in my life, I've been traded away for my father's gain. I never harbored any fantasies about him regretting how he treated me once he realized I ran away, but experiencing his ice-cold ruthlessness still feels like a kick in my gut.

He's right about one thing. He's not Papà anymore. Even that simple term carries a connotation of affection I no longer feel.

I am an object to him.

I have to trust I'm more than that for Damiano, but trusting anyone is difficult for me these days. I wish he'd pushed harder to get more information about Gemma. What are they going to do to her? Her betrayal will be punished. How harshly? I don't know. All I do know is I'm to blame for putting her in that position.

Since we hung up on my father, Damiano and I've been on our feet. He's figuring out the logistics of getting my father's drugs to Ibiza. I roam the halls and try to identify where Lazaro might break in from, even though Damiano has reassured me ten times over he'll never be able to get in.

When he sees me hovering by the living room window, he comes over and stops behind me. "The police have his photo," he says as he brushes my hair off my neck. "They've been instructed to bring him to me as soon as they see him anywhere on the island."

I look over my shoulder at him. "You're working with the police?"

"I've had the chief in my pocket for years. My point is he won't find you, Vale. He'll be dead before he lays eyes on you."

I want to believe him, but something holds me back. It's funny how things can change so quickly. Last night, when I was in his arms, safe and warm, I would have believed anything he said. If he asked me to stay with him then, I would have said yes. Now, my world feels like a glass plate spinning on a thin wooden pole. I don't know what to do with myself. Thinking about the future fills me with dread.

"Where's Martina?" I ask.

He glances in the direction of her room. "She's still asleep. When she wakes, don't tell her about Lazaro, all right? I'm afraid she won't take it well if she knows he might already be on the island. He killed her friend, and—"

"I understand." He doesn't need to explain it to me. I know exactly what Martina is feeling. "I'll keep her company."

Damiano's eyes soften. "I appreciate it. I've got a few things to review, will you be all right?"

"Go, I'm fine."

He curls his fist into my shirt at the small of my back, presses me into him, and brings our lips together. I give him what I have, but God, it feels all wrong. The closer Lazaro gets, the more I think about the past and the awful things I did.

The day drags on even once Martina wakes and we get busy in the kitchen. She teaches me how to make her favorite cake, and we spend hours baking all the layers and making the flavored creams. At one point, I have to pause and duck into the bathroom to collect myself. It's so absurd to be baking while a killer is probably on his way over. I take a few deep breaths to calm myself. Then I return to the kitchen and pour myself a large glass of wine.

When the evening comes and the skies begin to dim, we sit down for dinner. We're halfway through our grilled tuna steak when the doorbell rings.

I jolt out of my seat. Is it Lazaro? No, that's impossible. He wouldn't ring the doorbell.

Damiano settles me with a calm look. "I'll be right back," he says, lifting his napkin off his lap and putting it by his plate.

"Are you okay?" Martina asks, her face lined with concern.

I realize I'm still standing, so I sit back down. "Yeah, fine. Just a little jumpy."

My racing heartbeat slows only when Damiano reenters the room with Ras by his side.

"You're back," I say, noting Ras's tired eyes.

They lose their tiredness as soon as they land on me. He comes closer, shaking his head, as if I've sorely disappointed him. "Look." He sticks out his hand.

There's a very clear bite mark on his index finger. My eyes widen. "That's from Gemma?"

He drags a chair out and sinks into it. His eyes flash with a dark curiosity I hadn't seen in him before. "I've got a few long gashes on my back as well. I swear, she must spend her free time sharpening her nails into knives."

I arch a brow. "What did you expect? You ambushed her in the women's change room. I'd be more concerned if she didn't put up a fight."

He huffs a laugh. "I've never had a woman I haven't slept with rough me up like that."

Is it just me, or does he sound mildly impressed?

"Do you know what your father's going to do to her now that she's been caught helping?" Ras asks and looks down at the plate Martina places in front of him.

"No. He wouldn't tell us."

Damiano meets my gaze. "I'll find out. I just need a bit more time to secure the deal."

Would he be able to patiently wait if this was Martina we were talking about? I glance away. Ras doesn't look too happy with that answer either. He sticks his fork into the tuna and tears off a piece.

"How did she look?" I ask him. "Did she seem happy?"

Ras peers at me from under his brows. "She looked...fine." He clears his throat. "We didn't talk much until she got on the phone with you."

There has to be something I can do for my sister from my new position by Damiano's side.

But it's not up to me. It's up to him. He will be don, and it will be his word that matters, not mine.

"Finish up your food in my office," Damiano tells Ras as he gets up. "We have things to discuss."

I'm so absorbed with my worries I barely notice them leave. My wineglass is empty. I refill it nearly to the brim.

Why did I agree to involve Gemma in all of this? I should have run when Damiano offered me my freedom, instead of sticking around and thinking I can help. Now I've created problems for her and I don't know how to solve them. It's like everything I touch turns rotten. Damiano might not understand this yet, but I know it to be true.

I'm sick of it. Sick of being who I am. A coward, a fool, and a killer.

Rising from the table, I realize Martina is gone too. Wasn't she here when Ras and Damiano went to his office?

A foreboding feeling prickles the back of my neck. She probably went up to her room when she realized I wasn't in the mood to converse. Still, I decide to check on her. When I get to her bedroom door, it's silent on the other side. I knock and walk in. She's not there.

My feet move quickly as I go back down and check the kitchen, the next most likely place for her to be. It's empty. I grab a small cutting knife and slip it into my pocket, alarm bells ringing inside my head.

When I return to the living room, I see something move by the pool. I walk closer and closer to the glass doors leading outside. It's dark out there, with just the built-in lights giving the water a soft glow, but I can't see around the edges of the garden.

I flip the light switch. Suddenly, everything is illuminated, and that's when I see Martina.

It's like someone dropped me into a vat of thick tar. Every movement feels harder, every breath impossible to take. She's in Lazaro's grip, his knife pressed to her throat. Icy panic creeps into my lungs until I can't breathe. How did he get in? How is this happening?

I push the sliding door open and run toward them. "Martina!"

Lazaro smiles and squeezes her harder. He rarely smiles with teeth, but this time I see them. It looks grotesque on his face, like an alien going through the motions without understanding the emotion behind it.

I stop when I'm a few feet away. "Let her go."

He rakes his gaze down me before settling it back on my face. "Wife."

"Let. Her. Go. Lazaro."

"I'll have a scar for the rest of my life," he says, ignoring what I said. "The bullet went right through my chest."

Martina's pale and stiff with fear. Her worst nightmare's come alive. God, I'll do anything to get Lazaro away from her. I just need an opportunity.

"I wish it had gone through your heart," I whisper.

He chuckles dryly. "I didn't teach you how to use a gun yet. Don't worry, when we're home, I'll teach you everything I know."

I always thought there was a chance he'd be done with me after I betrayed him, but now I know I was wrong. He's not going to kill me. He's going to take me back, punish me, and have me kill again.

I can't do it. I *won't* do it.

Pounding footsteps sound behind me. I don't need to turn to know it's Damiano and Ras.

"Drop the knife, or I'll put a bullet in your head."

I hear Damiano but can't see him. I don't want to take my eyes off Martina even for a moment. He must be a few meters behind me.

"If my pulse stops for any reason, I blow up," Lazaro says simply, nodding toward the watch on his wrist. It must be tracking his heartbeat.

My eyes widen.

That smile is back on his face. "I'm not an amateur, Valentina. You managed to trick me once, I'll give you that, but it's never going to happen again."

I believe him. A strange sensation materializes inside my ribcage. I feared this moment so much, but now that it's here, my fear takes a back seat. I meet Martina's gaze and know what I must do.

"I'll go with you if you let Martina go," I say.

"She's staying with us until you and I are on my boat."

A boat? There's no beach here, just a sharp cliff that leads to the water. How did he get a boat here without it being detected by Damiano's guys?

Damiano tries to step closer, but I move out of his reach.

"Vale," he says under his breath.

I look at him over my shoulder and shake my head. A dozen emotions play across Damiano's face. I've made many choices in my past that I regret, but I'm not going to add another one to the list today. I will get Martina to safety, even if it's the last thing I do. He loves her so much—more than my parents ever loved me. I won't let him lose her.

Turning back to face Lazaro, I take a step forward. "Look," I say as I spread my arms wide. "I'm unarmed, I don't even have my phone with me. Take me to the boat and leave her be. If you say you'll release her, they won't shoot me."

Lazaro eyes the men behind me. The only advantage I have here is that he knows nothing about my relationship with Damiano. For all he knows, Damiano has been punishing me for my involvement with his sister's kidnapping all this time.

"Is that right?" he asks.

"Vale," Damiano grinds out. "What the—"

"Tell him you won't shoot me if he lets your sister go," I insist. He can't blow this chance.

I hear him heave a breath. "I won't shoot her."

Lazaro's knife glints in the light. "Good. I'll let your sister go when the time comes. Remember, if you kill me, we will all be dead. Don't follow us unless you want me to slit her throat."

He jerks his head to the side, telling me to go through the gate that leads out of the pool area. The lock on it is broken. There should have been a guard here, right?

As I step past the gate, my attention snags on the man lying on the ground. The guard is dead. Damiano and Ras don't follow. I can only imagine the torture this is for him to see his sister in danger.

"We don't have time to admire the scenery, Valentina," Lazaro says behind me. "Walk straight until you reach the cliff."

I follow his instructions, my heartbeat racing inside my chest. I keep looking over my shoulder to check on Martina, but it's dark outside, and all I catch are short glimpses of her terrified face. She must be in shock. Is Lazaro really going to let her go? I pray he will.

There's a rope ladder hanging off the edge of the cliff, and when I look down, I see a small motorboat anchored below. It bounces gently on the black water. That's how he's planning on getting away.

"Take the ladder," Lazaro commands.

There's no way I'm leaving her alone with him. "What about Martina?"

His blue eyes meet mine. "Go down, Valentina."

A drop of sweat rolls between my breasts. "No. Not until you let her go."

The air turns sticky and dense as Lazaro studies me with his cold, calculating gaze.

"She's the only one who's ever gotten away," he says finally. "A dark mark on my perfect record."

Fuck. He's going to kill her.

I can't let that happen.

I jerk the kitchen knife out of my pocket and press it against my wrist. "I know exactly where I need to cut myself so that I bleed out in minutes. I'll do it if you kill her."

Martina's features contort. "Vale, no!"

Lazaro sucks in a surprised breath. "You're bluffing."

The fact that he thinks that shows how little he understands me. "Let her go, or you'll never get me back."

I spent a long time being scared to do the right thing, but I'm not afraid anymore. This time, I'm going to do what's right, no matter what it costs me.

He grimaces. If I didn't know him any better, I'd think he was actually hurt by my words. "You're my wife," he snarls. "You belong to me."

"And you'll get me back as soon as you let her go."

His hard gaze, the gaze I've felt on myself so many times before, penetrates past the layers until he finally sees the truth of what I'm saying. He clicks with his tongue and pushes Martina away hard enough for her to fall to the ground. He steps over her and advances on me. "Drop the knife and get down the ladder, or I'll change my mind."

I do as he says, giving Martina one last look before I lower to the ground and place my foot on the first rung. She's crying silently, her face wet with tears.

The rope creaks and sways as I climb down, its rough surface harsh against my palms. Lazaro stands on the edge off the cliff, watching my every move, and when I'm nearly at the bottom of the cliff, he turns and starts his descent.

My feet touch the rocks the boat is tied to by a thick rope, and as I try to find my balance, I trip on something.

I glance down.

There's a fist-sized loose rock beside my foot. Without thinking twice, I bend down, pick it up, and hide it behind my back.

Lazaro jumps off the last rung and turns to face me. He jerks his head in the direction of the boat. "Climb in and sit down."

There are only two seats, side by side. He unties the rope while I take my seat. When he's done, he takes his spot behind the wheel.

I put the hand that's holding the rock between my thigh and the edge of the boat, hiding it from sight. "Where are we going?"

He turns the key in the ignition. "Back home."

He steers us out to sea. It's so dark, it takes me only thirty seconds to become disorientated. I have no idea what direction we're going in.

"New York isn't my home," I tell him. "It stopped being that when I got married to you."

A muscle in his jaw ticks. "I made mistakes with you, but I'll fix them."

"Mistakes? Forcing me to kill for you is more than a mistake," I say.

"That's not what I meant. I should have spent more time with you. We should have started working on a family."

I look at him in horror. That's what he thinks he did wrong? "I'll never give you a child, Lazaro. I'll cut it out of my womb before I bring your spawn into this world."

"You don't know what you're saying. But I'll fix you. I'll teach you how to see things my way. You'll never leave me again, Valentina. You're my wife. My partner. I've waited a long time to share my life with you, and I'll never let you go again. I love you."

I squeeze the rock in my palm. "You don't love anything."

"You're wrong."

"Do you really have an explosive on your body?"

He nods. "Our insurance in case they decide to come after us."

The clouds part to reveal a sliver of the moon. It's like a celestial eye, looking down at me and waiting to see if I'll do what I need to do.

I suck in a deep breath.

I'm never going back.

I lunge at him and slam the sharp edge of the rock into his temple. He shouts in pain and throws me off him, but I jump on him again. It's easier to fight him when I don't have any self-preservation left.

"Stop it," he roars.

I land another hit on his head. This one knocks him down. I don't wait to see if I did the job right this time, I just keep hitting him and hitting him until there's blood all over my hands.

When I stop, he groans weakly and blinks one eye at me. "We're a team. We're good together."

"No, we fucking aren't."

I take the rock with both hands and slam it right into the center of his face.

CHAPTER 35

DAMIANO

DESPERATION DRIPS INTO MY BLOODSTREAM. I've only felt like this once before—the day my sister disappeared in New York. Somehow now it's even worse. I froze when I saw the scene by the pool. I froze, because in that moment, I thought I'd have to make a choice—Vale or Mari—and I didn't know how I would choose.

My sister has always been the most important thing in my life. My joy, my mirror, my family. I told myself I'd never abandon her like my mother did. I've judged my mother for the choice she made my entire life. I could never understand her joining my father in death over living a life with us.

But now I finally understand.

In an impossible situation like this, there is no right or wrong.

Whatever you do, damnation awaits.

My gun is clutched in my hand as I peer past the pool gate where Lazaro, Vale, and Martina are standing. They're talking, but they're too far for me to hear them. When I see Vale press a knife to her wrist, my stomach turns to ice. I know what she's doing.

She's saving my sister.

She's doing my fucking job.

Cazzo. How the hell did this happen? I should have triple checked all of the cameras instead of trusting my men to get it right in Ras's absence. The pool camera isn't working. That's how Lazaro made it in.

Utter dismay settles over me like a heavy jacket and makes my limbs feel like lead. My mother's screams ring in my ears. I can't lose the two of them, but I'm powerless. I never thought I'd find myself here again.

Lazaro and Vale stop talking. Moonlight reflects off the blade that's angled against Vale's skin, and Martina's eyes are fixated on it. Even from this far, I can see how hard she's shaking.

Suddenly, their standoff ends. Lazaro shoves my sister to the ground and barks something to Vale. She starts moving to the edge of the cliff, Lazaro close behind her. I have a clear shot, but I can't take it. Not when he's made himself into a human bomb with an unknown payload.

As soon as Lazaro disappears over the cliff, I sprint to my sister.

"Dem!" She's crying as I take her into my arms. "He has Vale."

"I know. Are you hurt?"

"I'm fine. You need to help her. They're getting into his boat."

I hand her to a security guard and nod to Ras. We sprint around the house and jump down three stairs at a time until we're on my dock. Ras leaps into a speedboat with me right on his heels.

Vale did it. She saved Martina's life for the second time, but I can't let it be at the expense of her own. I should have been there by her side the entire time. Why did I leave her at the dinner table? I can't even remember what I needed to talk to Ras about anymore.

If I don't get her back, the world as I know it will end. There won't be any light in it without her.

As our boat speeds over the water, I rake my fingers through my hair. "Faster," I shout. We can't see Lazaro's boat, but they can't have gotten that far. They've got five minutes on us, tops. Once we catch up to them, bomb or not, I'll get Vale away from him, and then I'll put a bullet in his brain.

"There!" Ras yells as the clouds part.

In the distance, I see a tiny spec of a boat illuminated by the moon.

My chest expands. "We've got them. Don't slow down."

Once I save her, I'll make her my queen. I see it as clearly as if it's already happened. My brave Vale. She's perfect for me. We'll build our kingdom together, and she will rule by my side.

That's when it happens.

A ball of flames appears on the surface of the water, followed by an ear-splitting boom.

The sea burns.

And with it, the remains of Lazaro's boat.

My horror solidifies into a hard rock inside my stomach. No, that can't be real. She can't be *fucking burning*.

I fling my arm out and dig my fingers into Ras's shoulder. "Keep going," I rasp. "Get as close as possible." He lets out a grunt laced with frustration and speeds back up, moving in the direction of the flames.

The bomb. Lazaro wasn't lying about wearing one.

Did she kill him even though she knew it would mean her own death? No, Vale can't be dead. She. Can. Not. Be. Fucking. Dead. She wouldn't do that. She wanted to *live*, goddamn it. Didn't she know I'd track her down to the ends of the earth to get her back?

When we reach the burning debris, my heart sinks. There is no boat left. It's in pieces, torn apart by the blast.

"No. No!" I whip around, looking for something—anything —in the water that could be her. "Vale!"

Ras is turning the boat in place to shine the harsh spotlight on as much of the water as he can. It's hard to see anything.

I think I see a flash of skin by a floating piece of what's left of the hull. "Right there, go back," I yell.

Ras shines the light in that direction, and there's nothing there now, but there *was*. I'm sure of it. I saw her.

I leap off the boat. The water licks at my face, it's smell corrupted by gasoline and flames. I swim until I'm exactly in the spot I thought I saw her, and then I dive.

Ras keeps the light focused on me, which is the only reason I can see anything at all. I swim until I have no air left in my lungs, and then I come back up and do it all over again.

She has to be here somewhere. My lungs ache, and my chest feels like it's about to crack open.

Everything becomes so very clear in that moment.

I love this woman. I'll swim to the bottom of this sea if that's what it takes to bring her back to me. Please God, let me find her. If you do, I promise you, I'll never leave her side.

When I emerge out of the water to suck in another breath, I hear a weak voice somewhere to my right. At first, I think it's the oxygen deprivation affecting my hearing and making me imagine things. But then I hear it again.

Whipping around, I see her. She's treading water about thirty feet away, her hair plastered to her face.

I blink to make sure it's not a mirage. She's still there, and the wave of adrenaline that follows makes me feel like I could fucking fly.

"Vale!" My arms slice through the water. Twenty feet. Ten feet. Five.

As soon as her body is in my arms, I let out a gasp of relief. My head feels light. She burrows her face into the crook of my neck and cries.

～

The adrenaline doesn't recede until my feet hit solid ground. We climb out of the boat, and I lift her into my arms. Ras stays behind to tie up the boat and give us some privacy.

A few guards try to run up to me, but I scare them away with a look. I need a fucking minute to just hold her. Don't they understand that I nearly lost her in the waves?

Vale fists my soaking wet shirt and meets my gaze. "Is he dead?"

"You killed him, baby. I don't know how, but you killed him."

Her features contort. "I hit him with a rock," she whimpers. "I smashed it into his face."

I squeeze her tighter as guilt rages through me. It should have been me. "You did what you had to do."

She sniffs and wipes her hand under her nose. "He didn't think I could do it. Put my own life on the line to be free of him."

"You didn't do it just to be free. You saved Mari." My heartbeat finds an irregular rhythm. "I'll never forget that, Vale."

When we make it inside the house, my sister is waiting for us in the living room. She jumps off the couch and runs up to us, her eyes widening when she takes in our dripping clothes. "Oh thank God! Are you okay?"

I lower Vale to her feet and watch as they embrace. Seeing them together makes something shift inside my chest.

Vale smooths her hand over Martina's hair and kisses her temple. "I'm so sorry you had to go through that."

My sister's grip on her tightens. "Don't apologize. It wasn't your fault. What happened?"

Vale sucks in a breath. "I hit him with a rock I found. When I thought he was about to die, I dove into the water. The boat exploded above me."

She killed him with a *fucking* rock. Her gaze finds mine, and I see the horror of those few moments reflected within. She didn't want to hurt people anymore, but she had to do it.

I swear to God, it's the last time she'll ever have to do anything like that again.

We leave Mari and go upstairs to change. When Vale moves toward the shower in my room, I fight down the urge to follow her. I want to give her space, but she looks over her shoulder and beckons me forward. We strip out of our clothes and step into the shower.

When she turns on the water, I can't hold it in anymore. I have so much to say to her.

"I fucked up," I rasp. "I promised you I'd keep you safe, and I didn't."

She picks up the soap and runs it over my chest.

"I should have been totally focused on protecting you, but instead, half of my mind was on Sal and how I was going to bring him down. I failed you." I take the soap out of her hand and bring her fingertips to my lips. "But I'll never fail you again. Be with me. Give me another chance to show you how good we can be together."

She sighs. "I don't want to be your kept woman. My entire life I've been a little dinghy tossed around by waves created by far larger ships. It's time I set my own course."

I nudge her chin up. "I don't want a kept woman. I want a partner. An equal by my side. That's you. If I'm about to become a king, you will be my queen."

She blinks at me, and I can see she's not convinced yet. "Dons don't have partners."

"Maybe your father doesn't, but I'm not him, and the Casalesi have a strong tradition of putting women in powerful roles. You can do whatever you want. Choose a part of the empire to govern."

Some color returns to her cheeks. "I know how mafias work well enough to know you can't just bring a stranger into a clan and give her all this power."

I give her a soft smile. "A stranger, no. But I can give it to my wife."

Her mouth parts. "Are you proposing to me?"

"Yes."

"We've known each other for barely a month."

"My father proposed to my mother on their second date. They loved each other more than anyone I've ever known. It may have only been a month, but there isn't a sliver of doubt inside of me. You're the only woman I'll ever want. I love you, Vale."

Her eyelashes flutter, and she drops her gaze to my chest. "I need to think."

"Of course." I don't expect a response from her right now. She's been through a lot. But every day, I'll work on convincing her to be mine.

CHAPTER 36

VALENTINA

I SPEND the next few days in Damiano's bed nursing my countless bruises and shallow cuts. Martina brings me all my meals, Ras checks in at least once a day, and Damiano leaves my side for an hour at most. I sense he hates when he has to do it.

Despite my rough physical condition, I feel good. Light even. Lazaro won't ever find me again. The hold he had on me ever since he put that ring on my finger is gone.

Technically, I'm a widow, but I'll never think of myself as such. Lazaro will have no place in my history.

For so long, I thought he damaged me beyond repair, but now I'm not as pessimistic. By saving Martina, I think I may have saved myself. I don't feel like such an awful person anymore. When I look back on the woman I was, the one who tortured and killed those people, I see a broken soul trying her best to survive. It was the best I could do after being betrayed by those I trusted most. My parents. They put me into a horrific situation with no way out.

I'd never do that to my own kids.

My father was upset when Damiano told him about Lazaro. I was in the room while they talked, although my father didn't know I was there. He said it had to be done, but that he'd lost one of his best men.

When Damiano told him I was the one who killed Lazaro, he was silent. I don't think I'll ever get an apology out of him, but I don't need one. I've forgiven myself. I'll never forgive him.

On the other side of the enormous bedroom window is the sea. I climb out of bed and step out onto the balcony.

I've come here often over the last few days to stare at the glittering water and think about what Damiano said to me when we returned to the house the night Lazaro died.

He wants me to stay here. To marry me and make me his queen. He said he loved me, but I didn't say it back. The memory sends a rush of warmth through me, but it's chased away by a breeze. I place my forearms on the railing and exhale a breath.

I woke up before him this morning—a rarity—and I studied his body and the contours of his face. He's so handsome that sometimes it hurts to look at him. He has a little birthmark just above his right hip, and when I pressed my lips to it this morning, he stirred awake and made a sound I'll never forget. A happy sigh, mixed with a sleepy moan. I wanted to box that sound up and hide it away. A piece of him only I would get to keep.

I thought he'd pressure me to make a decision, but he

hasn't brought it up again. He comes and keeps me company. We watch movies, share meals, and talk about his day. More often, we have lengthy make-out sessions that leave me feeling hazy with arousal. He insists he won't do anything else with me until I'm back to one hundred percent. When I ask him questions about Sal or anything clan related, he gives me honest answers without holding anything back.

All of this plants ideas inside my head, which I'm sure is his intention. He's showing me what it could be like if I say yes. And honestly? He's starting to win me over.

It's all crazy. I've only just escaped a toxic marriage to a made man, and now I'm seriously considering saying yes to another.

But Damiano isn't Lazaro, and I'm no longer compelled to act on anyone's wishes but my own. If I agree to do this, it will be my choice. It will be a marriage of equals. There won't be any secrets or lies or wool pulled over my eyes.

When the door creaks open, I know it's him. The sound of his leather shoes on the hard wood floor is familiar by now. He steps onto the balcony and places a warm hand on the small of my back.

I turn to him. There are subtle changes to his face. The hard lines I remember so clearly that first night we met have softened. His eyes are no longer so dark. His lips quirk with a hint of a smile, and a hoard of butterflies comes alive inside my gut.

"What are you thinking about?" he asks in his deep voice.

I smile. "You."

His brow furrows, and he flicks his gaze away, seeming nervous for what must be the first time. "Should I be worried?"

"Maybe," I tease.

"I have something to show you that should score a few points in my favor."

"I've already seen your penis."

He snorts a laugh. "Not that." His arm snakes around my waist. "C'mon."

I'm eager to leave the confines of his room after spending three days in it, so I follow him zealously. His hand stays on my hip as we make it down the hall and descend the stairs.

When the living room comes into sight, my mouth falls open. I grip his forearm for support. "Gemma?"

My sister's sitting on the couch across from a glowering Ras, but when she hears me, she jumps to her feet and whirls around. "Vale!"

I can't believe my eyes. How is it possible that she's here? How did my father allow her to come?

My gaze finds Damiano's. He's looking very pleased with himself.

"You did this?" I ask him in an awed voice.

He doesn't answer, just smiles and nudges me forward.

That's when I know.

I'm going to marry this man.

∾

Around dusk, we all go outside to have dinner on the patio. The table is set for five. I settle in between Damiano and Gemma and take in the magnificent spread prepared by the cook. A board of Iberian ham, tomato spread, and bread, leafy salad with grilled goat cheese, sardines in olive oil, and shrimp ceviche. It all looks so good it makes my mouth water.

While Gemma argues with Ras over what wine we should drink—I don't recall her ever having strong opinions on the topic—Damiano takes it upon himself to fill my plate with food.

"I hope you're not planning on feeding me this time."

He shoots me a wicked look. "I'd need to get the rope first."

My subsequent laugh trails off when my gaze falls on Martina.

Judging by the dark shadows under her eyes, she's still not back to herself. Ras offers her some wine, and she nods. When Gemma whispers something to Martina, a small smile appears on the younger woman's face, but it's tinged with sadness. She needs to heal, and it will take some time. She carries a weight, just like I did. It's something she'll have to confront one day. When she's ready, we'll be here for her.

Once Gemma settles in beside me, I reach over and take her hand. It's still so surreal that she's here. Damiano flew her here in his private plane after managing to convince my father to allow her to visit for a few days. In exchange, he offered more favorable terms on the luxury counterfeit deal they're going to sign once Sal is out. They've begun negotiations so that when Damiano takes over, it can be ready to go into effect.

Damiano's smart—he figured out exactly how to manipulate my father. Tie it back to his business interests, and he can suddenly become a far more reasonable man.

Earlier, I tried to talk to Gemma about her engagement to Rafaele Messero, but she brushed me off. It seems it worries me more than it worries her. She wouldn't let me linger on the topic. Instead, she begged me to tell her about what happened between Lazaro and I. Eventually, I did. I told her everything. We cried together, clinging on to each other until our tears had dried. I've never seen her as angry as when I told her our parents knew all about it and refused to do anything. She said they'd never get away with doing something like that again, and I think she's right. Once Damiano's influence is cemented over my father, I'll be able to protect my siblings.

The conversation at the table flows with ease. We talk about lighthearted things up until Ras gets a call just as the plates are being cleared for dessert.

When he returns, his posture is rigid, and his lips are pressed into a thin line.

Damiano stands. "What happened?"

"We've received the first shipment from Garzolo. It's enough for us to cut the others off. They're waiting for your go-ahead."

I press my napkin to my lips. We've talked about Damiano's plan often enough for me to know this is the point of no return. As soon as he stops accepting drugs from Sal's supplier, Sal will know something's going on.

And then it'll become a game of who loses the confidence of the key clan members first.

I don't expect Damiano to turn to me, but he does. "I need to talk to you for a minute."

I follow him inside until we're in his office. He shuts the door behind him and comes to stand in front of me. "You know what will happen when I give that order."

"I do."

His eyes search my face. "I know it's only been a few days, but I need to know what you're thinking before I make this move. If you have anything you want to say, speak now."

I bring my fingers up to his cheek. "I think it's time you take back what's yours."

He inhales. It's an answer, but not the one he's looking for. "And you?"

A clock ticks loudly on the wall, and it only makes me realize how fast my pulse is racing. "And I'll be by your side for all of it. As your wife."

Damiano shuts his eyes and angles his face to kiss the tips of my fingers. He pulls me into his chest. "You don't know what this means to me."

When his lips find mine and his tongue slips into my mouth, it feels like coming home.

The first real home I've ever had.

"You know what I'll have to do to become the new don," he says after a while. "It won't be the first or last time."

He'll have to kill Sal with his bare hands. I was raised by a don, and I know what kind of life a position like that entails.

But it's not violence that scares me. It's the reasons behind it, and that's the difference between Damiano and everyone else. I trust his reasons will always be justified.

"It takes more than that to scare me off people I love," I say, slipping my arms around his neck.

Satisfaction unfurls across his face. "And that's why you are my perfect match."

EPILOGUE

DAMIANO

"THE FLOWERS GOT STUCK in traffic, but they'll be here in an hour. I couldn't find a priest who'd do it on such short notice, but there's a guy I know at the yacht club who's registered to do weddings, and I have him in the car," Ras says as he leans against the doorframe of my bedroom.

I adjust my tie in the mirror. Muffled female laughter reaches me from down the hall. Outside the balcony, a violin is being tuned.

"Not ideal, but it will do," I say.

Ras moves to the bar cart, pours whiskey into two glasses, and hands one to me. "How do you feel?"

"Like I'm getting married in two hours," I say.

He smirks. "*Cin cin.*"

We clink our glasses and drink.

My biggest regret is that I can't give Vale the wedding she deserves, which is why I told her that she'll have two—one now while her sister is here with us, and another once I take my place as don. I want to see her on the steps of the basilica in Naples where my parents got married.

There's a photo of that day resting on my nightstand. I move to look at it again. Most of our family photos burned in the fire, but over the years, Ras's father helped me find a few.

Whenever I see this particular photo, I'm struck with how normal my parents look. It's cropped closely on them, with just the basilica's entrance in the background and none of the guests in sight. My mother is in a white lace dress with a high neck, and my father is in a finely tailored suit. Beautiful, yes. But normal. Without knowing anything about the couple, it would be easy to imagine them as a common Italian family, instead of a don and donna of the *sistema*.

Their love for each other humanized them.

After falling for Vale, I think I finally see them as humans too. Flawed and imperfect, but capable of immense love.

When the time comes, we leave the bedroom and make our way to the gardens where the ceremony will take place. We'll get married under an arbor that Mari created a few years ago.

"It looks nice," I say to Ras, scanning the space.

"I wish I could take the credit, but it's mostly Gemma's work."

My brow arches. "You two are finally getting along?"

"Like oil and water," he says, glancing away and sliding his hands into his pockets.

I snicker. "You think I haven't noticed you eyeing her whenever she's not looking? Too bad she's engaged."

His response never makes it out of his mouth. The violin begins to play, and the ceremony starts.

My sister comes out first, followed by Gemma, both of them in pretty blue dresses. They each give me warm smiles and take their places opposite Ras.

When Vale appears at the end of the walkway, my heart jumps into my throat. There's a tremble in my hands, and I clench my fists by my side and force myself to breathe.

My God, this woman.

She floats down the walkway, her shoulders bared, and a bouquet in her arms. That dress on her is a wet dream, and I'm already considering how quickly I'll be able to peel it off her.

Mine. The word echoes in my head up until she stops before me and lifts her eyes to meet mine.

The garden, our friends, even the ground I stand on disappear. Everything but her blanks out. Inside those eyes is a promise of a future I never thought I'd have, and when her full lips quirk into a breathless smile, I grin and lift my face up to the azure sky.

I hope you're watching me right now.

∾

A FEW DAYS LATER

Vale's hair is bundled up in a towel as she steps out of the shower. I had intended on joining her there, but then I opened my goddamn mouth. I've spent the last few days in bed, thoroughly indulging my obsession with my wife. The plan was to continue to do that until dinner, but I've managed to piss her off and ruin the mood.

Her gaze finds me standing by the balcony, and she exhales a frustrated breath. "Did you really think I'd let you ship me off somewhere *days* after our wedding, Damiano? That's not how this is going to work." She stomps to the makeup vanity —a new addition to the room since she moved in—and huffs as she lowers into a chair. "I can't believe you."

I should have known she would react this way. Ras still hasn't given the order to cut Sal off. I wanted to wait until after our wedding before causing all hell to break loose. Putting that gold band on her finger became my priority as soon as she said she'd marry me, but now that she's finally mine, the fear of losing her is unlike any fear I've felt before.

Raking my fingers through my hair, I walk over to stand behind her. "I want to make sure you're safe."

"I'm safe by your side," she snaps. "Don't even try. I'm not leaving. Unless you want to sedate me and stuff me inside a trunk, I'm not going anywhere."

I place my hands on her delicate shoulders and meet her angry eyes in the mirror. "I'm not stuffing my beautiful wife into a trunk," I mutter. "Not again. It was only an idea."

"A bad one," she retorts. "Haven't I proven to you by now that I'm not helpless? I don't need saving. After these weeks on Ibiza, I've realized I'm far stronger than I ever gave myself credit for."

"Vale, you're the strongest person I know. It's not you being weak that I'm worried about. It's me."

Her expression softens at my confession. She puts her comb back down on the vanity and places her hand over mine. "If we're doing this, we're doing this together. I'm not going to be cooped up in some remote Italian villa while you fight for your throne and risk your life. You need me, Dem."

I lace her fingers with mine. I do need her. Her wisdom, her strength, and her courage. Just looking at her fills me with certainty there's only one way for this to end.

With our victory.

She stands and throws her arms around my neck. "I love you. No matter what happens, I'll love you through it all."

Warmth spreads through my chest. I wrap her damp hair around my fist and bring her lips to mine. She tastes so goddamn sweet.

When we break apart, I rest my forehead against hers. "Before I met you, I thought romantic love made people crazy and weak. I was right about the first. *Cazzo,* I'm so fucking crazy about you. But love doesn't make us weak. It's the opposite. It shows us what we absolutely can't lose— what's worth dying for. I'd die for you, Vale."

She kisses me again. "I'd prefer you live for me instead."

An hour later, I'm sitting in my office. My hair's still damp after I convinced Vale to take a second shower with me once we finished our conversation.

I pick up the phone and dial Napoletano.

He picks up on the third ring. "I hear congratulations are in order."

"How would you—" My eyes jump to the corners of the room. "Are you watching me right now?"

"Ras called me earlier."

I lean back in my chair and pinch the bridge of my nose. "Right."

There's a clipped chuckle. "How does it feel being a married man?"

"Excellent. Thinking about trying it?"

"No."

I wait for him to say more, but apparently that's all he's got on the topic, so after a moment, I continue. "I'm about to pull the trigger."

"The timing is right. There's a lot of discontent in the ranks. I think you'll find the support you need quicker than you expected."

"Good. Still, I have to plan for the worst." Spinning my pen over a knuckle, I release a breath. "I can't have the two people I care about most in one place. Vale insists on staying, but Mari is still...unwell. She hasn't fully recovered from what happened, and I want her someplace safe. Somewhere she'll be able to heal."

There's a long silence on the other end of the line that I suspect is underscored with distaste. He's probably pissed off I called him about this instead of something more suited for his skillset.

"Look, I know you're not a babysitter. I'm asking for a favor—"

"I'll take her."

There's no emotion in how he says the words, but the delivery is almost too flat. Like he's actively trying to keep his voice neutral.

A hint of unease latches onto my spine. I shrug it off. Napoletano is nearly impossible to read when you're talking to him face-to-face, let alone over the phone. The man is an enigma. It's one of the many reasons he's so fucking good at what he does. I hate the idea of sending Mari away, but besides Ras, he's the only one I can trust with her.

"I don't know how long it will be until things cool down."

"She can stay with me for as long as she needs."

I drop my head back and look at the plastered ceiling. It's the right thing to do, but that doesn't make it easy. "Thanks. Where will you take her?"

"Somewhere in Italy. It's best for me not to say. You'll be able to stay in touch over a secure line."

"All right."

"I'll come pick her up tomorrow morning."

That doesn't give me a lot of time to break the news to her, but I know she won't put up a fight like Vale did. She might grumble, but she'll go with Napoletano and stay with him until it's safe for her to come back.

"I owe you one," I say.

"Yes, you do."

We hang up, and I release a breath.

A guarantee of my sister's safety for a future favor.

I shrug. On paper, it's the simplest deal I've ever made.

Whatever Napoletano asks of me, it will be worth it to keep Mari safe.

And now that this is sorted, there's no more reason to delay. Time to put our plan into motion.

I send a text to Ras and drop my phone down on the desk.

It's the sound of the first domino falling.

THE END

BONUS SCENE

It's Damiano and Valentina's wedding night. Need I say more? ;)

Sign up here to receive it by email:
https://BookHip.com/RPZVCNS

ACKNOWLEDGMENTS

There are a few people without whom this book wouldn't exist, at least not in its current iteration. First, I have to thank my husband, because I've gotten so very lucky with him. Sometimes I have to pinch myself to believe he's real. His respect for my work makes this career—this act of endurance—possible. Beyond that, thank you for catching many typos and giving me excellent feedback on the story.

My dear friend Skyler, thank you for being my friend and work wife. Your energy, enthusiasm, and love for this insane rollercoaster journey we're on keeps me going through the toughest of times. You were my ideal reader for this manuscript and your beta feedback helped me craft Damiano into the delicious alpha that he is.

Heidi, you took this book to another level. Your dev edits made this story came alive like I couldn't even imagine, and I'm so proud of the final result. Grateful and humbled to be working with a master editor like you.

Big thank you to all of my author friends and mentors. You know who you are!

And finally, thank you dear reader for picking up this book and getting all the way through the end. I hope you fell in love with Valentina and Damiano the same way I did and I can't wait to give you more of The Fallen.

Love,

Gabrielle

Lightning Source UK Ltd.
Milton Keynes UK
UKHW040618031222
413194UK00002B/282

9 781088 047224